PENGUIN POETS

# THE PENGUIN BOOK
## CONTEMPORARY IRISH POETRY

Peter Fallon was born in 1951. In 1970, while a student at Trinity College, Dublin, he founded The Gallery Press. His books include *Winter Work* and *The News and Weather*. He lives in north Co. Meath.

Derek Mahon was born in Belfast in 1941 and graduated from Trinity College, Dublin, where he was recently writer in residence. He worked for some years in London as a journalist and screenwriter. His *Selected Poems*, published by Penguin in 1993, was awarded the 1992 *Irish Times*/Aer Lingus Irish Literature Prize for Poetry.

# THE PENGUIN BOOK OF
# CONTEMPORARY IRISH POETRY

*Edited by*
*Peter Fallon and Derek Mahon*

**PENGUIN BOOKS**

PENGUIN BOOKS

Published by the Penguin Group
Penguin Books Ltd, 27 Wrights Lane, London W8 5TZ, England
Penguin Putnam Inc., 375 Hudson Street, New York, New York 10014, USA
Penguin Books Australia Ltd, Ringwood, Victoria, Australia
Penguin Books Canada Ltd, 10 Alcorn Avenue, Toronto, Ontario, Canada M4V 3B2
Penguin Books (NZ) Ltd, Private Bag 102902, NSMC, Auckland, New Zealand

Penguin Books Ltd, Registered Offices: Harmondsworth, Middlesex, England

First published 1990
9 10 8

Printed in England by Clays Ltd, St Ives plc
Filmset in Linotron Ehrhardt

# CONTENTS

# CONTENTS

CONTENTS

viii

# CONTENTS

x

# CONTENTS

# CONTENTS

# CONTENTS

# INTRODUCTION

Among the contours of modern Irish poetry the work of Yeats is Everest. His poems and his other activities in the pursuit of a new national identity represent a monument which, more often than not, obscured the achievement of younger writers. The commanding features in the landscape of more recent Irish poetry are Louis MacNeice (1907–63) and Patrick Kavanagh (1904–67). Somewhere between 'the mountains and the gantries' of MacNeice's Belfast and the 'black hills' of Kavanagh's Shancoduff, contemporary Irish poetry has its figurative source.

By 'contemporary Irish poetry' we mean poems written by Irish men and women, in English and in Irish, in the course of the past thirty or forty years. MacNeice, Kavanagh and other poets like Austin Clarke (1896–1974), Denis Devlin (1908–59) and Padraic Fallon (1905–74) were still writing in the fifties and sixties, and John Hewitt in the eighties, but they belong to an older generation than the ones we hope to represent. The influence and perhaps even the development of Clarke, Devlin and Fallon may have been impeded by their publishing history. Clarke published no book of poems between 1938 and 1955; his *Collected Poems* appeared in 1974, the year of his death. Devlin was never a presence in print through the fifties, sixties and seventies; his *Collected Poems* appeared in 1989. Padraic Fallon's *Poems*, his first collection, appeared in 1974, shortly before he died. Clarke is something of a special case. His reputation has suffered many vicissitudes and, while the young Montague learned much from him, the tortured lyrics of *Night and Morning* (1938) and his too much neglected long poem, *Mnemosyne Lay in Dust* (1966), may now be seen as links in a chain connecting Joyce to Kinsella. Samuel Beckett (1906–89) and Francis Stuart (b. 1902) may be called 'contemporary', but the best of their strictly *poetic* work belongs to an earlier period. There have been advocates of Modernism like Thomas McGreevy (1894–1967) and George Reavey (1907–76), but theirs is not a tradition which flourishes in Ireland now.

From the beginning MacNeice was associated with the English tradition. His friendships, shared interests and collaborations with 'the Auden generation' ensured as much. For those shared concerns included a commitment to the making of poems 'expressive of the poet's immediate interests and his sense of the natural and *social* world' (*Modern Poetry*, 1938). He believed the poet to be the conscience of a community, 'its critical faculty, its generous instinct', and his poems refer to 'darkest Ulster', to London where he lived and worked, and to the West of Ireland, which represented for him a dream world, an imaginative hinterland. After his death he was adopted as what Michael Longley calls a 'progenitor' by a number of new poets who emerged in Northern Ireland in the sixties. His ironic inflections are audible in the early work of Michael Longley, James Simmons, Derek Mahon and Paul Muldoon. MacNiece is a superlative love poet, whose best work marries lyrical grace to philosophic weight. He saw the world as 'incorrigibly plural'; in it the question of 'one' and 'many' was unresolved. Poems and radio plays record versions of a quest, historical, personal and allegorical. Solutions lay in the writing itself. In *Autumn Journal* (1938), a poem of twenty-four cantos, he took the measure of his time. This long documentary places a private life in the context of world events.

In 1940 MacNeice returned to England from a visit to the United States because 'I thought I was missing history'. It was Kavanagh's proud boast that he 'lived in important places, times/When great events were decided'; but, for him, these historical milestones belonged to the chronicle of a particular parish. More than Mac-Neice, more than Yeats, Kavanagh may be seen as the true origin of much Irish poetry today. One poem, the sonnet 'Epic', gave single-handed permission for Irish poets to trust and cultivate their native ground and experience:

> I have lived in important places, times
> When great events were decided, who owned

That half a rood of rock, a no-man's land
Surrounded by our pitchfork-armed claims.
I heard the Duffys shouting 'Damn your soul'
And old McCabe stripped to the waist, seen
Step the plot defying blue cast-steel –
'Here is the march along these iron stones'
That was the year of the Munich bother. Which
Was more important? I inclined
To lose my faith in Ballyrush and Gortin
Till Homer's ghost came whispering to my mind.
He said: I made the Iliad from such
A local row. Gods make their own importance.

That whisper acted as a liberation to younger poets like John Montague and Seamus Heaney. Kavanagh's advocacy of parochialism over provincialism was widely heeded:

Parochialism and provincialism are opposites. The provincial has no mind of his own; he does not trust what his eyes see until he has heard what the metropolis – towards which his eyes are turned – has to say on any subject. This runs through all activities.

The parochial mentality on the other hand is never in any doubt about the social and artistic validity of his [*sic*] parish. All great civilizations are based on parochialism – Greek, Israelite, English. Parochialism is universal; it deals with the fundamentals.

To know fully even one field or one lane is a lifetime's experience. In the world of poetic experience it is depth that counts and not width. A gap in a hedge, a smooth rock surfacing a narrow lane, a view of a woody meadow, the stream at the junction of four small fields – these are as much as a man can fully experience.

Not since William Carleton (1794–1869), the novelist and short story writer, had rural Ireland possessed such an authentic annalist, and analyst.

Another crucial figure in the post-Yeatsian literary culture was the late Liam Miller, who founded the Dolmen Press in 1951. Previously Irish poets had tended to publish in London; but, with the establishment of Dolmen, a handful born in the late twenties (Thomas Kinsella, John Montague, Richard Murphy, Pearse Hutchinson) could begin to publish realistically, indeed more than handsomely, in Dublin, without immediate reference to London, for so long the arbiter in this field as in others. The Irish publishing industry is now a busy and extensive one.

Such was the centrality of Kinsella's role in this development, and such his iconic significance, that we decided to place him at the beginning of this anthology, although he is not quite the oldest contributor. His career has been prolific and idiosyncratic, if historically curative. From the grim formality of early poems like 'In the Ringwood' and 'Downstream' he has moved on to the grim informality of 'Death Bed' and 'Finistère', while his celebrated version of the eighth-century epic *Táin Bó Cuailgne* and his repossession of much forgotten matter in *An Duanaire*\* have established him at the forefront of the host of poets who translate from Irish. Even if his most recent work's intense subjectivity makes few concessions to the reader, his dedication has been exemplary, his performance constantly surprising. The same is true of his contemporaries Montague and Murphy – both of whom, like Kinsella, have turned their hands to the long poem or sequence as well as the short lyric. Montague's collages, *The Rough Field* and *The Dead Kingdom*, investigate his personal and historical experience of Northern Ireland, while Murphy's *The Battle of Aughrim* explores his own Anglo-Irish heritage.

The Northern experience has received a great deal of poetic coverage in the period with which we are concerned, to such an extent that it might almost seem abroad as if the only contemporary Irish poetry of particular interest had its origins there. The excellence and popularity of Seamus Heaney's work has much to do with this,

---

\* *An Duanaire: Poems of the Dispossessed 1600–1900* edited by Sean Ó Tuama with translations into English verse by Thomas Kinsella (Dolmen Press, 1981).

but the Northern phenomenon remains, in Kinsella's phrase, 'largely a journalistic entity'. There was never, contrary to received opinion, a Northern 'School' in any real sense, merely a number of individual talents. Too much has been made of the so-called Belfast 'Group'. Still, it is undeniable that in a traditionally philistine province, the individual talents of Heaney, Longley, Simmons and Mahon appeared more or less simultaneously and coincidentally with the present 'Troubles'. A second generation included Paul Muldoon, Ciaran Carson and Medbh McGuckian. Frank Ormsby, in his introduction to *Poets from the North of Ireland* (Blackstaff Press, 1979), echoes John Hewitt in suggesting that one reason for the intense activity in Northern Ireland in the sixties was the 1947 Education Act, which made increased educational opportunities available to all.

But, of course, Northern Irish poetry, prodigious though it has been, is only part of the picture, a fact taken for granted in Ireland itself if less obvious elsewhere. For contemporaneously with the now more than twenty-year-old Northern phenomenon the Republic has continued to produce first-rate poets (Michael Hartnett, Eiléan Ní Chuilleanáin, Paul Durcan, Nuala Ní Dhomhnaill) whose work, though keenly followed in Ireland, receives insufficient attention abroad. The density of local reference in Irish poetry, which might be offered as an explanation or excuse, has proved no obstacle in the case of Heaney.

If the present anthology can be said to have any polemical purpose, that purpose would be to correct imbalances created over the years by editors, publishers and critics, and to dispel the illusion that Irish poetry has been written exclusively by persons of Northern provenance, whether they live in Belfast, Dublin, Dingle or Berkeley, California. A glance at the contents pages tells a different story: as ever, poets from the North contribute to a national body of work which, in its turn, belongs to a global community. These poets are tied less to particular places – or parishes – than ever before. The notion of exile has for centuries permeated the Irish consciousness and while it was true of writers like Joyce and Beckett in the recent past, it is hardly true in the same sense for young poets like Michael O'Loughlin and Harry Clifton, who spend most of their lives outside

Ireland. Eamon Grennan, a poet born in Dublin but who teaches in New York State, returning each year to Ireland, has written of his *migrations*. You might say these writers *commute*.

The continuity and renewal of energy among poets born south of the Border reflect changed conditions in the Republic, much as Northern poetry reflects changed conditions there. This renewal has expressed itself in three principal ways: in a new urban working-class poetry, in an increasingly self-conscious feminist poetry, and in a new attention to the Irish language. All three are suggested here by, among others, O'Loughlin, Eavan Boland and Nuala Ní Dhomhnaill. Ní Dhomhnaill, indeed, has forged a unique Irish-language expression of the contemporary woman's psyche.

Kinsella, in his introduction to *The New Oxford Book of Irish Verse* (1986) and elsewhere, has written of the intimate fusion of Irish literature and history and described the phenomenon of two linguistic entities, two major bodies of poetry, in dynamic interaction.

More than ever before there is a vigorous exchange between contemporary Irish writers in Irish and English. Ní Dhomhnaill's work has been translated by Michael Hartnett and a dozen other poets and appears here in dual-language form, as does that of Michael Davitt (we have not commissioned any translations for this book; instead, we have drawn only on the work of poets already available in bilingual editions) whose magazine *Innti* has been a platform for the best new writing in Irish during the last two decades. Together with Paul Durcan, whose tabloid titles and bizarre narratives have proved so popular, Nuala Ní Dhomhnaill is one of the most admired younger poets in Ireland today. Both of them have worked to build an audience for their poetry through readings around the country and abroad. They enjoy high profile and uncommon attention. A number of other writers whose first publications were books of verse (Dermot Bolger and Sebastian Barry among them) have recently turned their energies with considerable success to other forms – fiction and drama – for which there is a readier critical and popular response.

Irish poets, of course, have always looked abroad. Now the new narrative devices of East European and South American fictions are evident in the poetry of Muldoon and Carson. Increasingly the give-and-take between Irish and American poetry is felt, sharing as it does a comparable relationship with the English language, and determined as their countries are by transatlantic neighbourhood. But ultimately Irish poetry, conditioned by historical experience, technical tradition and linguistic usage, speaks for itself in one or another of the many voices which have evolved over the years. It may be worth noting the frequent use of the conditional; again and again, one meets 'would' or 'might', 'as if' and 'seems', as if (see?) life has been carried on in some kind of suspense. The word most frequently dwelt on in this selection, though, is probably 'home', as if an uncertainty exists as to where that actually is. This book tries to suggest the map of achievement and variety by Irish poets in the last thirty or forty years. Confident of poetry's primary importance and primal power, they may be most at home in what Heaney christens in the title of his most recent book of essays, *The Place of Writing* (1989).

# THOMAS KINSELLA

## A Lady of Quality

In hospital where windows meet
With sunlight in a pleasing feat
    Of airy architecture
My love has sweets and grapes to eat,
The air is like a laundered sheet,
    The world's a varnished picture.

Books and flowers at her head
Make living-quarters of her bed
    And give a certain style
To our pillow-chat, the nonsense said
To bless the room from present dread
    Just for a brittle while.

For obvious reasons we ignore
The leaping season out-of-door,
    Light lively as a ferret,
Woodland walks, a crocused shore,
The transcendental birds that soar
    And tumble in high spirit

While under this hygienic ceiling
Where my love lies down for healing
    Tiny terrors grow,
Reflected in a look, revealing
That her care is spent concealing
    What, perhaps, I know:

The ever-present crack in time
Forever sundering the lime-
    Paths and the fragrant fountains,
Photographed last summer, from
The unknown memory we climb
    To find in this year's mountains.

'Ended and done with' never ceases,
Constantly the heart releases
    Wild geese to the past.
Look, how they circle poignant places,
Falling to sorrow's fowling-pieces
    With soft plumage aghast.

We may regret, and must abide.
Grief, the hunter's, fatal stride
    Among the darkening hearts
Has gone too long on either side.
Our trophied love must now divide
    Into its separate parts

And you go down with womankind
Who in her beauty has combined
    And focused human hungers,
With country ladies who could wind
A nation's love-affair with mind
    Around their little fingers,

And I communicate again
Recovered order to my pen
    To find a further answer
As, having looked all night in vain,
A weary prince will sigh and then
    Take a familiar dancer.

Now the window's turning dark
And ragged rooks across the Park
    Mix with the branches; all

The clocks about the building mark
The hour. The random is at work
    On us: two petals fall,

A train lifts up a lonely cry . . .
Our fingertips together lie
    Upon the counterpane.
It will be hard, it seems, and I
Would wish my heart to justify
    What qualities remain.

# In the Ringwood

As I roved out impatiently
Good Friday with my bride
To drink in the rivered Ringwood
The draughty season's pride
A fell dismay held suddenly
Our feet on the green hill-side.

The yellow Spring on Vinegar Hill,
The smile of Slaney water,
The wind that swept the Ringwood,
Grew dark with ancient slaughter.
My love cried out and I beheld her
Change to Sorrow's daughter.

'Ravenhair, what rending
Set those red lips a-shriek,
And dealt those locks in black lament
Like blows on your white cheek,
That in your looks outlandishly
Both woe and fury speak?'

As sharp a lance as the fatal heron
There on the sunken tree
Will strike in the stones of the river
Was the gaze she bent on me.
O her robe into her right hand
She gathered grievously.

'Many times the civil lover
Climbed that pleasant place,
Many times despairing
Died in his love's face,
His spittle turned to vinegar,
Blood in his embrace.

Love that is every miracle
Is torn apart and rent.
The human turns awry
The poles of the firmament.
The fish's bright side is pierced
And good again is spent.

Though every stem on Vinegar Hill
And stone on the Slaney's bed
And every leaf in the living Ringwood
Builds till it is dead
Yet heart and hand, accomplished,
Destroy until they dread.

Dread, a grey devourer,
Stalks in the shade of love.
The dark that dogs our feet
Eats what is sickened of.
The End that stalks Beginning
Hurries home its drove.'

I kissed three times her shivering lips.
I drank their naked chill.
I watched the river shining
Where the heron wiped his bill.
I took my love in my icy arms
In the Spring on Ringwood Hill.

# Downstream

*Drifting to meet us on the darkening stage*
*A pattern shivered; whorling in its place*
*Another held us in a living cage*
*Then broke to its reordered phase of grace.*

*

Again in the mirrored dusk the paddles sank.
  We thrust forward, swaying both as one.
  The ripples widened to the ghostly bank

Where willows, with their shadows half undone,
  Hung to the water, mowing like the blind.
  The current seized our skiff. We let it run

Grazing the reeds, and let the land unwind
  In stealth on either hand. Dark woods: a door
  Opened and shut. The clear sky fell behind,

The channel shrank. Thick slopes from shore to shore
  Lowered a matted arch. I thought of roots
  Crawling full of pike on the river-floor

To cage us in, sensed the furred night-brutes
  Halt in their trails, twitching their tiny brushes.
  What plopped in the reeds and stirred between the shoots?

Then I remembered how among those bushes
  A man one night fell sick and left his shell
  Collapsed, half eaten, like a rotted thrush's

To frighten stumbling children. 'You could tell',
  My co-shadow murmured, 'by the hands
  He died in terror.' And the cold of hell,

A limb-lightness, a terror in the glands,
  Pierced again as when that story first
  Froze my blood: the soil of other lands

Drank lives that summer with a body thirst;
  Nerveless by the European pit
  – Ourselves through seven hundred years accurst –

We saw the barren world obscurely lit
  By tall chimneys flickering in their pall,
  The haunt of swinish man – each day a spit

That, turning, sweated war, each night a fall
  Back to the evil dream where rodents ply,
  Man-rumped, sow-headed, busy with whip and maul

Among nude herds of the damned. It seemed that I,
  Coming to conscience on that lip of dread,
  Still dreamed, impervious to calamity,

Imagining a formal drift of the dead
  Stretched calm as effigies on velvet dust,
  Scattered on starlit slopes with arms outspread

And eyes of silver – when that story thrust
  Pungent horror and an actual mess
  Into my very face, and taste I must.

Then hungry joy and sickening distress
  Fumbled together by the brimming flood,
  And night consumed a hopeless loneliness.

Like mortal jaws, the alleys of the wood
  Fell-to behind us. At its heart, a ghost
  Glimmered briefly with my gift of blood

– Spreadeagled on a rack of leaves, almost
  Remembering. It looked full at the sky,
  Calmly encountering the starry host,

Meeting their silver eyes with silver eye.
  An X of wavering flesh, a skull of light,
  Extinguished in our wake without a sigh.

Then the current shuddered in its flight
    And swerved on pliant muscle; we were sped
    Through sudden peace into a pit of night:

The Mill-Hole, whose rocky fathoms fed
    On moss and pure depth and the cold fin
    Turning in its heart. The river bed

Called to our flesh. Across the watery skin,
    Breathless, our shell trembled. The abyss . . .
    We shipped our oars in dread. Now, deeper in,

Something shifted in sleep, a quiet hiss
    As we slipped by. Adrift . . . A milk-white breast . . .
    A shuffle of wings betrayed with a feathery kiss

A soul of white with darkness for a nest.
    The creature bore the night so tranquilly
    I lifted up my eyes. There without rest

The phantoms of the overhanging sky
    Occupied their stations and descended;
    Another moment, to the starlit eye,

The slow, downstreaming dead, it seemed, were blended
    One with those silver hordes, and briefly shared
    Their order, glittering. And then impended

A barrier of rock that turned and bared
    A varied barrenness as toward its base
    We glided – blotting heaven as it towered –

Searching the darkness for a landing place.

# Wormwood

I have dreamt it again: standing suddenly still
In a thicket, among wet trees, stunned, minutely
Shuddering, hearing a wooden echo escape.

A mossy floor, almost colourless, disappears
In depths of rain among the tree shapes.
I am straining, tasting that echo a second longer.

If I can hold it . . . familiar if I can hold it . . .
A black tree with a double trunk – two trees
Grown into one – throws up its blurred branches.

The two trunks in their infinitesimal dance of growth
Have turned completely about one another, their join
A slowly twisted scar, that I recognize . . .

A quick arc flashes sidewise in the air,
A heavy blade in flight. A wooden stroke:
Iron sinks in the gasping core.

                              I will dream it again.

# *from* Nightwalker

\*

The foot of the tower. An angle where the darkness
Is complete. The parapet is empty.
A backdrop of constellations, crudely done
And mainly unfamiliar; they are arranged
To suggest a chart of the brain. Music far off.
In the part of the little harbour that can be seen
The moon is reflected in low water.
Beyond, the lamps on the terrace.

                           The music fades.
                  Snuggle into the skull.
Total darkness wanders among my bones.
Lung-tips flutter. Wavelets lap the shingle.
From the vest's darkness, smell of my body:
                  Chalk dust and flowers . . .
Faint brutality. Shoes creak in peace.
Brother Burke flattens his soutane
Against the desk.
             And the authorities
Used the National Schools to try to conquer
The Irish national spirit, at the same time
Exterminating what they called our 'jargon'
– The Irish language; in which Saint Patrick, Saint Bridget
And Saint Columcille taught and prayed!
Edmund Ignatius Rice founded our Order
To provide schools that were national in more than name.
Pupils from our schools played their part,
As you know, in the fight for freedom. And you will be called
In your different ways – to work for the native language,
To show your love by working for your country.
Today there are Christian Brothers' boys
Everywhere in the Government – the present Taoiseach
Sat where one of you is sitting now.

It wasn't long before Her Majesty
Gave us the famine – the starvation, as Bernard Shaw,
A godless writer, called it more accurately.
                              A hand is laid on my brow.
A voice breathes: You will ask are we struck dumb
By the unsimplifiable. Take these . . .
Bread of certainty; scalding soup of memories,
For my drowsy famine – martyrs in a dish
Of scalding tears: food of dragon men
And my own dragon half. Fierce pity!
                              The Blessed Virgin smiles
From her waxed pedestal, like young Victoria;
A green snake wriggles under her heel
Beside a vase of tulips.
                              Adolescents,
Celibates, we offer up our vows
To God and Ireland in Her name, grateful
That by our studies here they may not lack
Civil servants in a state of grace.
                              A glass partition rattles
In the draught. Rain against the windows.
A shiver clothes the flesh
                              bittersweet.
                              A seamew passes over,
Whingeing:
                *Éire, Éire . . . is there none*
*To hear? Is all lost?*
                              Not yet all; a while still
Your voice . . .
                *Alas, I think I will dash myself*
*At the stones. I will become a wind on the sea*
*Or a wave of the sea again, or a sea sound.*
*At the first light of the sun I stirred on my rock;*
*I have seen the sun go down at the end of the world;*
*Now I fly across the face of the moon.*
                              A dying language echoes

Across a century's silence.
                              It is time,
Lost soul, I turned for home.
                              Sad music steals
Over the scene.
                    Hesitant, cogitating, exit.

# Hen Woman

The noon heat in the yard
smelled of stillness and coming thunder.
A hen scratched and picked at the shore.
It stopped, its body crouched and puffed out.
The brooding silence seemed to say 'Hush . . .'

The cottage door opened,
a black hole
in a whitewashed wall so bright
the eyes narrowed.
Inside, a clock murmured 'Gong . . .'

(I had felt all this before . . .)

She hurried out in her slippers
muttering, her face dark with anger,
and gathered the hen up jerking
languidly. Her hand fumbled.
Too late. Too late.

It fixed me with its pebble eyes
(seeing what mad blur?).
A white egg showed in the sphincter;
mouth and beak opened together;
and time stood still.

Nothing moved: bird or woman,
fumbled or fumbling – locked there
(as I must have been) gaping.

\*

There was a tiny movement at my feet,
tiny and mechanical; I looked down.
A beetle like a bronze leaf
was inching across the cement,
clasping with small tarsi

13

a ball of dung bigger than its body.
The serrated brow pressed the ground humbly,
lifted in a short stare, bowed again;
the dung-ball advanced minutely,
losing a few fragments,
specks of staleness and freshness.

*

A mutter of thunder far off
– time not quite stopped.
I saw the egg had moved a fraction:
a tender blank brain
under torsion, a clean new world.

As I watched, the mystery completed.
The black zero of the orifice
closed to a point
and the white zero of the egg hung free,
flecked with greenish brown oils.

It slowly turned and fell.
Dreamlike, fussed by her splayed fingers,
it floated outward, moon-white,
leaving no trace in the air,
and began its drop to the shore.

*

I feed upon it still, as you see;
there is no end to that which,
not understood, may yet be noted
and hoarded in the imagination,
in the yolk of one's being, so to speak,
there to undergo its (quite animal) growth,
dividing blindly,
twitching, packed with will,
searching in its own tissue
for the structure

in which it may wake.
Something that had – clenched
in its cave – not been
now was: an egg of being.
Through what seemed a whole year it fell
– as it still falls, for me,
solid and light, the red gold beating
in its silvery womb,
alive as the yolk and white
of my eye; as it will continue
to fall, probably, until I die,
through the vast indifferent spaces
with which I am empty.

\*

It smashed against the grating
and slipped down quickly out of sight.
It was over in a comical flash.
The soft mucous shell clung a little longer,
then drained down.
She stood staring, in blank anger.
Then her eyes came to life, and she laughed
and let the bird flap away.
'It's all the one.
There's plenty more where that came from!'

Hen to pan!
It was a simple world.

# Ancestor

I was going up to say something,
and stopped. Her profile against the curtains
was old, and dark like a hunting bird's.

It was the way she perched on the high stool,
staring into herself, with one fist
gripping the side of the barrier around her desk
– or her head held by something, from inside.
And not caring for anything around her
or anyone there by the shelves.
I caught a faint smell, musky and queer.

I may have made some sound – she stopped rocking
and pressed her fist in her lap; then she stood up
and shut down the lid of the desk, and turned the key.
She shoved a small bottle under her aprons
and came toward me, darkening the passageway.

Ancestor . . . among sweet- and fruit-boxes.
Her black heart . . .
                            Was that a sigh?
– brushing by me in the shadows,
with her heaped aprons, through the red hangings
to the scullery, and down to the back room.

# Nuchal

*a fragment*

'. . . down among the roots like a half-
buried vase brimming
over with pure water,
a film of clear brilliancy
spilling down its sides
rippling with reflections
of the four corners of the garden.
Fish-spirits slip down shimmering
into the grass; the grass
welcomes them with a hiss
of movement and voices
– its own snake-spirits.

On the last of the grass,
dreaming on one outstretched arm,
the woman lies smiling in her sleep.
Her arm dips over the brink
with the fingers trailing ladylike
in the water
   – the rivulet
simply wanders up to her,
making to go past out of the garden,
meets her fingers
– and four sunlit ripples
lengthen out from them;
the stream divides and subdivides
into four, moistening and softening
the first downward curve of the hill.

She has dreamed so long already
– it is monstrous . . .
     four great rivers
creep across the plain

toward the four corners of
                    that vast domain:

Eastward, a quiet river feeds the soil
till the soft banks crumble, caked with oil.
A sudden shine, out of eternal spring:
a crop of gold, with many a precious thing
– bdellium, seeking the pearl in its own breast,
the flower-figured onyx, the amethyst . . .

Southward (it seems of melted gold) a stream
rolls toward the summer in a fiery gleam,
leaving a honey of fertility
to sweeten the salt marsh in some degree.

A third runs Westward in its deeper bed,
tigrish, through narrow gorges, winy red,
as though some heart toward which it ran (a vein)
drew it onward through that cruel terrain.

Lastly, a milk-white river, faring forth
in a slow flood, laughing to the North.

Four rivers reaching toward th'encircling sea,
that bitter river,
                    where every . . .'

# Endymion

At first there was nothing. Then a closed space.
Such light as there was showed him sleeping.
I stole nearer and bent down; the light grew brighter,
and I saw it came from the interplay of our two beings.
It blazed in silence as I kissed his eyelids.
I straightened up and it faded, from his pallor
and the ruddy walls with their fleshy thickenings
– great raw wings, curled – a huge owlet-stare –
as a single drop echoed in the depths.

# All is Emptiness, and I Must Spin

A vacancy in which, apparently
I hang
         with severed senses

                    *

I have been in places . . .

The floors crept,
an electric terror
waited everywhere
– just one touch!

We were made to separate
and strip. My urine flowed
with mild excitement.
Our hands touched lightly
in farewell.

Permit me, with drunken pleasure . . .

                    *

How bring oneself to judge, or think,
so hurled onward!
                    inward!

After a while, in the utter darkness,
there was a slight but perceptible
movement of the air.
It was not Death, but Night . . .
mountain coolness; a tiny
freshness of dew on the face
– tears of self forming.

I was lying in utter darkness
in a vaulted place. Cold air
crept over long-abandoned floors,

bearing a taint of remote iron
and dead ash: the interior
of some extinct . . .
                    A distant door
clangs. Echo of voices.

                    *

The sterile: it is a whole matter in itself.
Fantastic millions of
fragile

in every single

# The Route of the Táin

Gene sat on a rock, dangling our map.
The others were gone over the next crest,
further astray. We ourselves, irritated,
were beginning to turn down toward the river
back to the car, the way we should have come.

We should have trusted our book –
after they tried a crossing, and this river too
'rose against them' and bore off
a hundred of their charioteers toward the sea
*They had to move along the river Colptha*
*up to its source*
    there:
where the main branch sharpens away gloomily
to a gash in the hill opposite;
*then to Bélat Ailiúin*
      by that pathway
climbing back and forth out of the valley
over to Ravensdale.

Scattering in irritation . . . who had set out
so cheerfully to celebrate our book;
cheerfully as we made and remade it
through a waste of hours, content to 'enrich the present
honouring the past', each to his own just function . . .
Wandering off, ill-sorted,
like any beasts of the field,
one snout honking disconsolate,
another burrowing in its pleasures . . .

When not far above us a red fox
ran at full stretch out of the bracken
and panted across the hillside toward the next ridge.
Where he vanished – a faint savage sharpness

out of the earth – an inlet of the sea
shone in the distance at the mouth of the valley
beyond Omeath: grey waters crawled with light.

For a heartbeat, in alien certainty,
we exchanged looks. We should have known it, by now:
the process, the whole tedious
enabling ritual! Flux brought to fullness
– saturated – the clouding over – dissatisfaction
spreading slowly like an ache: something
reduced shivering suddenly into meaning
along new boundaries
                              – through a forest,
by a salt-dark shore,
by a standing stone on a dark plain,
by a ford running blood,
and along this gloomy pass, with someone ahead
calling and waving on the crest, against a heaven
of dismantling cloud – transfixed
by the same figure (stopped, pointing)
on the rampart at Cruachan
where it began . . .
the morning sunlight pouring on us all
as we scattered over the mounds
disputing over useless old books,
assembled in cheerful speculation
around a prone block, *Miosgán Medba*,
– Queen Medb's *turd* . . . ? – and rattled our maps,
joking together in growing illness
or age or fat; before us
the route of the Táin, over men's dust,
toward these hills that seemed to grow
darker as we drove nearer.

# Death Bed

Motionless – his sons –
we watched his brows draw together with strain.
The wind tore at the leather walls of our tent;
two grease lamps fluttered
at the head and foot of the bed.
Our shadows sprang here and there.

At that moment our sign might
have coursed across the heavens,
and we had spared no one to watch.

\*

Our people are most vulnerable to loss
when we gather like this to one side,
around some death,

and try to weave it into our lives
– who can weave nothing but our ragged
routes across the desert.

And it is those among us
who most make the heavens their business
who go most deeply into this death-weaving.

As if the star might
spring from the dying mouth
or shoot from the agony of the eyes.

'We must not miss it,
however it comes.'
– If it comes.

\*

He stretched out his feet
and seemed to sink deeper in the bed,
and was still.

Sons no longer,
we pulled down his eyelids
and pushed the chin up gently to close his mouth,
and stood under the flapping roof.
Our shelter sheltered under the night.

*

Hides, furs and skins,
are our shelter and our garments.

We can weave nothing.

# Finistère

One . . .

I smelt the weird Atlantic.
Finistère . . .
          Finisterre . . .

The sea surface darkened. The land behind me,
and all its cells and cists, grew dark.
From a bald boulder on the cairn top
I spied out the horizon to the northwest
and sensed that minute imperfection again.
Where the last sunken ray withdrew . . .
A point of light?

A maggot of the possible
wriggled out of the spine
into the brain.

We hesitated before that wider sea
but our heads sang with purpose
and predatory peace.

And whose excited blood was that
fumbling our movements? Whose ghostly hunger
tunnelling our thoughts full of passages
smelling of death and clay and faint metals
and great stones in the darkness?

At no great distance out in the bay
the swell took us into its mercy,
grey upheaving slopes of water
sliding under us, collapsing,
crawling onward, mountainous.

Driven outward a day and a night
we held fast, numbed by the steady
might of the oceanic wind.

We drew close together, as one,
and turned inward, salt chaos
rolling in silence all around us,
and listened to our own mouths
mumbling in the sting of spray:
    – Ill wind end well
    mild mother
    on wild water pour peace

    who gave us our unrest
    whom we meet and unmeet
    in whose yearning shadow
    we erect our great uprights
    and settle fulfilled
    and build and are still
    unsettled, whose goggle gaze
    and holy howl we have scraped
    speechless on slabs of stone
    poolspirals opening on
    closing spiralpools
    and dances drilled in the rock
    in coil zigzag angle and curl
    river ripple earth ramp
    suncircle moonloop . . .
    in whose outflung service
    we nourished our hunger
    uprooted and came

    in whale hell

                gale gullet

    salt hole

            dark nowhere

   calm queen

             pour peace

The bad dream ended at last.
In the morning, in a sunny breeze,
bare headlands rose fresh out of the waves.
We entered a deep bay, lying open
to all the currents of the ocean.
We were further than anyone had ever been
and light-headed with exhaustion and relief
– three times we misjudged and were nearly driven
on the same rock.
                              (I had felt all this before . . .)
We steered in along a wall of mountain
and entered a quiet hall of rock echoing
to the wave-wash and our low voices.
I stood at the prow. We edged to a slope of stone.
I steadied myself. 'Our Father . . .', someone said
and there was a little laughter. I stood
searching a moment for the right words.
They fell silent. I chose the old words once more
and stepped out. At the solid shock
a dreamy power loosened at the base of my spine
and uncoiled and slid up through the marrow.
A flow of seawater over the rock fell back
with a she-hiss, plucking at my heel.
My tongue stumbled


Who
      is a breath
that makes the wind
that makes the wave
that makes     this     voice?

Who
      is the bull with seven scars
the hawk on the cliff
the salmon sunk in his pool
the pool sunk in her soil

the animal's fury
the flower's fibre
a teardrop in the sun?

Who
        is the word that spoken
the spear springs
        and pours out terror
the spark springs
        and burns in the brain?

When men meet on the hill
dumb as stones in the dark
        (the craft knocked behind me)
who is the jack of all light?
Who goes in full into
the moon's interesting conditions?
Who fingers the sun's sink hole?
        (I went forward, reaching out)

# The Oldest Place

We approached the shore. Once more.

                              Repeated memory
shifted among the green-necked confused waves.
The sea wind and spray tugged and refreshed us,
but the stale reminder of our sin still clung.

We would need to dislodge
the flesh itself, to dislodge that
– shrivel back to the first drop
and be spat back shivering into
the dark beyond our first father.

                    *

We fished and fowled and chopped at the forest,
cooked and built, ploughed and planted,
danced and drank, all as before.
But worked inland, and got further.

And there was something in the way the land behaved:
passive, but responding. It grew under our hands.
We worked it like a dough to our requirements
yet it surprised us more than once
with a firm life of its own, as if
it used us.

              Once, as we were burying
one of our children, the half-dug grave
dampened, and overbrimmed, and the water
ran out over the land and would not stop
until the place had become a lake.

                    *

Year followed year.
The first skin blemishes appeared,
and it almost seemed we had been waiting for them.
The sickness and the dying began again.

To make things easier, we decided
to come together in one place.
We thought of the bare plain we found first,
with the standing stone: miles of dead clay
without a trace of a root or a living thing.
We gathered there and the sick died
and we covered them. Others fell sick
and we covered them, fewer and fewer.
A day came when I fell down by the great stone
alone, crying, at the middle of the stinking plain.

*

Night fell, and I lay there face down,
and I dreamed that my ghost stood up
and faint starry shadows everywhere
lifted themselves up and began
searching about among themselves for something,
hesitant at first, but quickly certain,
and all turning
               – muscular nothingnesses,
demons, animal-heads, wrestling vaguely toward me
reaching out terrible gifts into my face,
clawfuls of dripping cloth
and gold and silver things.
They passed through me . . .

               To the stone,
and draped it with their gifts, murmuring,
and dropped them about its base.
With each gift, the giver
sighed and melted away,
the black stone packed more
with dark radiance.

             And I dreamed
that my ghost moved toward it, hand on heart,
the other hand advanced . . .

                              And its glare
gathered like a pulse, and struck
on the withered plain of my own brain.

                    *

A draped black shaft under the starlight,
with bars and blocks and coils of restless metal
piled about it, and eyes hovering
above those abnormal stirrings.
A little higher, where there might have been branches,
a complex emptiness shimmered in front of the stars.

A shawl shifted on the top, dangled
black and silver, a crumpled face
with forehead torn crisscross, begging,
with tongue flapping,
and dropped to earth.

# Tao and Unfitness at Inistiogue on the River Nore

## *Noon*

The black flies kept nagging in the heat.
Swarms of them, at every step, snarled
off pats of cow dung spattered in the grass.

Move, if you move, like water.

The punts were knocking by the boathouse, at full tide.
Volumes of water turned the river curve
hushed under an insect haze.

                            Slips of white,
trout bellies, flicked in the corner of the eye
and dropped back onto the deep mirror.

Respond. Do not interfere. Echo.

Thick green woods along the opposite bank
climbed up from a root-dark recess
caved with mud-whitened leaves.

                   *

In a matter of hours all that water is gone,
except for a channel near the far side.
Muck and shingle and pools where the children
wade, stabbing flatfish.

## *Afternoon*

Inistiogue itself is perfectly lovely,
like a typical English village, but a bit sullen.
Our voices echoed in sunny corners
among the old houses; we admired
the stonework and gateways, the interplay
of roofs and angled streets.

33

The square, with its 'village green', lay empty.
The little shops had hardly anything.
The Protestant church was guarded by a woman
of about forty, a retainer, spastic
and indistinct, who drove us out.

An obelisk to the Brownsfoords and a Victorian
Celto-Gothic drinking fountain, erected
by a Tighe widow for the villagers,
'erected' in the centre. An astronomical-looking
sundial stood sentry on a platform
on the corner where High Street went up out of the square.

We drove up, past a long-handled water pump
placed at the turn, with an eye to the effect,
then out of the town for a quarter of a mile
above the valley, and came to the dead gate
of Woodstock, once home of the Tighes.

\*

The great ruin presented its flat front
at us, sunstruck. The children disappeared.
Eleanor picked her way around a big fallen branch
and away along the face toward the outbuildings.
I took the grassy front steps and was gathered up
in a brick-red stillness. A rook clattered out of the dining room.

A sapling, hooked thirty feet up
in a cracked corner, held out a ghost-green
cirrus of leaves. Cavities
of collapsed fireplaces connected silently
about the walls. Deserted spaces, complicated
by door-openings everywhere.

There was a path up among bushes and nettles
over the beaten debris, then a drop, where bricks
and plaster and rafters had fallen into the kitchens.
A line of small choked arches . . . The pantries, possibly.

Be still, as though pure.

A brick, and its dust, fell.

## Nightfall

The trees we drove under in the dusk
as we threaded back along the river through the woods
were no mere dark growth, but a flitting-place
for ragged feeling, old angers and rumours . . .

Black and Tan ghosts up there, at home
on the Woodstock heights: an iron mouth
scanning the Kilkenny road: the house
gutted by the townspeople and burned to ruins . . .

The little Ford we met, and inched past, full of men
we had noticed along the river bank during the week,
disappeared behind us into a fifty-year-old night.
Even their caps and raincoats . . .

Sons, or grandsons. Poachers.
                              Mud-tasted salmon
slithering in a plastic bag around the boot,
bloodied muscles, disputed since King John.

The ghosts of daughters of the family
waited in the uncut grass as we drove
down to our mock-Austrian lodge and stopped.

*

We untied the punt in the half-light, and pushed out
to take a last hour on the river, until night.
We drifted, but stayed almost still.
The current underneath us
and the tide coming back to the full
cancelled in a gleaming calm, punctuated
by the plop of fish.

Down on the water . . . at eye level . . . in the little light
remaining overhead . . . the mayfly passed in a loose drift,
thick and frail, a hatch slow with sex,
separate morsels trailing their slack filaments,
olive, pale evening dun, imagoes, unseen eggs
dropping from the air, subimagoes, the river filled
with their nymphs ascending and excited trout.

Be subtle, as though not there.

We were near the island – no more than a dark mass
on a sheet of silver – when a man appeared in midriver
quickly and with scarcely a sound, his paddle touching
left and right of the prow, with a sack behind him.
The flat cot's long body slid past effortless
as a fish, sinewing from side to side,
as he passed us and vanished.

# JOHN MONTAGUE

## The Trout

Flat on the bank I parted
Rushes to ease my hands
In the water without a ripple
And tilt them slowly downstream
To where he lay, tendril light,
In his fluid sensual dream.

Bodiless lord of creation
I hung briefly above him
Savouring my own absence
Senses expanding in the slow
Motion, the photographic calm
That grows before action.

As the curve of my hands
Swung under his body
He surged, with visible pleasure.
I was so preternaturally close
I could count every stipple
But still cast no shadow, until

The two palms crossed in a cage
Under the lightly pulsing gills.
Then (entering my own enlarged
Shape, which rode on the water)
I gripped. To this day I can
Taste his terror on my hands.

# Like Dolmens Round My Childhood, the Old People

Like dolmens round my childhood, the old people.

Jamie MacCrystal sang to himself,
A broken song without tune, without words;
He tipped me a penny every pension day,
Fed kindly crusts to winter birds.
When he died, his cottage was robbed,
Mattress and money box torn and searched.
Only the corpse they didn't disturb.

Maggie Owens was surrounded by animals,
A mongrel bitch and shivering pups,
Even in her bedroom a she-goat cried.
She was a well of gossip defiled,
Fanged chronicler of a whole countryside:
Reputed a witch, all I could find
Was her lonely need to deride.

The Nialls lived along a mountain lane
Where heather bells bloomed, clumps of foxglove.
All were blind, with Blind Pension and Wireless,
Dead eyes serpent-flicked as one entered
To shelter from a downpour of mountain rain.
Crickets chirped under the rocking hearthstone
Until the muddy sun shone out again.

Mary Moore lived in a crumbling gatehouse,
Famous as Pisa for its leaning gable.
Bag-apron and boots, she tramped the fields
Driving lean cattle from a miry stable.
A by-word for fierceness, she fell asleep
Over love stories, *Red Star* and *Red Circle*,
Dreamed of gypsy love rites, by firelight sealed.

Wild Billy Eagleson married a Catholic servant girl
When all his Loyal family passed on:
We danced round him shouting 'To Hell with King Billy,'
And dodged from the arc of his flailing blackthorn.
Forsaken by both creeds, he showed little concern
Until the Orange drums banged past in the summer
And bowler and sash aggressively shone.

Curate and doctor trudged to attend them,
Through knee-deep snow, through summer heat,
From main road to lane to broken path,
Gulping the mountain air with painful breath.
Sometimes they were found by neighbours,
Silent keepers of a smokeless hearth,
Suddenly cast in the mould of death.

Ancient Ireland, indeed! I was reared by her bedside,
The rune and the chant, evil eye and averted head,
Fomorian fierceness of family and local feud.
Gaunt figures of fear and of friendliness,
For years they trespassed on my dreams,
Until once, in a standing circle of stones,
I felt their shadows pass

Into that dark permanence of ancient forms.

# Woodtown Manor

*for Morris Graves*

### 1

Here the delicate dance of silence,
The quick step of the robin,
The sudden skittering rush of the wren:
Minute essences move in and out of creation
Until the skin of soundlessness forms again.

Part order, part wilderness,
Water creates its cadenced illusion
Of glaucous, fluent growth;
Fins raised, as in a waking dream,
Bright fish probe their painted stream.

Imaginary animals harbour here:
The young fox coiled in its covert,
Bright-eyed and mean, the baby bird:
The heron, like a tilted italic,
Illuminating the gospel of the absurd.

And all the menagerie of the living marvellous:
Stone shape of toad,
Flicker of insect life,
Shift of wind touched grass
As though a beneficent spirit stirred.

### 2

Twin deities hover in Irish air
Reconciling poles of east and west;
The detached and sensual Indian God,
Franciscan dream of gentleness:
Gravity of Georgian manor
Approves, with classic stare,
Their dual disciplines of tenderness.

# All Legendary Obstacles

All legendary obstacles lay between
Us, the long imaginary plain,
The monstrous ruck of mountains
And, swinging across the night,
Flooding the Sacramento, San Joaquin,
The hissing drift of winter rain.

All day I waited, shifting
Nervously from station to bar
As I saw another train sail
By, the *San Francisco Chief* or
*Golden Gate*, water dripping
From great flanged wheels.

At midnight you came, pale
Above the negro porter's lamp.
I was too blind with rain
And doubt to speak, but
Reached from the platform
Until our chilled hands met.

You had been travelling for days
With an old lady, who marked
A neat circle on the glass
With her glove, to watch us
Move into the wet darkness
Kissing, still unable to speak.

# King & Queen

Jagged head
of warrior, bird
of prey, surveying space

side by side
they squat, the pale
deities of this place

giant arms
slant to the calm
of lap, kneebone;

blunt fingers
splay to caress
a rain-hollowed stone

towards which
the landscape of five parishes
tends, band after band

of terminal,
peewit haunted,
cropless bogland.

JOHN MONTAGUE

# Last Journey

I.M. *James Montague*

We stand together
on the windy platform;
how crisp the rails
running out of sight
through the wet fields!

Carney, the station master,
is peering over
his frosted window:
the hand of the signal
points down.

Crowned with churns
a cart creaks up the
incline of Main Street
to the sliding doors
of the Co-Op.

A smell of coal,
the train is coming . . .
you climb slowly in,
propped by my hand to
a seat, back to the engine,

and we leave, waving
a plume of black smoke
over the rushy meadows,
small hills & hidden villages –
Beragh, Carrickmore,

Pomeroy, Fintona –
placenames that sigh
like a pressed melodeon
across this forgotten
Northern landscape.

# A Lost Tradition

All around, shards of a lost tradition:
From the Rough Field I went to school
In the Glen of the Hazels. Close by
Was the bishopric of the Golden Stone;
The cairn of Carleton's homesick poem.

Scattered over the hills, tribal-
And placenames, uncultivated pearls.
No rock or ruin, dun or dolmen
But showed memory defying cruelty
Through an image-encrusted name.

The heathery gap where the Rapparee,
Shane Barnagh, saw his brother die –
On a summer's day the dying sun
Stained its colours to crimson:
So breaks the heart, Brish-mo-Cree.

The whole landscape a manuscript
We had lost the skill to read,
A part of our past disinherited;
But fumbled, like a blind man,
Along the fingertips of instinct.

The last Gaelic speaker in the parish
When I stammered my school Irish
One Sunday after mass, crinkled
A rusty litany of praise:
*Tá an Ghaeilge againn arís . . .*[1]

*Tír Eoghain*: Land of Owen,
Province of the O'Niall;
The ghostly tread of O'Hagan's
Barefoot gallowglasses marching
To merge forces in Dun Geanainn

Push southward to Kinsale!
Loudly the war-cry is swallowed
In swirls of black rain and fog
As Ulster's pride, Elizabeth's foemen,
Founder in a Munster bog.

[1] We have the Irish again.

# A Grafted Tongue

(Dumb,
bloodied, the severed
head now chokes to
speak another tongue –

As in
a long suppressed dream,
some stuttering garb-
led ordeal of my own)

An Irish
child weeps at school
repeating its English.
After each mistake

The master
gouges another mark
on the tally stick
hung about its neck

Like a bell
on a cow, a hobble
on a straying goat.
To slur and stumble

In shame
the altered syllables
of your own name:
to stray sadly home

And find
the turf-cured width
of your parents' hearth
growing slowly alien:

In cabin
and field, they still
speak the old tongue.
You may greet no one.

To grow
a second tongue, as
harsh a humiliation
as twice to be born.

Decades later
that child's grandchild's
speech stumbles over lost
syllables of an old order.

# The Wild Dog Rose

### I

I go to say goodbye to the *cailleach*[1]
that terrible figure who haunted my childhood
but no longer harsh, a human being
merely, hurt by event.

            The cottage,
circled by trees, weathered to admonitory
shapes of desolation by the mountain winds,
straggles into view. The rank thistles
and leathery bracken of untilled fields
stretch behind with – a final outcrop –
the hooped figure by the roadside,
its retinue of dogs

               which give tongue
as I approach, with savage, whining cries
so that she slowly turns, a moving nest
of shawls and rags, to view, to stare
the stranger down.

              And I feel again
that ancient awe, the terror of a child
before the great hooked nose, the cheeks
dewlapped with dirt, the staring blue
of the sunken eyes, the mottled claws
clutching a stick

             but now hold
and return her gaze, to greet her,
as she greets me, in friendliness.
Memories have wrought reconciliation
between us, we talk in ease at last,
like old friends, lovers almost,
sharing secrets

         of neighbours
she quarrelled with, who now lie
in Garvaghey graveyard, beyond all hatred;
of my family and hers, how she never married,
though a man came asking in her youth.
'You would be loath to leave your own,'
she sighs, 'and go among strangers' –
his parish ten miles off.

         For sixty years
since she has lived alone, in one place.
Obscurely honoured by such confidences,
I idle by the summer roadside, listening,
while the monologue falters, continues,
rehearsing the small events of her life.
The only true madness is loneliness,
the monotonous voice in the skull
that never stops
         because never heard.

## 2

And there
where the dog rose shines in the hedge
she tells me a story so terrible
that I try to push it away,
my bones melting.

         Late at night
a drunk came beating at her door
to break it in, the bolt snapping
from the soft wood, the thin mongrels
rushing to cut, but yelping as
he whirls with his farm boots
to crush their skulls.

         In the darkness
they wrestle, two creatures crazed

with loneliness, the smell of the
decaying cottage in his nostrils
like a drug, his body heavy on hers,
the tasteless trunk of a seventy year
old virgin, which he rummages while
she battles for life

     bony fingers
reaching desperately to push
against his bull neck. 'I prayed
to the Blessed Virgin herself
for help and after a time
I broke his grip.'

    He rolls
to the floor, snores asleep,
while she cowers until dawn
and the dogs' whimpering starts
him awake, to lurch back across
the wet bog.

     3

    And still
the dog rose shines in the hedge.
Petals beaten wide by rain, it
sways slightly, at the tip of a
slender, tangled, arching branch
which, with her stick, she gathers
into us.

    'The wild rose
is the only rose without thorns,'
she says, holding a wet blossom
for a second, in a hand knotted
as the knob of her stick.
'Whenever I see it, I remember
the Holy Mother of God and
all she suffered.'

                    Briefly
the air is strong with the smell
of that weak flower, offering
its crumbled yellow cup
and pale bleeding lips
fading to white

                        at the rim
of each bruised and heart-
shaped petal.

---

[1] An old woman, a hag.

# At Last

A small sad man with a hat
he came through the customs at Cobh
carrying a roped suitcase and
something in me began to contract

but also to expand. We stood,
his grown sons, seeking for words
which under the clouding mist
turn to clumsy, laughing gestures.

At the mouth of the harbour lay
the squat shape of the liner
hooting farewell, with the waves
striking against Spike Island's grey.

We drove across Ireland that day,
lush river valleys of Cork, russet
of the Central Plain, landscapes
exotic to us Northerners, halting

only in a snug beyond Athlone
to hear a broadcast I had done.
How strange in that cramped room
the disembodied voice, the silence

after, as we looked at each other!
Slowly our eyes managed recognition.
'Well done' he said, raising his glass:
father and son at ease, at last.

# Herbert Street Revisited

*for Madeleine*

### I

A light is burning late
in this Georgian Dublin street:
someone is leading our old lives!

And our black cat scampers again
through the wet grass of the convent garden
upon his masculine errands.

The pubs shut: a released bull,
Behan shoulders up the street,
topples into our basement, roaring 'John!'

A pony and donkey cropped flank
by flank under the trees opposite;
short neck up, long neck down,

as Nurse Mullen knelt by her bedside
to pray for her lost Mayo hills,
the bruised bodies of Easter Volunteers.

Animals, neighbours, treading the pattern
of one time and place into history,
like our early marriage, while

tall windows looked down upon us
from walls flushed light pink or salmon
watching and enduring succession.

### 2

As I leave, you whisper,
'don't betray our truth'
and like a ghost dancer,
invoking a lost tribal strength

53

I halt in tree-fed darkness

to summon back our past,
and celebrate a love that eased
so kindly, the dying bone,
enabling the spirit to sing
of old happiness, when alone.

### 3

So put the leaves back on the tree,
put the tree back in the ground,
let Brendan trundle his corpse down
the street singing, like Molly Malone.

Let the black cat, tiny emissary
of our happiness, streak again
through the darkness, to fall soft
clawed into a landlord's dustbin.

Let Nurse Mullen take the last
train to Westport, and die upright
in her chair, facing a window
warm with the blue slopes of Nephin.

And let the pony and donkey come –
look, someone has left the gate open –
like hobbyhorses linked in
the slow motion of a dream

parading side by side, down
the length of Herbert Street,
rising and falling, lifting
their hooves through the moonlight.

# A Flowering Absence

How can one make an absence flower,
lure a desert to sudden bloom?
Taut with terror, I rehearse a time
when I was taken from a sick room:
as before from your flayed womb.

And given away to be fostered
wherever charity could afford.
I came back, lichened with sores,
from the care of still poorer
immigrants, new washed from the hold.

I bless their unrecorded names,
whose need was greater than mine,
wet nurses from tenement darkness
giving suck for a time,
because their milk was plentiful

Or their own children gone.
They were the first to succour
that still terrible thirst of mine,
a thirst for love and knowledge,
to learn something of that time

Of confusion, poverty, absence.
Year by year, I track it down
intent for a hint of evidence,
seeking to manage the pain –
how a mother gave away her son.

I took the subway to the hospital
in darkest Brooklyn, to call
on the old nun who nursed you
through the travail of my birth
to come on another cold trail.

*Sister Virgilius, how strange!*
*She died, just before you came.*
*She was delirious, rambling of all*
*her old patients; she could well*
*have remembered your mother's name.*

Around the bulk of St Catherine's
another wild, raunchier Brooklyn:
as tough a territory as I've known,
strutting young Puerto Rican hoods,
flash of blade, of bicycle chain.

Mother, my birth was the death
of your love life, the last man
to flutter near your tender womb:
a neonlit barsign winks off & on,
*motherfucka, thass your name.*

There is an absence, real as presence.
In the mornings I hear my daughter
chuckle, with runs of sudden joy.
Hurt, she rushes to her mother,
as I never could, a whining boy.

All roads wind backwards to it.
An unwanted child, a primal hurt.
I caught fever on the big boat
that brought us away from America
— away from my lost parents.

Surely my father loved me,
teaching me to croon, *Ragtime Cowboy*
*Joe, swaying in his saddle*
*as he sings*, as he did, drunkenly
dropping in from the speakeasy.

So I found myself shipped back
to his home, in an older country,
transported to a previous century,

where his sisters restored me,
natural love flowering around me.

And the hurt ran briefly underground
to break out in a schoolroom
where I was taunted by a mistress
who hunted me publicly down
to near speechlessness.

*So this is our brightest infant?*
*Where did he get that outlandish accent?*
*What do you expect, with no parents,*
*sent back from some American slum:*
*none of you are to speak like him!*

Stammer, impediment, stutter:
she had found my lode of shame,
and soon I could no longer utter
those magical words I had begun
to love, to dolphin delight in.

And not for two stumbling decades
would I manage to speak straight again.
Grounded for the second time
my tongue became a rusted hinge
until the sweet oils of poetry

eased it and light flooded in.

# The Locket

Sing a last song
for the lady who has gone,
fertile source of guilt and pain.
*The worst birth in the annals of Brooklyn*,
that was my cue to come on,
my first claim to fame.

Naturally, she longed for a girl,
and all my infant curls of brown
couldn't excuse my double blunder
coming out, both the wrong sex,
and the wrong way around.
Not readily forgiven.

So you never nursed me
and when all my father's songs
couldn't sweeten the lack of money,
*when poverty comes through the door
love flies up the chimney*,
your favourite saying.

Then you gave me away,
might never have known me,
if I had not cycled down
to court you like a young man,
teasingly untying your apron,
drinking by the fire, yarning

Of your wild, young days
which didn't last 'ong, for you,
lovely Molly, the belle of your small town,
landed up mournful and chill
as the constant rain that lashes it,
wound into your cocoon of pain.

Standing in that same hallway,
*don't come again*, you say, roughly,
*I start to get fond of you, John,*
*and then you are up and gone;*
the harsh logic of a forlorn woman
resigned to being alone.

And still, mysterious blessing,
I never knew, until you were gone,
that, always around your neck,
you wore an oval locket
with an old picture in it,
of a child in Brooklyn.

# Deer Park

A flourish of silver
trumpets as the royal
favourite is prepared
for the swansdown bed.

Fingers and toes
palpable, succulent
as those pert curves
of mouth, snub nose.

The string of pearls
on her stomach folds
luminously pendent
like rare raindrops

While a pair of pure-
bred hunting hounds
snuffle her plump
and perfumed hands.

A candid light streams
from such guileless,
dimpled nakedness, such
cherubic openness!

And the fillet of
gold she bears so
demurely in honour
of her sovereign master,

Upon her piled strands
of auburn Irish hair,
looped to reveal her
golden neck collar.

A king's treasure
of roseate flesh
caught on canvas
for a king's pleasure

With a full quiver
of arrows, a dangling
brace of pheasant
all stamped: royal property.

# RICHARD MURPHY

## Sailing to an Island

The boom above my knees lifts, and the boat
Drops, and the surge departs, departs, my cheek
Kissed and rejected, kissed, as the gaff sways
A tangent, cuts the infinite sky to red
Maps, and the mast draws eight and eight across
Measureless blue, the boatmen sing or sleep.

We point all day for our chosen island,
Clare, with its crags purpled by legend:
There under castles the hot O'Malleys,
Daughters of Granuaile, the pirate queen
Who boarded a Turk with a blunderbuss,
Comb red hair and assemble cattle.
Across the shelved Atlantic groundswell
Plumbed by the sun's kingfisher rod,
We sail to locate in sea, earth and stone
The myth of a shrewd and brutal swordswoman
Who piously endowed an abbey.
Seven hours we try against wind and tide,
Tack and return, making no headway.
The north wind sticks like a gag in our teeth.

Encased in a mirage, steam on the water,
Loosely we coast where hideous rocks jag,
An acropolis of cormorants, an extinct
Volcano where spiders spin, a purgatory
Guarded by hags and bristled with breakers.

The breeze as we plunge slowly stiffens:
There are hills of sea between us and land,
Between our hopes and the island harbour.

A child vomits. The boat veers and bucks.
There is no refuge on the gannet's cliff.
We are far, far out: the hull is rotten,
The spars are splitting, the rigging is frayed,
And our helmsman laughs uncautiously.
What of those who must earn their living
On the ribald face of a mad mistress?
We in holiday fashion know
This is the boat that belched its crew
Dead on the shingle in the Cleggan disaster.

Now she dips, and the sail hits the water.
She luffs to a squall; is struck; and shudders.
Someone is shouting. The boom, weak as scissors,
Has snapped. The boatman is praying.
Orders thunder and canvas cannonades.
She smothers in spray. We still have a mast;
The oar makes a boom. I am told to cut
Cords out of fishing-lines, fasten the jib.
Ropes lash my cheeks. Ease! Ease at last:
She swings to leeward, we can safely run.
Washed over rails our Clare Island dreams,
With storm behind us we straddle the wakeful
Waters that draw us headfast to Inishbofin.

The bows rock as she overtakes the surge.
We neither sleep nor sing nor talk,
But look to the land where the men are mowing.
What will the islanders think of our folly?

The whispering spontaneous reception committee
Nods and smokes by the calm jetty.
Am I jealous of these courteous fishermen
Who hand us ashore, for knowing the sea

Intimately, for respecting the storm
That took nine of their men on one bad night
And five from Rossadillisk in this very boat?
Their harbour is sheltered. They are slow to tell
The story again. There is local pride
In their home-built ships.
We are advised to return next day by the mail.

But tonight we stay, drinking with people
Happy in the monotony of boats,
Bringing the catch to the Cleggan market,
Cultivating fields, or retiring from America
With enough to soak till morning or old age.

The bench below my knees lifts, and the floor
Drops, and the words depart, depart, with faces
Blurred by the smoke. An old man grips my arm,
His shot eyes twitch, quietly dissatisfied.
He has lost his watch, an American gold
From Boston gas-works. He treats the company
To the secretive surge, the sea of his sadness.
I slip outside, fall among stones and nettles,
Crackling dry twigs on an elder tree,
While an accordion drones above the hill.

Later, I reach a room, where the moon stares
Cobwebbed through the window. The tide has ebbed,
Boats are careened in the harbour. Here is a bed.

# The Last Galway Hooker

Where the Corrib river chops through the Claddagh
To sink in the tide-race its rattling chain
The boatwright's hammer chipped across the water

Ribbing this hooker, while a reckless gun
Shook the limestone quay-wall, after the Treaty
Had brought civil war to this fisherman's town.

That 'tasty' carpenter from Connemara, Cloherty,
Helped by his daughter, had half-planked the hull
In his eightieth year, when at work he died,

And she did the fastening, and caulked her well,
The last boat completed with old Galway lines.
Several seasons at the drift-nets she paid

In those boom-years, working by night in channels
With trammel and spillet and an island crew,
Tea-stew on turf in the pipe-black forecastle,

Songs of disasters wailed on the quay
When the tilt of the water heaved the whole shore.
'She was lucky always the *Ave Maria*,'

With her brown barked sails, and her hull black tar,
Her forest of oak ribs and the larchwood planks,
The cavern-smelling hold bulked with costly gear,

Fastest in the race to the gull-marked banks,
What harbour she hived in, there she was queen
And her crew could afford to stand strangers drinks,

Till the buyers failed in nineteen twenty-nine,
When the cheapest of fish could find no market,
Were dumped overboard, the price down to nothing;

Until to her leisure a fisher priest walked
By the hungry dockside, full of her name,
Who made a cash offer, and the owners took it.

Then like a girl given money and a home
With no work but pleasure for her man to perform
She changed into white sails, her hold made room

For hammocks and kettles, the touch and perfume
Of priestly hands. So now she's a yacht
With pitch-pine spars and Italian hemp ropes,

Smooth-running ash-blocks expensively bought
From chandlers in Dublin, two men get jobs
Copper-painting her keel and linseeding her throat,

While at weekends, nephews and nieces in mobs
Go sailing on picnics to the hermit islands,
Come home flushed with health having hooked a few dabs.


Munich, submarines, and the war's demands
Of workers to feed invaded that party
Like fumes of the diesel the dope of her sails,

When the Canon went east into limed sheep-lands
From the stone and reed patches of lobstermen
Having sold her to one on Cleggan Quay,

Who was best of the boatsmen from Inishbofin,
She his best buy. He shortened the mast, installed
A new 'Ailsa Craig', made a hold of her cabin,

Poured over the deck thick tar slightly boiled;
Every fortnight he drained the sump in the bilge
'To preserve the timbers.' All she could do, fulfilled.

The sea, good to gamblers, let him indulge
His fear when she rose winding her green shawl
And his pride when she lay calm under his pillage:

And he never married, was this hooker's lover,
Always ill-at-ease in houses or on hills,
Waiting for weather, or mending broken trawls:

Bothered by women no more than by the moon,
Not concerned with money beyond the bare need,
In this boat's bows he sheathed his life's harpoon.

A neap-tide of work, then a spring of liquor
Were the tides that alternately pulled his soul,
Now on a pitching deck with nets to hand-haul,

Then passing Sunday propped against a barrel
Winding among words like a sly helmsman
Till stories gathered around him in a shoal.

She was Latin blessed, holy water shaken
From a small whiskey bottle by a surpliced priest,
Madonnas wafered on every bulkhead,

Oil-grimed by the diesel, and her luck lasted
Those twenty-one years of skill buoyed by prayers,
Strength forged by dread from his drowned ancestors.

She made him money and again he lost it
In the fisherman's fiction of turning farmer:
The cost of timber and engine spares increased,

Till a phantom hurt him, ribs on a shore,
A hulk each tide rattles that will never fish,
Sunk back in the sand, a story finished.


We met here last summer, nineteen fifty-nine,
Far from the missiles, the moon-shots, the money,
And we drank looking out on the island quay,

When his crew were in London drilling a motorway.
Old age had smoothed his barnacled will,
One calm evening he sold me the *Ave Maria*.

Then he was alone, stunned like a widower –
Relics and rowlocks pronging from the wall,
A pot of boiling garments, winter everywhere,

Especially in his bones, watching things fall,
Hooks of three-mile spillets, trammels at the foot
Of the unused double-bed – his mind threaded with all

The marline of his days twined within that boat,
His muscles' own shackles then staying the storm
Which now snap to bits like frayed thread.


So I chose to renew her, to rebuild, to prolong
For a while the spliced yards of yesterday.
Carpenters were enrolled, the ballast and the dung

Of cattle he'd carried lifted from the hold,
The engine removed, and the stale bilge scoured.
De Valera's daughter hoisted the Irish flag

At her freshly adzed mast this Shrove Tuesday,
Stepped while afloat between the tackle of the *Topaz*
And the *St John*, by Bofin's best boatsmen,

All old as himself. Her skilful sailmaker,
Her inherited boatwright, her dream-tacking steersman
Picked up the tools of their interrupted work,

And in memory's hands this hooker was restored.
Old men my instructors, and with all new gear
May I handle her well down tomorrow's sea-road.

RICHARD MURPHY

# *from* The Battle of Aughrim

## *Casement's Funeral*

After the noose, and the black diary deeds
Gossiped, his fame roots in prison lime:
The hanged bones burn, a revolution seeds.
Now Casement's skeleton is flying home.

A gun salutes, the troops slow-march, our new
Nation atones for her shawled motherland
Whose welcome gaoled him when a U-boat threw
This rebel quixote soaked on Banna Strand.

Soldiers in green guard the draped catafalque
With chalk remains of once ambiguous bone
Which fathered nothing till the traitor's dock
Hurt him to tower in legend like Wolfe Tone.

From gaol yard to the Liberator's tomb
Pillared in frost, they carry the freed ash,
Transmuted relic of a death-cell flame
Which purged for martyrdom the diarist's flesh.

On the small screen I watch the packed cortège
Pace from High Mass. Rebels in silk hats now
Exploit the grave with an old comrade's speech:
White hair tossed, a black cape flecked with snow.

## *Slate*

Slate I picked from a nettlebed
Had history, my neighbour said.

To quarry it, men had to row
Five miles, twelve centuries ago.

An inch thick, it hung watertight
Over monks' litany by candlelight:

Till stormed by Viking raids, it slipped.
Four hundred years overlapped.

Pirates found it and roofed a fort
A mile west, commanding the port.

Red-clawed choughs perched on it saw
Guards throw priests to the sea's jaw.

Repaired to succour James the Shit
The battle of Aughrim shattered it.

Through centuries of penal gale
Hedge-scholars huddled where it fell.

Pegged above a sea-wormed rafter
It rattled over landlord's laughter.

Windy decades pined across
Barrack roof, rebellion, moss.

This week I paved my garden path
With slate St Colman nailed on lath.

## Rapparees

Out of the earth, out of the air, out of the water
And slinking nearer the fire, in groups they gather:
Once he looked like a bird, but now a beggar.

This fish rainbows out of a pool: 'Give me bread!'
He fins along the lake-shore with the starved.
Green eyes glow in the night from clumps of weed.

The water is still. A rock or the nose of an otter
Jars the surface. Whistle of rushes or bird?
It steers to the bank, it lands as a pikeman armed.

With flint and bundles of straw a limestone hall
Is gutted, a noble family charred in its sleep,
And they gloat by moonlight on a mound of rubble.

The highway trees are gibbets where seventeen rot
Who were caught last week in a cattle-raid.
The beasts are lowing. 'Listen!' 'Stifle the guard!'

In a pinewood thickness an earthed-over charcoal fire
Forges them guns. They melt lead stripped from a steeple
For ball. At the whirr of a snipe each can disappear

Terrified as a bird in a gorse-bush fire,
To delve like a mole or mingle like a nightjar
Into the earth, into the air, into the water.

## *Luttrell's Death*

Luttrell, Master of Luttrellstown
Sat in a gold and red sedan
The burden of a hungry urchin
And a weak old man
Barefoot on cobbles in the midnight rain,
Up torchlit quays from a coffee shop
Where after supper, the silver cup
Lifted, a fop had said,
'It's time to bury Aughrim's dead.'

A poor smell of ordure
Seeped through his embroidered chair,
He slid the glass open for air,
Waved off a beggar groping at the door
And watched six black dray-horses cross
The river. 'Let the traitor pass.'
He felt his pocket full of pebbles
Which he used at Mass in straw-roofed chapels
To lob at little girls.

The chair slewed at his town house,
Flambeaus, footmen in place,
And plunked him down.
He'd sold his country to preserve his class,
The gutters hissed: but that was done
Twenty-six years ago, he said,
Had they not buried Aughrim's dead?
Standing under grey cut stone
A shadow cocked a gun.

No one betrayed his assassin
Although the Duke of Bolton
Offered three hundred pounds' reward.
The crowd spat on Henry Luttrell's coffin.
Eighty years after his murder
Masked men, inspired by Wolfe Tone,
Burst open his tomb's locks,
Lit a stub of wax
And smashed the skull with a pickaxe.

## Patrick Sarsfield's Portrait

Sarsfield, great-uncle in the portrait's grime,
Your emigration built your fame at home.
Landlord who never racked, you gave your rent
To travel with your mounted regiment.

Hotly you duelled for our name abroad
In Restoration wig, with German sword,
Wanting a vicious murder thrust to prove
Your Celtic passion and our Lady's love.

Gallant at Sedgemoor, cutting down for James
The scythe-armed yokels Monmouth led like lambs,
You thought it needed God's anointed king
To breathe our Irish winter into spring.

Your ashwood lance covered the Boyne retreat:
When the divine perfidious monarch's rout
From kindred enemy and alien friend
Darkened the land, you kindled Ireland.

At Limerick besieged, you led the dance:
'If this had failed, I would have gone to France.'
When youths lit brandy in a pewter dish
You were their hazel nut and speckled fish.

A French duke scoffed: 'They need no cannonballs
But roasted apples to assault these walls.'
Sarsfield, through plague and shelling you held out;
You saved the city, lost your own estate.

Shunning pitched battle was your strategy:
You chose rapparee mountain routes to try
The enemy's morale, and blew his train
Of cannon skywards in the soft night rain.

Your king, who gave St Ruth supreme command,
Mistrusted you, native of Ireland.
'Await further orders,' you were told
At Aughrim, when your plan was overruled.

You stood, while brother officers betrayed
By going, and six thousand Irish died.
Then you assumed command, but veered about:
Chose exile in your courteous conqueror's boat.

'Change kings with us, and we will fight again,'
You said, but sailed off with ten thousand men;
While women clutched the hawsers in your wake,
Drowning – it was too late when you looked back.

Only to come home stronger had you sailed:
Successes held you, and the French prevailed.
Coolly you triumphed where you wanted least,
On Flemish cornfield or at Versailles feast.

Berwick the bastard sired by James the Shit
Immortalized you with no head but grit.
He took your widow Honor for his wife
When serving the Sun King you lost your life.

We loved you, horseman of the white cockade,
Above all, for your last words, 'Would to God
This wound had been for Ireland.' Cavalier,
You feathered with the wild geese our despair.

# Seals at High Island

The calamity of seals begins with jaws.
Born in caverns that reverberate
With endless malice of the sea's tongue
Clacking on shingle, they learn to bark back
In fear and sadness and celebration.
The ocean's mouth opens forty feet wide
And closes on a morsel of their rock.

Swayed by the thrust and backfall of the tide,
A dappled grey bull and a brindled cow
Copulate in the green water of a cove.
I watch from a cliff-top, trying not to move.
Sometimes they sink and merge into black shoals;
Then rise for air, his muzzle on her neck,
Their winged feet intertwined as a fishtail.

She opens her fierce mouth like a scarlet flower
Full of white seeds; she holds it open long
At the sunburst in the music of their loving;
And cries a little. But I must remember
How far their feelings are from mine marooned.
If there are tears at this holy ceremony
Theirs are caused by brine and mine by breeze.

When the great bull withdraws his rod, it glows
Like a carnelian candle set in jade.
The cow ripples ashore to feed her calf;
While an old rival, eyeing the deed with hate,
Swims to attack the tired triumphant god.
They rear their heads above the boiling surf,
Their terrible jaws open, jetting blood.

At nightfall they haul out, and mourn the drowned,
Playing to the sea sadly their last quartet,
An improvised requiem that ravishes

74

Reason, while ripping scale up like a net:
Brings pity trembling down the rocky spine
Of headlands, till the bitter ocean's tongue
Swells in their cove, and smothers their sweet song.

# The Reading Lesson

Fourteen years old, learning the alphabet,
He finds letters harder to catch than hares
Without a greyhound. Can't I give him a dog
To track them down, or put them in a cage?
He's caught in a trap, until I let him go,
Pinioned by 'Don't you want to learn to read?'
'I'll be the same man whatever I do.'

He looks at a page as a mule balks at a gap
From which a goat may hobble out and bleat.
His eyes jink from a sentence like flushed snipe
Escaping shot. A sharp word, and he'll mooch
Back to his piebald mare and bantam cock.
Our purpose is as tricky to retrieve
As mercury from a smashed thermometer.

'I'll not read anymore.' Should I give up?
His hands, long-fingered as a Celtic scribe's,
Will grow callous, gathering sticks or scrap;
Exploring pockets of the horny drunk
Loiterers at the fairs, giving them lice.
A neighbour chuckles. 'You can never tame
The wild duck: when his wings grow, he'll fly off.'

If books resembled roads, he'd quickly read:
But they're small farms to him, fenced by the page,
Ploughed into lines, with letters drilled like oats:
A field of tasks he'll always be outside.
If words were bank-notes, he would filch a wad;
If they were pheasants, they'd be in his pot
For breakfast, or if wrens he'd make them king.

# Gate Lodge

Two Irish yews, prickly green, poisonous,
Divide my entrance, tapering in trim gloom.
Old rookery buildings, pitch-pine resinous,
Wake up shell-shocked, welcoming you back home.

Barefoot a child skips from my hearth to touch
The wrought obsequious latch of lip-service;
Taking you in, between double gates, to reach
Beyond the ruts your mother's peerless place.

I face my forebear's relic, a neat sty
That hovelled with his brogue some grateful clod
Unearthed by famine; and I hear go by
Your souper choir school voice defrauding God.

Pigeon park, pheasant wood and snipe bog lie
Within my scope: your shotgun territory.

# PEARSE HUTCHINSON

## Málaga

*for Sammy Sheridan*

The scent of unseen jasmine on the warm night beach.

The tram along the sea road all the way from town
through its wide open sides drank unseen jasmine down.
Living was nothing all those nights but that strong flower,
whose hidden voice on darkness grew to such mad power
I could have sworn for once I travelled through full peace
and even love at last had perfect calm release
only by breathing in the unseen jasmine scent,
that ruled us and the summer every hour we went.

The tranquil unrushed wine drunk on the daytime beach.
Or from an open room all that our sight could reach
was heat, sea, light, unending images of peace;
and then at last the night brought jasmine's great release –
not images but calm uncovetous content,
the wide-eyed heart alert at rest in June's own scent.

In daytime's humdrum town from small child after child
we bought cluster on cluster of the star flower's wild
white widowed heads, re-wired on strong weed stalks they'd
    trimmed
to long green elegance; but still the whole month brimmed
at night along the beach with a strong voice like peace;
and each morning the mind stayed crisp in such release.

Some hint of certainty, still worth longing I could teach,
lies lost in a strength of jasmine down a summer beach.

# Be Born a Saint

*for Claude Tarnaud and Henriette de Champrel*

Be born a saint; or keep,
as natural and faithful as your nails,
a retinue of calm conformities,
and social artifice: both minor, and enough
to keep the prophets of the great hypocrisies
from rice-bowl-breaking, and from breaking
your glasses, or your fall –
or inviting you in only as a good turn,
something like a bragitóir,[1] your most grim
bousingot imprecation indulgently laughed 'with',
your lightest nonsense owlishly revered.

Be born a saint: with private means; or keep
some social graces, though society
appears ungracious; hating and noli me tangere
will seldom get you hated, but regarded
as an Untouchable – or an intangible –
oftener than you know, if less than you imagine;
when some rare force,
hateless, eager, and unhateable,
arrives and offers – by that time response
may be impossible, almost atrophied, a helpless
vaginismus, too slow. Unless, of course, you
become the bragitóir gone berserk, become literal:
burn down the Bourse, assault the Minister
of Picot-Edging in their brand of fact,
not only the kind in your own mind and poem.

Be born a saint; or keep
some calm irrelevant conformities: or else
love will take a turn for the worse
with every noble and ideally sensible refusal
to accept the loan of a tie from the cloakroom attendant,

with every wine-gum sucked furtively
all through Vexilla Regis,
with every pompous cliché in defence of love.
That's unattractive advice
from slow-learnt cowardice.

Failures in bravery are often listless: that learning
can hardly set me scrabbling in the glory-hole
for a greening evening-suit one size too large
the Minister of Civilization gave me years
before I disliked anyone; easier to wait,
beside the bed of delicately dying love,
for a typhoon or amazing medicine.
Love takes a long and garrulous time to die.

---

[1] In medieval Ireland, a buffoon who entertained his audience by farting.

# Look, No Hands

*for Ernie Hughes*

*Lengua sin manos, cuemo osas fablar?*
– Poema del Cid

I blame old women for buying paper roses,
yet pluck a dandelion: by the time
it reaches my lapel it's turned to paper.

I hate the winter, and blame drinkers
for hiding in dark pubs when the sun shines outside,
and could be enjoyed at sidewalk tables;
yet every time I visit a crowded beach
I bring a sun-ray lamp along.

I praise trust above all,
yet cannot let a friend post a letter
in case he might stop on the way for a drink.

I admire a stone for its hardness,
resembling it only in barrenness;
admire a butterfly's brightness,
resembling it only in brittleness.

I like speed, summer, the country roads,
but never could master a bike.
Believing in God because of the need to praise –
though fear alone, so far, makes me long to pray –
if granted another hundred years
I might learn
　　　　　　how to say prayers.

# Fleadh Cheoil[1]

Subtle capering on a simple thought,
the vindicated music soaring out
each other door in a mean twisting main street,
flute-player, fiddler and penny-whistler
concentrating on one sense only
such a wild elegance of energy gay and sad
few clouds of lust or vanity could form;
the mind kept cool, the heart kept warm;
therein the miracle, three days and nights
so many dances played and so much drinking done,
so many voices raised in singing but none
in anger nor any fist in harm –
Saint Patrick's Day in Cambridge Circus might
have been some other nation's trough of shame.

Hotel-back-room, pub-snug, and large open lounges
and the mean street like a Latin fête,
music for once taking all harm out –
from even the bunting's pathetic blunderings,
and the many mean publicans making money fast,
hand over fat fist, pouring the flat
western porter from black-chipped white enamel,
Dervorgilla's penitent chapel
crumbling arch archaic but east,
only music now releasing her people
like Sweeney's cousins on a branch unable
to find his words, but using music
for all articulateness.

But still the shabby county-town was full,
en fête; on fire with peace – for all
the black-and-white contortionists bred
from black and white enamel ever said.
From Easter Snow and Scartaglin

the men with nimble fingers came
in dowdy Sunday suits,
from Kirkintilloch and Ladbroke Grove came back
in flashy ties and frumpish hats,
to play an ancient music, make it new.
A stranger manner of telling than words can do,
a strange manner, both less and more than words or Bach,
but like, that Whitsuntide, stained-glass in summer,
high noon, rose window, Benedictbeuern pleasure,
and Seán Ó Neachtain's loving singing wood,
an Nollaig sa tSamhradh.[2]

Owls and eagles, clerks and navvies,
ex-British Tommies in drab civvies,
and glorious-patriots whose wild black brindled hair
stood up for the trench-coats they had no need to wear
that tranquil carnival weekend,
when all the boastful maladies got cured –
the faction-fighting magniloquence,
devoid of charity or amorous sense,
the sun-shunning pubs, the trips to Knock.

One said to me: 'There's heart in that',
pointing at: a thick-set man of middle age,
a thick red drinker's face,
and eyes as bright as good stained-glass,
who played on and on and on
a cheap tin-whistle, as if no race
for petty honours had ever come to pass
on earth, or his race to a stale pass;
tapping one black boot on a white flag,
and us crowding, craning, in at the door,
gaining, and storing up, the heart in that.
With him a boy about eighteen,
tall and thin, but, easy to be seen,
Clare still written all over him
despite his eighteen months among the trim

scaffoldings and grim digs of England;
resting his own tin-whistle for his mentor's riff,
pushing back, with a big red hand, the dank mousy quiff,
turning to me to say, 'You know what I think of it,
over there?

       Over there, you're free.'
Repeating the word 'free', as gay and sad as his music,
repeating the word, the large bright eyes convinced
of what the red mouth said, convinced beyond
shaming or furtiveness, a thousand preachers,
mothers and leader-writers wasting their breath
on the sweet, foggy, distant-city air.
Then he went on playing as if there never were
either a famed injustice or a parish glare.

*Ennis*

[1] A music festival.

[2] Christmas in Summer.

84

# Gaeltacht[1]

Bartley Costello, eighty years old,
sat in his silver-grey tweeds on a kitchen chair,
at his door in Carraroe, the sea only yards away,
smoking a pipe, with a pint of porter beside his boot:
'For the past twenty years I've eaten nothing only
periwinkles, my own hands got them off those rocks.
You're a quarter my age, if you'd stick to winkles
you'd live as long as me, and keep as spry.'

In the Liverpool Bar, at the North Wall,
on his way to join his children over there,
an old man looked at me, then down at his pint
of rich Dublin stout. He pointed at the black glass:
'Is lú í an Ghaeilge ná an t-uisce sa ngloine sin.'[2]

Beartla Confhaola, prime of his manhood,
driving between the redweed and the rock-fields,
driving through the sunny treeless quartz glory of Carna,
answered the foreigners' glib pity, pointing at the
small black cows: 'You won't get finer anywhere
than those black porry cattle.' In a pub near there,
one of the locals finally spoke to the townie:
'Labhraim le stráinséirí. Creidim gur chóir bheith
ag labhairt le stráinséirí.'[3] Proud as a man who'd claim:
'I made an orchard of a rock-field,
bougainvillaea clamber my turf-ricks.'

A Dublin tourist on a red-quarter strand
hunting firewood found the ruins of a boat,
started breaking the struts out – an old man came,
he shook his head, and said:
'Áá, a mhac: ná bí ag briseadh báid.'[4]

The low walls of rock-fields in the west
are a beautiful clean whitegrey. There are chinks between

the neat stones to let the wind through safe,
you can see the blue sun through them.
But coming eastward in the same county,
the walls grow higher, darkgrey:
an ugly grey. And the chinks disappear:
through those walls you can see nothing.

Then at last you come to the city,
beautiful with salmon basking becalmed black below
a bridge over the pale-green Corrib; and ugly
with many shopkeepers looking down on men like
Bartley Costello and Beartla Coñfhaola because they
speak in Irish, eat periwinkles, keep
small black porry cattle, and on us
because we are strangers.

[1] An Irish-speaking area.

[2] The Irish is less than the water in that glass.

[3] I speak with strangers. I believe it's right to be speaking with strangers.

[4] Ah, son: don't be breaking a boat.

# Bright After Dark

*for Sebastian Ryan*

In the first country,
what you must do when the cow stops giving milk
is climb, after dark, a certain hill,
and play the flute: to kill your scheming neighbour's curse.
If you can find a silver flute to play,
the spell will break all the faster, the surer.
But silver is not essential. But: the job must
be done after dark:
otherwise, it won't work.

In the second country,
when you send a child out of the house at night,
after dark, you must, if you wish it well,
take, from the fire, a burnt-out cinder
and place it on the palm of the child's hand
to guard the child against the dangers of the dark.
The cinder, in this good function, is called aingeal,
meaning angel.

In the third country,
if you take a journey at night, above all
in the blind night of ebony, so good for witches to work in,
you dare not rely on fireflies for light,
for theirs is a brief, inconstant glow. What you must hope
is that someone before you has dropped grains of maize
on the ground to light your way; and you must drop
grains of maize for whoever comes after you:
for only maize can light the way on a dark night.

# The Frost is All Over

*for Michael Hartnett*

To kill a language is to kill a people.
The Aztecs knew far better: they took over
their victims' language, kept them carving
obsidian beauties, weeded their religion
of dangerous gentleness, and winged them blood-flowers
(that's a different way to kill a people).
The Normans brought and grew, but Honor Croome
could never make her Kerryman verse English:
Traherne was in the music of his tears.

We have no glint or caution who we are:
our patriots dream wolfhounds in their portraits,
our vendors pose in hunting-garb, the nightmare
forelock tugging madly at some lost leash.
The Vikings never hurt us, xenophilia
means bland servility, we insult
ourselves and Europe with artificial trees,
and coins as gelt of beauty now
as, from the start, of power.

Like Flemish words on horseback, tongue survives
in turns of speech the telly must correct;
our music bows and scrapes on the world's platforms,
each cat-gut wears a rigorous bow-tie.
The frost, we tell them, is all over, and they love
our brogue so much they give us guns to kill
ourselves, our language, and all the other gooks.

Bobrowski would have understood, he found
some old, surviving words of a murdered language,
and told a few friends; but he knew how to mourn,
a rare talent, a need not many grant.

To call a language dead before it dies
means to bury it alive; some tongues do die
from hours or days inside the coffin, and when
the tearful killers dig it up they find
the tongue, like Suarez, bitten to its own bone.
Others explode in the church, and stain the bishop,
whose priest could speak no Gaelic to his 'flock'
but knew to sink a splendid tawny goblet
as deep as any master of the hunt.

Is Carleton where the tenderness must hide?
Or would they have the Gaelic words, like insects,
crawl up the legs of horses, and each bite,
or startle, be proclaimed a heritage?
Are those who rule us, like their eager voters,
ghosts yearning for flesh? Ghosts are cruel,
and ghosts of suicides more cruel still.
To kill a language is to kill one's self.

*Summer 1973*

# Amhrán na mBréag[1]

*after the Irish of Micheál Mharcais Ó Conghaile*

In the middle of the wood I set sail
as the bee and the bat were at anchor just off shore
I found in the sea's rough shallows a nest of bees
In a field's ear I saw
a mackerel milking a cow
I saw a young woman in Greece boiling the city of Cork over the
    kitchen fire
Last night, in a serpent's ear, I slept sound
I saw an eel with a whip in her hand whipping a shark ashore
MacDara's Island told me he never saw more
wonders:
a kitten washing a salmon in the river
the music-mast of a ship being
conceived in a cat's arse
a badger in the nest of an eagle milking a cow
and a sparrow wielding a hammer putting a keel on a boat.

[1] The Song of Lies.

# A True Story Ending in False Hope

*for Martin Collins*

The barman vaulted the counter
landing with a fine clatter
beside our musical table;
he nearly upset the pints
of all the dominical couples.
'We'll have no music here,'
he roared, bursting a blood-vessel.
We weren't, in fact, a steel-band,
*or* a demolition-squad,
so Justin gestured the tin-whistle
towards the married couples:
'Does anyone mind this
                                  music?'
Some said they didn't,
the rest sang dumb,
but one old woman spoke up loudly:
'We like it,' she cried,
'it brightens things up a bit here.'
The barman burst another vessel.
'Out! Out!' he shouted.
'We'll finish our drink,' said the Corkman,
the Corkman who'd *asked* for the music,
*and* we did,
*but* we left –
uttering suitable imprecations.

We crossed the unmusical road,
skirting a public jax
that hadn't yet turned into a ghost,
boarded a chopper for heaven,
and played and drank till closing-time,
thinking how musical
Ireland
            will
                  be.

# ANTHONY CRONIN

## Responsibilities

My window shook all night in Camden Town
Where through the cutting's murk the sibilant engines
Pounded past, slowly, gasping in the rain.
Three o'clock was a distant clanking sound.

On Primrose Hill the gasfire in my room
Hissed for more money while the sofa bristled.
The unopened wardrobe stared sepulchrally.
It probably was my predecessor's tomb.

Daily I strolled through leaves to look for letters,
A half of bitter or a chance encounter.
My state was ecstasy, illusion, hunger,
And I was often lectured by my betters.

What wonder that I seldom rose till three
When light was leaking from the grimy primrose
That is the western sky of winter London,
Light in the head, lugubrious, cynical, free.

The past, implausible and profitless,
Is yet a part of us, though I suppose
Gide has the right of it: who have no sense
Of their own history know most happiness.

And yet I set that autumn sunlight down,
That delicate, pale ochre and that haze;
My eye so idle and the afternoon
So still and timeless with the haze withdrawn.

I could disown them like a thirties poet
And yet I set inexplicables down,
And scattered images of London when
With a true love I could most truly know it.

The cavernous Rowtons where the footsteps grew
Unsteadily down each corridor and passed,
The stages marked on all my bootless journeys:
A pub, a railing and a short way through.

I groped through bombsites on the Finchley Road,
Fog in the stomach, blanketed in cold.
Next morning when the gears began to groan
Whatever else I had, I had no load.

No more than when in Hammersmith one morning
The sun lit up the Broadway through the fog.
Incarnadine, transported I was stalking
Beside the early buses in that dawning.

Nightly the wagons splashed along Watling Street,
Battened down, bound for the pool or for the smoke,
Waiting for lifts I did not know myself
An avatar, a prehistoric beat.

I saw the landscape of old England like
A man upon the moon: amazing shapes,
Wheels, pulleys, engines, slag-heaps, bricks and dirt,
And furnace sunsets frowning through the smoke.

And heard the poets of old England too
In Watney's pubs repeating cricket scores
And Dylan stories, talk of our medium
And principles and programmes (radio).

The past, predestined, populous and over
Clings in the dampening leaves, the smell of petrol,
On the brown northern heights where I remember
Highgate and Hampstead in a fine October.

# Lines for a Painter

*to Patrick Swift*

The tree grew under your hand one day,
So many shades of green growing over the white
Canvas, as through the actual leaves outside the window
And through the open window onto the canvas fell the light.

And I sat on the bed trying unsuccessfully to write,
Envying you the union of the painter's mind and hand,
The contact of brush with canvas, the physical communion,
The external identity of the object and the painting you had
    planned;

For among the shards of memory nothing that day would grow
Of its own accord,
And I thought I could never see, as you saw the tree on the canvas,
One draughtsman's word.

Only inside the mind,
In the rubble of thought,
Were the pro-and-con, prose-growing, all too argumentative
Poems I sought.

Whereas there in Camden Town
In the petrol fumes and gold of a London summer was the tree you
    drew,
As you might find anywhere, inside or outside the studio, something
Which was itself, not you.

Well envying I have said,
But that evening as we walked
Through the cooling twilight down
To the pub and talked

I saw what in truth I had envied –
Not in fact
That you were released from any obligation,
Or that the act

Of painting was less or more objective
Than thinking the word –
But that, like poems, your painting
Was of course the reward

Of the true self yielding to appearances
Outside its power
While still in the dominion of love asseverating
Its absolute hour.

# Elegy for the Nightbound

Tonight in the cold I know most of the living are waiting
For a miracle great as if suddenly ageing money
Repented its rule of the world, all, all of us failing
To find the word which unlocks and would give us something
Better than truth or justice.
And always we find ourselves wanting though all of us enter
The world as a humble supplicant and a lover
And the dream of the child is to grow at last to the stature
His love has attained.
I awoke one night in the mountains
And heard through the falling rain and the breathable darkness
The whispering world say, singular third person
We only know what you did we can never know what you wanted,
And not only wicked but foolish, Lord, are the fallen.
And now in the night when the city, gentle with neon,
Calls me from paper where love is an abstract perfection
To the village of friends who are gathered which none ever leaves
I must work out from the fractions of conversation
The total I answer for which is the total I am.

Yet tonight as the twig-breaking winter creeps in through the
    garden
And the blasphemous Irish are fighting on Hammersmith Broadway
The living pray to the living to recognize difference:
For who can believe that we are but the sum of our actions?
Only the saint and the dead and the deer and the dog.
We are what we want when we love though the wallpaper hates us
And tomorrows founder around a November in fog.
Though nothing remains as you turn to me now at the table
But a circumstance harder to cheat than the words and the white
Page upon which I will put down the poem I'm able
Instead of the one I will never be able to write,
I remember this evening how cold it was there in the evenings,
Two thousand feet up, the rain goose-flesh on the lake,

And the trees were black, the mountains gone and the rain still
   falling around me
Later when I the singular lay awake.

# *from* R.M.S. Titanic

## 1

Trembling with engines, gulping oil, the river
Under the factories glowering in the dark
Is home of the gulls and homeless; cold
Lights on the sucking tideway, scurf and sewage,
Gobbets of smoke and staleness and the smell,
The seaweed sour and morning smell of sea.

Here in the doss the river fog is dawn.
Under the yellow lights it twists like tapeworm,
Wreathes round the bulbs and, with the scent of urine,
Creeps down the bare board corridors, becomes
The sour, sweet breath of old men, sleepless, coughing.

Lights on the glistening metal, numinous fog
Feathering to mist, thin garlands hung
On the wet back of the Mersey. Out to sea
A great dawn heaves and tugs the tide past Crosby.

## 2

On the bog road the blackthorn flowers, the turf-stacks,
Chocolate brown, are built like bricks but softer,
And softer too the west of Ireland sky.
Turf smoke is chalked upon the darker blue
And leaves a sweet, rich, poor man's smell in cloth.
Great ragged rhododendrons sprawl through gaps

And pink and white the chestnut blossom tops
The tumbled granite wall round the demesne.
The high, brass-bound De Dion coughing past,
O'Connor Don and the solicitor,
Disturbs the dust but not the sleeping dogs.

Disturb the memories in an old man's head.
We only live one life, with one beginning.
The coming degradations of the heart
We who awake with all our landfalls staring
Back at us in the dawn, must hold our breath for.

The west is not awake to where Titanic
Smokes in the morning, huge against the stars.

# TOM MAC INTYRE

## The Yellow Bittern

*after the Irish of Cathal Buidhe Mac Giolla Gunna (eighteenth century)*

Sickens my gut, Yellow Bittern,
to see you stretched there,
whipped, not by starvation
but the want of a jar;
Troy's fall was skittles to this,
you flattened on bare stones,
you harmed no one, pillaged no crop,
your preference always – the wee drop.

Sours my spit, Yellow Bittern,
thought of you done for,
heard your shout many's the night,
you mudlarkin', and no want of a jar;
at that game I'll shape a coffin,
so all claim, but look at this,
a darlin' bird downed like a thistle,
*causa mortis* – couldn't wet his whistle.

Sands my bones, Yellow Bittern,
your last earthlies under a bush,
rats next, rats for the wakin',
pipes in their mouths and them all smokin';
Christ's sake, if you'd only sent word,
tipped me the wink you were in a bind,
dunt of a crowbar, the ice splitter-splatter,
nothing to stop another week on the batter.

Heron, blackbird, thrush, you've had it too:
sorry, mates, I'm occupied,
I'm blinds down for the Yellow Bittern,
a blood relation on the mother's side;
whole-hog merchants, we lived it up,
*carpe'd* our *diem*, hung out our sign,
collared life's bottle disregarding the label,
angled our elbows met under the table

while the wife moaned with the rest,
'Give it up – you're finished – a year' –
I told her she lied,
my staple and staff was the regular jar;
now, naked proof, this lad with a gullet
who, forced on the dry, surely prayed for a bullet,
No, friends, drink it up – and piss it down,
warm them worms waitin' undergroun'.

# Sweet Killen Hill

*after the Irish of Peadar Ó Doirnín (eighteenth century)*

Flower of the flock,
any time, any land,
plenty your ringlets,
plenty your hand,
sunlight your window,
laughter your sill,
and I must be with you
on sweet Killen Hill.

Let sleep renege me,
skin lap my bones,
love and tomorrow
can handle the reins,
you my companion
I'd never breathe ill,
and I guarantee bounty
on sweet Killen Hill.

You'll hear the pack yell
as puss devil-dances,
hear cuckoo and thrush
pluck song from the branches,
see fish in the pool
doing their thing,
and the bay as God made it
from sweet Killen Hill.

Pulse of my life,
we come back to *mise*,
why slave for McArdle —
that bumbailiff's issue,

I've a harp in a thousand,
love-songs at will,
and the air is cadenza
on sweet Killen Hill.

Gentle one, lovely one,
come to me,
now sleep the clergy,
now sleep their care,
sunrise will find us
but sunrise won't tell
that love lacks surveillance
on sweet Killen Hill.

# JAMES SIMMONS

## The Archæologist

Portrush. Walking dead streets in the dark.
Winter. A cold wind off the Atlantic
rattling metal in the amusement park.

Rain. The ornate dancehall, empty on the rocks,
bright paint worn thin, posters half torn away,
sweet-stalls, boarded up and locked with padlocks.

Returned to the scene, at once I see again
myself, when ten years younger, and a girl,
preserved in an almost perfect state by the brain.

That is her window, high on the side wall.
Beneath it figures, projected by the mind,
are moving. I am about to call.

I give her name and wait. She is called down.
Without taking thought I know what I want to do.
Love, like electric current, lights the town.

Nothing is tawdry, all our jokes are funny,
the pin-table is brighter than Shakespeare's works,
my handful of warm coins is sufficient money.

Imaginative reconstruction shed
some light upon a vanished way of life.
I cannot live like them, and they are dead.

The cold makes me simpler and breaks the spell:
I don't mind crying, but I hate to shiver,
and walk quickly back to my hotel.

# Written, Directed by and Starring . . .

The scripts I used to write for the young actor –
me – weren't used. And now I couldn't play
the original parts and, as director,
I'd turn myself, if I applied, away.

My break will come; but now the star's mature
his parts need character and 'love' is out.
He learns to smile on birth and death, to endure:
it's strange I keep the old scripts lying about.

Looking them over I've at times forgot
they've never been put on. I seem to spend
too much time reading through a final shot
where massed choirs sing, they kiss, and then THE END.

It's hard to start upon this middle phase
when my first period never reached the screen,
and there's no end now to my new screen-plays,
they just go on from scene to scene to scene.

The hero never hogs the screen because
his wife, his children, friends, events intrude.
When he's not on the story doesn't pause –
not if he dies. I don't see why it should.

# The End of the Affair

We could count the times we went for a walk
or the times we danced together in the past
months – if not the times of making love and talk.
Our first separation will be our last.

I suppose we never discussed what we have known:
that I am to go home, that you will stay.
All the mutual tenderness that has grown,
sweet as it is, is not to get in the way

of the work before us, mine and yours.
What has been given is being taken away,
and we aren't looking for loopholes and cures,
freely absenting ourselves from this felicity

to tell our story under plain covers
in bed, or by example, till everyone understands
that joy will not be bound. Artists and lovers
start and complete their work with empty hands.

To leave my wife and children for love's sake
and marry you would be a failure of nerve.
I remember love and all that goes to make
the marriage, the affairs, that I deserve.

# Stephano Remembers

We broke out of our dream into a clearing
and there were all our masters still sneering.
My head bowed, I made jokes and turned away,
living over and over that strange day.

The ship struck before morning. Half past four,
on a huge hogshead of claret I swept ashore
like an evangelist aboard his god:
his will was mine, I laughed and kissed the rod,
and would have walked that foreign countryside
blind drunk, contentedly till my god died;
but finding Trinculo made it a holiday:
two Neapolitans had got away,
and that shipload of scheming toffs we hated
was drowned. Never to be humiliated
again, 'I will no more to sea,' I sang.
Down white empty beaches my voice rang,
and that dear monster, half fish and half man,
went on his knees to me. Oh, Caliban,
you thought I'd take your twisted master's life;
but a drunk butler's slower with a knife
than your fine courtiers, your dukes, your kings.
We were distracted by too many things . . .
the wine, the jokes, the music, fancy gowns.
We were no good as murderers, we were clowns.

# A Long Way After Ronsard

*for Eileen*

When time has made you wrinkled, sore and slow,
and let my caged abilities fly free,
will you feel proud when many people know
I longed for you and you rejected me?

Deaf to my wit, my anger and my prayers,
you didn't even want to lead me on.
Those nights frustration hounded me upstairs
and kept the pencil in my hand till dawn.

Reading these poems will you see how vile
you were to me, and what a paltry choice
he was – that smoother man? Or will you smile,
'Poor Jim is famous'? . . . I can hear your voice.

# West Strand Visions

The man alone at the third-floor window
is the man alone at the cliff's edge.
Below him gulls are cutting each other's
invisible paths of flight. Bent sideways
in his cockpit above the dog-fight
alone he observes engaging bi-planes
locked in each other's sights and strategies,
diving, swerving and climbing heavily,
and droning earthward in flames.

The man watching the pony-girl waving
on the West Strand to her three assistants
and suddenly rearing her horse and wheeling
off at a canter, followed by donkeys
into the grey curtain of rain,
is the man watching barbarians gather,
Tamburlaine, was it, or Genghis Khan,
shaggy in robes strange to the watcher,
returned from reconnoitring,
deciding and acting on God's plan.

The man who watches neglected children
leaping in yellow light of sunset
by waters whipped by wind, majestic
ten yards out and fierce,
but gentle in the shallows,
is me, estranged from mystery,
trying to hear what they say,
envying no one in the world but they
who never use words like 'beauty',
shouting in apparent ecstasy
a pane of glass and fifty yards away.

# Claudy

*for Harry Barton, a song*

The Sperrins surround it, the Faughan flows by,
at each end of Main Street the hills and the sky,
the small town of Claudy at ease in the sun
last July in the morning, a new day begun.

How peaceful and pretty if the moment could stop,
McIlhenny is straightening things in his shop,
and his wife is outside serving petrol, and then
a girl takes a cloth to a big window pane.

And McCloskey is taking the weight off his feet,
and McClelland and Miller are sweeping the street,
and, delivering milk at the Beaufort Hotel,
young Temple's enjoying his first job quite well.

And Mrs McLaughlin is scrubbing her floor,
and Artie Hone's crossing the street to a door,
and Mrs Brown, looking around for her cat,
goes off up an entry – what's strange about that?

Not much – but before she comes back to the road
that strange car parked outside her house will explode,
and all of the people I've mentioned outside
will be waiting to die or already have died.

An explosion too loud for your eardrums to bear,
and young children squealing like pigs in the square,
and all faces chalk-white and streaked with bright red,
and the glass and the dust and the terrible dead.

For an old lady's legs are ripped off, and the head
of a man's hanging open, and still he's not dead.
He is screaming for mercy, and his son stands and stares
and stares, and then suddenly, quick, disappears.

And Christ, little Katherine Aiken is dead,
and Mrs McLaughlin is pierced through the head.
Meanwhile to Dungiven the killers have gone,
and they're finding it hard to get through on the phone.

# For Thomas Moore

When the young have grown tired
and the old are abused,
when beauty's degraded
and brilliance not used,
when courage is clumsy
and strength misapplied
we wish that our seed
in the dark womb had died.

But when youth finds its singers
and old men find peace
and beauty finds servants
and genius release,
when courage has wisdom
and strength mends our wrongs
we will sing unembarrassed
your marvellous songs.

# Rogation Day: Portrush

*for Derek Mahon*

I stop to consult my diary and think how queer
that in my day farmers can be sincere
kneeling in stiff suits, their rough hands
joined, praying for swaying cornlands,
a big yield, reward for labour, a reply
from the dumb planets and the gaseous sky.

Upstairs my hands grip the shoulders
of a kindly lady. Between the unholy boulders
of her thighs I play Moses with my loins.
Below, when the spinning disc stops, coins
flow in *Sportsland*. Someone has picked the right slot
in the one-armed bandit. I hear the jackpot,

and I ejaculate and the girl-friend sighs.
The farmers stand and rub their eyes
for this is a miracle and all the walls are glass.
They can see through the church and up my ass,
and the boy waging his penny in the one-armed thief.
Lord I am lucky: help thou their unbelief.

# From the Irish

Most terrible was our hero in battle blows:
hands without fingers, shorn heads and toes
were scattered. That day there flew and fell
from astonished victims eyebrow, bone and entrail,
like stars in the sky, like snowflakes, like nuts in May,
like a meadow of daisies, like butts from an ashtray.

Familiar things, you might brush against or tread
upon in the daily round, were glistening red
with the slaughter the hero caused, though he had gone.
By proxy his bomb exploded, his valour shone.

## Westport House, Portrush

They have emptied the heart of Westport,
dismantled the great stairwell
and inserted three narrow holiday homes
into the gutted shell
where my parents often welcomed
us children and many beside,
where my children engendered children,
where my father and grandmother died.

Sweet pea, night stock and roses
once made the backyard sweet,
and each year blue lobelia
on the front wall next the street.
Aunt Molly's rosewood piano
was being played all day long.
There was always music. Michael Stephens
began his career of song.

What has happened? No brash invader,
not one soul worth your hate,
but a local builder, a gombeen
with money to speculate,
bought Westport from my former wife
who'd accepted the house in lieu
of alimony. She needed cash
and was lucky to get it too,

for half the slates were missing,
carpets faded and frayed,
the frames of the windows rotting off.
We couldn't afford a maid.
It is hard to sustain a mansion
on a lecturer's modest pay
unless you can make and mend yourself.
It was sinking gradually.

The rusted hinge of the garage door,
where carriages once had passed,
burst from the rotten wood and fell
and was left to lie and was lost.
The windows rattled in shrunken frames
and the garden by that late stage
was hidden in briars, weeds and grass.
They flung rubbish over the hedge.

Great herring gulls still strut the roof,
eyes bright and hurling down
what sounds like lyrical abuse
that echoes round the town.
There's style and courage in those cries,
ferocious love and hate,
indifference to vicissitude
I cannot emulate.

JAMES SIMMONS

# The Pleasant Joys of Brotherhood

*to the tune of 'My Lagan Love'*

I love the small hours of the night
when I sit up alone.
I love my family, wife and friends.
I love them and they're gone.
A glass of Power's, a well-slacked fire,
I wind the gramophone.
The pleasant joys of brotherhood
I savour on my own.

An instrument to play upon,
books, records on the shelf,
and albums crammed with photographs:
I *céilí* [1] by myself.
I drink to passion, drink to peace,
the silent telephone.
The pleasant joys of brotherhood
I savour on my own.

[1] Friendly visit, social evening.

117

# DESMOND O'GRADY

## *from* The Dark Edge of Europe

### I

A twist of cloth on the flat stones
Close by her heel in the rocky ford,
The peasant woman, bowed, unaware
Of the age on her back, the ache in her bones,
Washes away by the bend in the road
At the heel of the hill, a rag in her hair.

Farther behind in a yard full of haycocks
Her man and his son untackle the cart,
Stable the oxen, hang up the harness,
Their day done. One knocks
The crusted clay from the belly part
Of a shovel. The other stands in silence.

The valley suspends its diurnal labour.
Lake and island hang in the sky.
The sun, blocked by the broken wall
Of a castle, sinks with a stone's languor
Into the evening. The caught eye
Swivels to a hawk's impending fall.

By the butt of an ancient tree a boy,
My guide, squats sucking a stalk;
His head, his noble historical head,
Cocked like an animal's, his mind's eye
Fixed upon nothing. Out on the dark
Edge of Europe my love lies dead.

# Professor Kelleher and the Charles River

The Charles river reaps here like a sickle. April
Light sweeps flat as ice on the inner curve
Of the living water. Overhead, far from the wave, a dove
White gull heads inland. The spring air, still
Lean from winter, thaws. Walking, John
Kelleher and I talk on the civic lawn.

West, to our left, past some trees, over the ivy walls,
The clock towers, pinnacles, the pillared university yard,
The Protestant past of Cambridge New England selfconsciously
    dead
In the thawing clay of the Old Burying Ground. Miles
East, over the godless Atlantic, our common brother,
Ploughing his myth-muddy fields, embodies our order.

But here, while the students row by eights and fours on the river –
As my father used to row on the Shannon when, still a child,
I'd cross Thomond Bridge every Sunday, my back to the walled
And turreted castle, listening to that uncle Mykie deliver
His version of history – I listen now to John Kelleher
Unravel the past a short generation later.

Down at the green bank's nerve ends, its roots half in the river,
A leafing tree gathers refuse. The secret force
Of the water worries away the live earth's under-surface.
But his words, for the moment, hold back time's being's destroyer
While the falling wave on both thighs of the ocean
Erodes the coasts, at its dying conceptual motion.

Two men, one young, one old, stand stopped acrobats in the blue
Day, their bitch river to heel. Beyond,
Some scraper, tower or ancestral house's gable end.
Then, helplessly, as in some ancient dance, the two
Begin their ageless struggle, while the tree's shadow
With all its arms, crawls on the offal-strewn meadow.

Locked in their mute struggle there by the blood-loosed tide
The two abjure all innocence, tear down past order –
The one calm, dispassionate, clearsighted, the other
Wild with ecstasy, intoxicated, world mad.
Surely some new order is at hand;
Some new form emerging where they stand.

Dusk. The great dim tide of shadows from the past
Gathers for the end – the living and the dead.
All force is fruitful. All opposing powers combine.
Aristocratic privilege, divine sanction, anarchy at last
Yield the new order. The saffron sun sets.
All shadows procession in an acropolis of lights.

DESMOND O'GRADY

# Reading the Unpublished Manuscripts of Louis MacNeice at Kinsale Harbour

One surely tires eventually of the frequent references – the gossip,
praise, the blame, the intimate anecdote – to those
who, for one unpredictable reason or other (living
abroad, difference of age, chance, the friends one chose,
being detained too long at the most opportune moment) one
never, face to tactile face, has met; but who
had the way things fall fallen favourably, once met, for some
right physic force, would have been polar, kindred you –
though time, space, human nature, sometimes contract
to force the action done that makes abstraction fact.

Here in this mock of a room which might have been yours, might
    have been
the place of our eventual meeting, I find a berth temporarily
(so long too late) among your possessions. Alone,
except for your face in the framed photos,
I sit with your manuscripts spread over my knees,
reliving the unpublished truths of your autobiography.
On the shelves and table, desk, floor, your books
and papers, your bundles of letters – as if you were just moving in
or out, or had been already for years –
like a poem in the making you'll never now finish.
Through the windows I see down to the hook of Old Kinsale
    Harbour.
Mid-summer. Under the sun the sea as smooth as a dish.
Below on the quays the fishermen wind up the morning's business:
stacking the fishboxes, scraping the scales from their tackle and
    hands.
Behind this house the hills shovel down on the town's slate roofs
the mysterious green mounds of their history.
Flaming fir, clouted holly.
Not an Irish harbour at all, but some other –
the kind you might find along the Iberian coast, only greener.

Down to here, down to this clay of contact between us, Hugh
    O'Neill once marched
from way up your part of the country, the North, the winter of
    sixteen
hundred and one, to connect with the long-needed Spaniards three
    months
under siege in the Harbour. Having played the English their own
    game and watched
all his life for his moment, he lost our right lot in one bungled night
and with it the thousands of years of our past and our future. He
    began
what divides the North they brought your ash back to, from the
    South I have left
for Rome – where O'Neill's buried exiled. And here, then, this
    moment, late
as the day is (what matter your physical absence) I grow towards
    your knowing,
towards the reassurance of life in mortality, the importance, the
    value of dying.

# *from* The Dying Gaul

## 30

The hour at last come round
   the stroke that scores the kill
taken, there follows a painless,
   partly nostalgic withdrawal –
a drag to the sideline – to a clean piece
   of this world's dying ground.

Lean legs nerve like an athlete's.
   Raised kneecaps gleam altar marble.
Thigh shanks knot. The curled
   weighty balls bag low and the gentle
penis limps childless. Tousled,
   his head's like a young brown bull's.

Reclining, at repose upon
   one unwound nude haunch,
pelvis and dragged out legs
   draining, his belly's bunch
about the navel wrinkles.
   Life strains on his taut right arm.

The blood clots, the nerve
   sings and all his joints
jamb stuck. His grounded gaze,
   like the madman's private smile, confronts
the process's revelation – the ways
   death consummates, like love.

# *from* Hellas

*for Andrea Giustozzi*

### I

Here, because of the shock, the sudden
rage of our disappointment,
because brute thoroughness of execution
brought quick death, sorry wedding,
Greece and you have been in all our thoughts,
on all our tongues. Over morning coffee,
late over drinks in the radio-reporting
night – the daily newspapers scattered
like blasted doves about the room –
we have talked of your dark present,
your unforeseeable future, the past's example.
Even when alone in the street,
on a bus, reading, at work,
you and Greece have been raging in silent riot
through my head like the despaired history
of my own country.

One night, at Patrick Creagh's house,
Vassilykos, stranded, arrived with his woman.
Three men with our women, our several
pasts, fragmented emotions, we imagined
the same hour in Athens shocked
groups, watching and watched, sat
behind barred windows, bolted doors,
like Jews in a ghetto.
Vassilykos, his name on the list of arrests
in *Le Monde*, talked Greece and her past
in postmortem and Patrick and I
spoke her poems out loud, turn
around, like a requiem.

There in that house of so many unspoken
remembrances (that one day we can all
share for a brief, intense while)
the spirits of Greece, living and dead,
were amongst and around us: Cavafy,
Elytis, Aeschylus, Archilochus,
Amphis and Gatsos, Menander, Sophocles,
Socrates, Plato, Seferis and Ritsos . . .
And our thoughts! Our thoughts!

Afterwards, going home through the dark
to the late night news –
the shock, like a death, or final
departure, still harder than marble
or honour back of the eyeballs –
an old song came into my head
from my own country:
Mise Éire
Sine mé ná an Cailleach Béara
Mór mo glór
Mé do rug Cuchulainn crógach
Mór mo náire
Mo chlann féin do dhíol a mháthair
Mise Éire
Uaigni mé ná an Cailleach Béara –
I am Ireland
I am older than the Hag of Baer Island
Great my pride
It was I bore brave Cuchulainn
Great my shame
My own family sold their mother
I am Ireland
I am lonelier than the Hag of Baer Island.

# *from* Lines in a Roman Schoolbook

### 2

This introspective exile here today
am minded of my elsewhere: its occasions
twenty-five decades ago when poets were hedge-
school masters in my fields and kept alive
the way of life that's ours by conversation –
just as that other hedge-school master talked
in his muddled marketplace under the Attic sun
and paid the price extorted. The best seems always
based on solid dialogue as when, when young,
our elders passed on to us what they knew,
then passed us on to those who knew the more –
for space shapes no restriction round its star.

### 4

In the valleys of the future we shall walk
and talk through, growing on good conversation
and the memories of good conversation; in the last
library of memory, reflection, thought we settle in
overlooking the valley of darkness and light; in the seed
time of our time, on our way home to the last town,
we may pause, like that ancient anonymous traveller,
at the entrance to the theatre of the last valley
prepared to conduct our last discourse; to say:
We talked and told each other all we knew,
as ours with theirs and theirs, since that Greek start,
taught those after us to do the same for their part.

# Purpose

I looked at my days and saw that
with the first affirmation of summer
I must leave all I knew: the house,
the familiarity of family,
companions and memories of childhood,
a future cut out like a tailored suit,
a settled life among school friends.

I looked face to face at my future:
I saw voyages to distant places,
saw the daily scuffle for survival
in foreign towns with foreign tongues
and small rented rooms on companionless
nights with sometimes the solace
of a gentle anonymous arm on the pillow.

I looked at the faces about me
and saw my days' end as a returned ship,
its witness singing in the rigging.

I saw my life and I walked out to it,
as a seaman walks out alone at night from
his house down to the port with his bundled
belongings, and sails into the dark.

# The Great Horse Fair

Crouched on their women woven saddle rugs,
heated in parley,
the Chieftains hold Council
at our annual Great Horse Fair.

Taller than rooftrees
each Chieftain's standard
at the place of assembly.
Curved the great felt tents,
richly embroidered at sunrise.
Deft the design of the dyed thread
with intricate needlework.
Like the morning sky's stars before dawn
the bonfires burn by the tent mouths.
In thousands the handcarved
bright daubed covered wagons
ring the camp site.
Untackled,
their upright shafts forest the morning.
Throng of our tribesmen;
with free speech for each free man
at the Chief's deliberations.

Sheepswool the cloak of the Horsemaster
tossed back off scaled armour;
gold-mounted the leather
scabbards his longsword.
Beside him his helmet of bronze squares,
plumed ermine
mounted on red felt.

Tethered the ponies,
their posts driven upright
in rich red earth:
palominos and piebalds,

chestnuts and bays, sorrels and roans.
Harness on racks by pegged tent flaps:
embossed leather saddle work,
broad saddle cloths of appliquéd felt stuff
sweeps the ground with bright tassels.
Glint of sandcast harness brasses.
Sweat polished leather.
Silver studded chestband, bridle,
snaffle-bit, cheek bars –
links of red quartz, green onyx, blue topaz.

Regal their longhaired tall women:
blonde blue-eyed, ravenhead olive-eyed,
green-eyed redhead;
handwoven bright plaid shawls on their shoulders
against dawn's chill,
gold thread woven in the plaits of their hair.
Silver flash of hammered marriage bracelets
each one her own man's handspan broad on the forearm,
slender snake bracelets
coiled round bare biceps;
finger rings, earrings and throatbands of goldwork,
embossed leather belts at the waist
with mounted precious medallions.
Rawhide the sandals
and studded with silver their soft leather anklets.
And the Chieftains in Council . . .

'Now that they've lost their grasslands
they're pushing in from the east on our pasture.
We're overgrazing twice yearly.
No wonder our grass is failing.
Thieving herds in the ploughlands
destroy the young grain crop.
Herdsmen and homesteaders at each other's throats.
Refugees and old mercenaries
returned from the wars in the mountains

stake claim to lands we've long redivided.
We're too many people with too many herds.
Both growing yearly. We're overpopulated
and everyone squabbles over too little land.'

'There's only one obvious solution:
Some of us have to move out.
The question is where?'

The south is a military block.
East we're outnumbered. North
there's nothing but forest and swamp;
no grazing for horses and cattle.
That was the year
we shoved out west
on our general journey . . .

# BRENDAN KENNELLY

## My Dark Fathers

My dark fathers lived the intolerable day
Committed always to the night of wrong,
Stiffened at the hearthstone, the woman lay,
Perished feet nailed to her man's breastbone.
Grim houses beckoned in the swelling gloom
Of Munster fields where the Atlantic night
Fettered the child within the pit of doom,
And everywhere a going down of light.

And yet upon the sandy Kerry shore
The woman once had danced at ebbing tide
Because she loved flute music, and still more
Because a lady wondered at the pride
Of one so humble. That was long before
The green plant withered by an evil chance;
When winds of hunger howled at every door
She heard the music dwindle and forgot the dance.

Such mercy as the wolf receives was hers
Whose dance became a rhythm in a grave,
Achieved beneath the thorny savage furze
That yellowed fiercely in a mountain cave.
Immune to pity, she, whose crime was love,
Crouched, shivered, searched the threatening sky,
Discovered ready signs, compelled to move
Her to her innocent appalling cry.

Skeletoned in darkness, my dark fathers lay
Unknown, and could not understand
The giant grief that trampled night and day,
The awful absence moping through the land.
Upon the headland, the encroaching sea
Left sand that hardened after tides of Spring,
No dancing feet disturbed its symmetry
And those who loved good music ceased to sing.

Since every moment of the clock
Accumulates to form a final name,
Since I am come of Kerry clay and rock,
I celebrate the darkness and the shame
That could compel a man to turn his face
Against the wall, withdrawn from light so strong
And undeceiving, spancelled in a place
Of unapplauding hands and broken song.

# The Limerick Train

Hurtling between hedges now, I see
Green desolation stretch on either hand
While sunlight blesses all magnanimously.

The gods and heroes are gone for good and
Men evacuate each Munster valley
And midland plain, gravelly Connaught land

And Leinster town. Who, I wonder, fully
Understands the imminent predicament,
Sprung from rooted suffering and folly?

Broken castles tower, lost order's monument,
Splendour crumbling in sun and rain,
Witnesses to all we've squandered and spent,

But no Phoenix rises from that ruin
Although the wild furze in yellow pride
Explodes in bloom above each weed and stone,

Promise ablaze on every mountainside
After the centuries' game of pitch-and-toss
Separates what must live from what has died.

A church whips past, proclaiming heavy loss
Amounting to some forty thousand pounds;
A marble Christ unpaid for on His Cross

Accepts the Limerick train's irreverent sound,
Relinquishes great power to little men –
A river flowing still, but underground.

Wheels clip the quiet counties. Now and then
I see a field where like an effigy
In rushy earth, there stands a man alone

Lifting his hand in salutation. He
Disappears almost as soon as he is seen,
Drowned in distant anonymity.

We have travelled far, the journey has been
Costly, tormented odyssey through night;
And now, noting the unmistakable green,

The pools and trees that spring into the sight,
The sheep that scatter madly, wheel and run,
Quickly transformed to terrified leaping white,

I think of what the land has undergone
And find the luminous events of history
Intolerable as staring at the sun.

Only twenty miles to go and I'll be
Home. Seeing two crows low over the land,
I recognize the land's uncertainty,

The unsensational surrender and
Genuflexion to the busy stranger
Whose power in pocket brings him power in hand.

Realizing now how dead is anger
Such as sustained us at the very start
With possibility in time of danger,

I know why we have turned away, apart
(I'm moving still but so much time has sped)
From the dark realities of the heart.

From my window now, I try to look ahead
And know, remembering what's been done and said
That we must always cherish, and reject, the dead.

# Dream of a Black Fox

The black fox loped out of the hills
And circled for several hours,
Eyes bright with menace, teeth
White in the light, tail dragging the ground.
The woman in my arms cringed with fear,
Collapsed crying, her head hurting my neck.
She became dumb fear.

The black fox, big as a pony,
Circled and circled,
Whimsical executioner,
Torment dripping like saliva from its jaws.
Too afraid to show my fear,
I watched it as it circled;
Then it leaped across me,
Its great black body breaking the air,
Landing on a wall above my head.

Turning then, it looked at me.

And I saw it was magnificent,
Ruling the darkness, lord of its element,
Scorning all who are afraid,
Seeming even to smile
At human pettiness and fear.

The woman in my arms looked up
At this lord of darkness
And as quickly hid her head again.
Then the fox turned and was gone
Leaving us with fear
And safety –
Every usual illusion.

Quiet now, no longer trembling,
She lay in my arms,
Still as a sleeping child.

I knew I had seen fear,
Fear dispelled by what makes fear
A part of pure creation,
Some incomparable thing,
A thing so utterly itself
It might have taught me
Mastery of myself,
Dominion over death,
But was content to leap
With ease and majesty
Across the valleys and the hills of sleep.

# Bread

Someone else cut off my head
In a golden field.
Now I am re-created

By her fingers. This
Moulding is more delicate
Than a first kiss,

More deliberate than her own
Rising up
And lying down.

Even at my weakest, I am
Finer than anything
In this legendary garden

Yet I am nothing till
She runs her fingers through me
And shapes me with her skill.

The form that I shall bear
Grows round and white.
It seems I comfort her

Even as she slits my face
And stabs my chest.
Her feeling for perfection is

Absolute.
So I am glad to go through fire
And come out

Shaped like her dream.
In my way
I am all that can happen to men.
I came to life at her fingerends.
I will go back into her again.

# The Swimmer

For him the Shannon opens
Like a woman.
He has stepped over the stones

And cut the water
With his body
But this river does not bleed for

Any man. How easily
He mounts the waves, riding them
As though they

Whispered subtle invitations to his skin,
Conspiring with the sun
To offer him

A white, wet rhythm. The deep beneath
Gives full support
To the marriage of wave and heart,

The waves he breaks turn back to stare
At the repeated ceremony
And the hills of Clare

Witness the fluent weddings
The flawless congregation
The choiring foam that sings

To limbs which must, once more,
Rising and falling in the sun,
Return to shore.

Again he walks upon the stones,
A new music in his heart,
A river in his bones

Flowing forever through his head
Private as a grave
Or as the bridal bed.

# The Island

I

Consider the sea's insatiate lust
And my power of resistance.

The waves' appetite
Gives me reason to exist,

This undermining
This daily assault on my body

Keeps me singing
Like the larks that rise from my heather.

The sea would swallow me whole
But I am a shelter
For music that startles the sky.
In my fields and furrows
Is rhythm to rival the sea.

Is this why we fight?
Does my hidden music
Draw the sea to my throat

To suck my secrets into itself?
Must two kinds of music
Clash and devour
Till the crack of whatever doom lies in store?

I am always about to surrender
When the sea withdraws from my shore

And leaves me to hear my own music again.
Nothing stranger!
I am consoled
By the voices of creatures
Whose wings are made of my pain.

## 2

This morning my fields sigh with relief
Because they have survived a storm.
When the sea explodes in rage or grief

What can they do but take it as it comes?
My fields are not interested
In suicide or martyrdom

But in green joyful endurance,
In those changes that are mine also.
If I could imagine a happy man

He would be like my fields before
And after storm.
He would live close to the battered shore

But flourish in his own way.
He would accept the sky's changes
Absorb its fury

Be an image of repose in its light.
But I know nothing of men
And must content myself with

Green peace that knows how to survive.
Worse storms, I know, are gathering
But my fields will live.

# Proof

I would like all things to be free of me,
Never to murder the days with presupposition,
Never to feel they suffer the imposition
Of having to be this or that. How easy
It is to maim the moment
With expectation, to force it to define
Itself. Beyond all that I am, the sun
Scatters its light as though by accident.

The fox eats its own leg in the trap
To go free. As it limps through the grass
The earth itself appears to bleed.
When the morning light comes up
Who knows what suffering midnight was?
Proof is what I do not need.

# SEAMUS HEANEY

## Bogland

*for T. P. Flanagan*

We have no prairies
To slice a big sun at evening –
Everywhere the eye concedes to
Encroaching horizon,

Is wooed into the cyclops' eye
Of a tarn. Our unfenced country
Is bog that keeps crusting
Between the sights of the sun.

They've taken the skeleton
Of the Great Irish Elk
Out of the peat, set it up
An astounding crate full of air.

Butter sunk under
More than a hundred years
Was recovered salty and white.
The ground itself is kind, black butter

Melting and opening underfoot,
Missing its last definition
By millions of years.
They'll never dig coal here,

Only the waterlogged trunks
Of great firs, soft as pulp.
Our pioneers keep striking
Inwards and downwards,

Every layer they strip
Seems camped on before.
The bogholes might be Atlantic seepage.
The wet centre is bottomless.

# Anahorish

My 'place of clear water',
the first hill in the world
where springs washed into
the shiny grass

and darkened cobbles
in the bed of the lane.
*Anahorish*, soft gradient
of consonant, vowel-meadow,

after-image of lamps
swung through the yards
on winter evenings.
With pails and barrows

those mound-dwellers
go waist-deep in mist
to break the light ice
at wells and dunghills.

# The Tollund Man

## 1

Some day I will go to Aarhus
To see his peat-brown head,
The mild pods of his eye-lids,
His pointed skin cap.

In the flat country nearby
Where they dug him out,
His last gruel of winter seeds
Caked in his stomach,

Naked except for
The cap, noose and girdle,
I will stand a long time.
Bridegroom to the goddess,

She tightened her torc on him
And opened her fen,
Those dark juices working
Him to a saint's kept body,

Trove of the turfcutters'
Honeycombed workings.
Now his stained face
Reposes at Aarhus.

## 2

I could risk blasphemy,
Consecrate the cauldron bog
Our holy ground and pray
Him to make germinate

The scattered, ambushed
Flesh of labourers,
Stockinged corpses
Laid out in the farmyards,

Tell-tale skin and teeth
Flecking the sleepers
Of four young brothers, trailed
For miles along the lines.

### 3

Something of his sad freedom
As he rode the tumbril
Should come to me, driving,
Saying the names

Tollund, Grauballe, Nebelgard,
Watching the pointing hands
Of country people,
Not knowing their tongue.

Out there in Jutland
In the old man-killing parishes
I will feel lost,
Unhappy and at home.

# Summer Home

### 1

Was it wind off the dumps
or something in heat

dogging us, the summer gone sour,
a fouled nest incubating somewhere?

Whose fault, I wondered, inquisitor
of the possessed air.

To realize suddenly,
whip off the mat

that was larval, moving –
and scald, scald, scald.

### 2

Bushing the door, my arms full
of wild cherry and rhododendron,
I hear her small lost weeping
through the hall, that bells and hoarsens
on my name, my name.

O love, here is the blame.

The loosened flowers between us
gather in, compose
for a May altar of sorts.
These frank and falling blooms
soon taint to a sweet chrism.

Attend. Anoint the wound.

### 3

O we tented our wound all right
under the homely sheet

and lay as if the cold flat of a blade
had winded us.

More and more I postulate
thick healings, like now

as you bend in the shower
water lives down the tilting stoups of your breasts.

### 4

With a final
unmusical drive
long grains begin
to open and split

ahead and once more
we sap
the white, trodden
path to the heart.

### 5

My children weep out the hot foreign night.
We walk the floor, my foul mouth takes it out
On you and we lie stiff till dawn
Attends the pillow, and the maize, and vine

That holds its filling burden to the light.
Yesterday rocks sang when we tapped
Stalactites in the cave's old, dripping dark –
Our love calls tiny as a tuning fork.

# Funeral Rites

## I

I shouldered a kind of manhood
stepping in to lift the coffins
of dead relations.
They had been laid out

in tainted rooms,
their eyelids glistening,
their dough-white hands
shackled in rosary beads.

Their puffed knuckles
had unwrinkled, the nails
were darkened, the wrists
obediently sloped.

The dulse-brown shroud,
the quilted satin cribs:
I knelt courteously
admiring it all

as wax melted down
and veined the candles,
the flames hovering
to the women hovering

behind me.
And always, in a corner,
the coffin lid,
its nail-heads dressed

with little gleaming crosses.
Dear soapstone masks,
kissing their igloo brows
had to suffice

before the nails were sunk
and the black glacier
of each funeral
pushed away.

2

Now as news comes in
of each neighbourly murder
we pine for ceremony,
customary rhythms:

the temperate footsteps
of a cortège, winding past
each blinded home.
I would restore

the great chambers of Boyne,
prepare a sepulchre
under the cupmarked stones.
Out of side-streets and by-roads

purring family cars
nose into line,
the whole country tunes
to the muffled drumming

of ten thousand engines.
Somnambulant women,
left behind, move
through emptied kitchens

imagining our slow triumph
towards the mounds.
Quiet as a serpent
in its grassy boulevard

the procession drags its tail
out of the Gap of the North
as its head already enters
the megalithic doorway.

### 3

When they have put the stone
back in its mouth
we will drive north again
past Strang and Carling fjords

the cud of memory
allayed for once, arbitration
of the feud placated,
imagining those under the hill

disposed like Gunnar
who lay beautiful
inside his burial mound,
though dead by violence

and unavenged.
Men said that he was chanting
verses about honour
and that four lights burned

in corners of the chamber:
which opened then, as he turned
with a joyful face
to look at the moon.

# Punishment

I can feel the tug
of the halter at the nape
of her neck, the wind
on her naked front.

It blows her nipples
to amber beads,
it shakes the frail rigging
of her ribs.

I can see her drowned
body in the bog,
the weighing stone,
the floating rods and boughs.

Under which at first
she was a barked sapling
that is dug up
oak-bone, brain-firkin:

her shaved head
like a stubble of black corn,
her blindfold a soiled bandage,
her noose a ring

to store
the memories of love.
Little adulteress,
before they punished you

you were flaxen-haired,
undernourished, and your
tar-black face was beautiful.
My poor scapegoat,

I almost love you
but would have cast, I know,
the stones of silence.
I am the artful voyeur

of your brain's exposed
and darkened combs,
your muscles' webbing
and all your numbered bones:

I who have stood dumb
when your betraying sisters,
cauled in tar,
wept by the railings,

who would connive
in civilized outrage
yet understand the exact
and tribal, intimate revenge.

# Exposure

It is December in Wicklow:
Alders dripping, birches
Inheriting the last light,
The ash tree cold to look at.

A comet that was lost
Should be visible at sunset,
Those million tons of light
Like a glimmer of haws and rose-hips,

And I sometimes see a falling star.
If I could come on meteorite!
Instead I walk through damp leaves,
Husks, the spent flukes of autumn,

Imagining a hero
On some muddy compound,
His gift like a slingstone
Whirled for the desperate.

How did I end up like this?
I often think of my friends'
Beautiful prismatic counselling
And the anvil brains of some who hate me

As I sit weighing and weighing
My responsible *tristia*.
For what? For the ear? For the people?
For what is said behind-backs?

Rain comes down through the alders,
Its low conducive voices
Mutter about let-downs and erosions
And yet each drop recalls

The diamond absolutes.
I am neither internee nor informer;
An inner émigré, grown long-haired
And thoughtful; a wood-kerne

Escaped from the massacre,
Taking protective colouring
From bole and bark, feeling
Every wind that blows;

Who, blowing up these sparks
For their meagre heat, have missed
The once-in-a-lifetime portent,
The comet's pulsing rose.

# A Postcard from North Antrim

*in memory of Sean Armstrong*

A lone figure is waving
From the thin line of a bridge
Of ropes and slats, slung
Dangerously out between
The cliff-top and the pillar rock.
A nineteenth-century wind.
Dulse-pickers. Sea campions.

A postcard for you, Sean,
And that's you, swinging alone,
Antic, half-afraid,
In your gallowglass's beard
And swallow-tail of serge:
*The Carrick-a-Rede Rope Bridge*
Ghost-written on sepia.

Or should it be your houseboat
Ethnically furnished,
Redolent of grass?
Should we discover you
Beside those warm-planked, democratic wharves
Among the twilights and guitars
Of Sausalito?

Drop-out on a come-back,
Prince of no-man's land
With your head in clouds or sand,
You were the clown
Social worker of the town
Until your candid forehead stopped
A pointblank teatime bullet.

Get up from your blood on the floor.
Here's another boat

In grass by the lough shore,
Turf smoke, a wired hen-run –
Your local, hoped for, unfound commune.
Now recite me *William Bloat*,
Sing of *the Calabar*

Or of Henry Joy McCracken
Who kissed his Mary Ann
On the gallows at Cornmarket.
Or Ballycastle Fair.
'Give us the raw bar!'
'Sing it by brute force
If you forget the air.'

Yet something in your voice
Stayed nearly shut.
Your voice was a harassed pulpit
Leading the melody
It kept at bay,
It was independent, rattling, non-transcendent
Ulster – old decency

And Old Bushmills,
Soda farls, strong tea,
New rope, rock salt, kale plants,
Potato-bread and Woodbine.
Wind through the concrete vents
Of a border check-point.
Cold zinc nailed for a peace line.

Fifteen years ago, come this October,
Crowded on your floor,
I got my arm round Marie's shoulder
For the first time.
'Oh, Sir Jasper, do not touch me!'
You roared across at me,
Chorus-leading, splashing out the wine.

# Casualty

## I

He would drink by himself
And raise a weathered thumb
Towards the high shelf,
Calling another rum
And blackcurrant, without
Having to raise his voice,
Or order a quick stout
By a lifting of the eyes
And a discreet dumb-show
Of pulling off the top;
At closing time would go
In waders and peaked cap
Into the showery dark,
A dole-kept breadwinner
But a natural for work.
I loved his whole manner,
Sure-footed but too sly,
His deadpan sidling tact,
His fisherman's quick eye
And turned observant back.

Incomprehensible
To him, my other life.
Sometimes, on his high stool,
Too busy with his knife
At a tobacco plug
And not meeting my eye,
In the pause after a slug
He mentioned poetry.
We would be on our own
And, always politic
And shy of condescension,

I would manage by some trick
To switch the talk to eels
Or lore of the horse and cart
Or the Provisionals.

But my tentative art
His turned back watches too:
He was blown to bits
Out drinking in a curfew
Others obeyed, three nights
After they shot dead
The thirteen men in Derry.
PARAS THIRTEEN, the walls said,
BOGSIDE NIL. That Wednesday
Everybody held
His breath and trembled.

2

It was a day of cold
Raw silence, wind-blown
Surplice and soutane:
Rained-on, flower-laden
Coffin after coffin
Seemed to float from the door
Of the packed cathedral
Like blossoms on slow water.
The common funeral
Unrolled its swaddling band,
Lapping, tightening
Till we were braced and bound
Like brothers in a ring.

But he would not be held
At home by his own crowd
Whatever threats were phoned,
Whatever black flags waved.

I see him as he turned
In that bombed offending place,
Remorse fused with terror
In his still knowable face,
His cornered outfaced stare
Blinding in the flash.

He had gone miles away
For he drank like a fish
Nightly, naturally
Swimming towards the lure
Of warm lit-up places,
The blurred mesh and murmur
Drifting among glasses
In the gregarious smoke.
How culpable was he
That last night when he broke
Our tribe's complicity?
'Now you're supposed to be
An educated man,'
I hear him say. 'Puzzle me
The right answer to that one.'

### 3

I missed his funeral,
Those quiet walkers
And sideways talkers
Shoaling out of his lane
To the respectable
Purring of the hearse . . .
They move in equal pace
With the habitual
Slow consolation
Of a dawdling engine,
The line lifted, hand
Over fist, cold sunshine

On the water, the land
Banked under fog: that morning
I was taken in his boat,
The screw purling, turning
Indolent fathoms white,
I tasted freedom with him.
To get out early, haul
Steadily off the bottom,
Dispraise the catch, and smile
As you find a rhythm
Working you, slow mile by mile,
Into your proper haunt
Somewhere, well out, beyond . . .

Dawn-sniffing revenant,
Plodder through midnight rain,
Question me again.

# The Harvest Bow

As you plaited the harvest bow
You implicated the mellowed silence in you
In wheat that does not rust
But brightens as it tightens twist by twist
Into a knowable corona,
A throwaway love-knot of straw.

Hands that aged round ashplants and cane sticks
And lapped the spurs on a lifetime of game cocks
Harked to their gift and worked with fine intent
Until your fingers moved somnambulant:
I tell and finger it like braille,
Gleaning the unsaid off the palpable,

And if I spy into its golden loops
I see us walk between the railway slopes
Into an evening of long grass and midges,
Blue smoke straight up, old beds and ploughs in hedges,
An auction notice on an outhouse wall –
You with a harvest bow in your lapel,

Me with the fishing rod, already homesick
For the big lift of these evenings, as your stick
Whacking the tips off weeds and bushes
Beats out of time, and beats, but flushes
Nothing: that original townland
Still tongue-tied in the straw tied by your hand.

*The end of art is peace*
Could be the motto of this frail device
That I have pinned up on our deal dresser –
Like a drawn snare
Slipped lately by the spirit of the corn
Yet burnished by its passage, and still warm.

# An Ulster Twilight

The bare bulb, a scatter of nails,
Shelved timber, glinting chisels:
In a shed of corrugated iron
Eric Dawson stoops to his plane

At five o'clock on a Christmas Eve.
Carpenter's pencil next, the spoke-shave,
Fretsaw, auger, rasp and awl,
A rub with a rag of linseed oil.

A mile away it was taking shape,
The hulk of a toy battleship,
As waterbuckets iced and frost
Hardened the quiet on roof and post.

Where is he now?
There were fifteen years between us two
That night I strained to hear the bells
Of a sleigh of the mind and heard him pedal

Into our lane, get off at the gable,
Steady his Raleigh bicycle
Against the whitewash, stand to make sure
The house was quiet, knock at the door

And hand his parcel to a peering woman:
'I suppose you thought I was never coming.'
Eric, tonight I saw it all
Like shadows on your workshop wall,

Smelled wood shavings under the bench,
Weighed the cold steel monkey-wrench
In my soft hand, then stood at the road
To watch your wavering tail-light fade

And knew that if we met again
In an Ulster twilight we would begin
And end whatever we might say
In a speech all toys and carpentry,

A doorstep courtesy to shun
Your father's uniform and gun,
But – now that I have said it out –
Maybe none the worse for that.

# *from* Station Island

## 7

I had come to the edge of the water,
soothed by just looking, idling over it
as if it were a clear barometer

or a mirror, when his reflection
did not appear but I sensed a presence
entering into my concentration

on not being concentrated as he spoke
my name. And though I was reluctant
I turned to meet his face and the shock

is still in me at what I saw. His brow
was blown open above the eye and blood
had dried on his neck and cheek. 'Easy now,'

he said, 'it's only me. You've seen men as raw
after a football match . . . What time it was
when I was wakened up I still don't know

but I heard this knocking, knocking, and it
scared me, like the phone in the small hours,
so I had the sense not to put on the light

but looked out from behind the curtain.
I saw two customers on the doorstep
and an old landrover with the doors open

parked on the street so I let the curtain drop;
but they must have been waiting for it to move
for they shouted to come down into the shop.

She started to cry then and roll round the bed,
lamenting and lamenting to herself,
not even asking who it was. "Is your head

astray, or what's come over you?" I roared, more
to bring myself to my senses
than out of any real anger at her

for the knocking shook me, the way they kept it up,
and her whingeing and half-screeching made it worse.
All the time they were shouting, "Shop!

Shop!" so I pulled on my shoes and a sportscoat
and went back to the window and called out,
"What do you want? Could you quieten the racket

or I'll not come down at all." "There's a child not well.
Open up and see what you have got – pills
or a powder or something in a bottle,"

one of them said. He stepped back off the footpath
so I could see his face in the street lamp
and when the other moved I knew them both.

But bad and all as the knocking was, the quiet
hit me worse. She was quiet herself now,
lying dead still, whispering to watch out.

At the bedroom door I switched on the light.
"It's odd they didn't look for a chemist.
Who are they anyway at this time of the night?"

she asked me, with the eyes standing in her head.
"I know them to see," I said, but something
made me reach and squeeze her hand across the bed

before I went downstairs into the aisle
of the shop. I stood there, going weak
in the legs. I remember the stale smell

of cooked meat or something coming through
as I went to open up. From then on
you know as much about it as I do.'

'Did they say nothing?' 'Nothing. What would they say?'
'Were they in uniform? Not masked in any way?'
'They were barefaced as they would be in the day,

shites thinking they were the be-all and the end-all.'
'Not that it is any consolation,
but they were caught,' I told him, 'and got jail.'

Big-limbed, decent, open-faced, he stood
forgetful of everything now except
whatever was welling up in his spoiled head,

beginning to smile. 'You've put on weight
since you did your courting in that big Austin
you got the loan of on a Sunday night.'

Through life and death he had hardly aged.
There always was an athlete's cleanliness
shining off him and except for the ravaged

forehead and the blood, he was still that same
rangy midfielder in a blue jersey
and starched pants, the one stylist on the team,

the perfect, clean, unthinkable victim.
'Forgive the way I have lived indifferent –
forgive my timid circumspect involvement,'

I surprised myself by saying. 'Forgive
my eye,' he said, 'all that's above my head.'
And then a stun of pain seemed to go through him

and he trembled like a heatwave and faded.

# Clearances

*in memoriam M.K.H., 1911–1984*

> *She taught me what her uncle once taught her:*
> *How easily the biggest coal block split*
> *If you got the grain and hammer angled right.*
>
> *The sound of that relaxed alluring blow,*
> *Its co-opted and obliterated echo,*
> *Taught me to hit, taught me to loosen,*
>
> *Taught me between the hammer and the block*
> *To face the music. Teach me now to listen,*
> *To strike it rich behind the linear black.*

## 1

A cobble thrown a hundred years ago
Keeps coming at me, the first stone
Aimed at a great-grandmother's turncoat brow.
The pony jerks and the riot's on.
She's crouched low in the trap
Running the gauntlet that first Sunday
Down the brae to Mass at a panicked gallop.
He whips on through the town to cries of 'Lundy!'

Call her 'The Convert'. 'The Exogamous Bride'.
Anyhow, it is a genre piece
Inherited on my mother's side
And mine to dispose with now she's gone.
Instead of silver and Victorian lace,
The exonerating, exonerated stone.

## 2

Polished linoleum shone there. Brass taps shone.
The china cups were very white and big –
An unchipped set with sugar bowl and jug.

The kettle whistled. Sandwich and teascone
Were present and correct. In case it run,
The butter must be kept out of the sun.
And don't be dropping crumbs. Don't tilt your chair.
Don't reach. Don't point. Don't make noise when you stir.

It is Number 5, New Row, Land of the Dead,
Where grandfather is rising from his place
With spectacles pushed back on a clean bald head
To welcome a bewildered homing daughter
Before she even knocks. 'What's this? What's this?'
And they sit down in the shining room together.

### 3

When all the others were away at Mass
I was all hers as we peeled potatoes.
They broke the silence, let fall one by one
Like solder weeping off the soldering iron:
Cold comforts set between us, things to share
Gleaming in a bucket of clean water.
And again let fall. Little pleasant splashes
From each other's work would bring us to our senses.

So while the parish priest at her bedside
Went hammer and tongs at the prayers for the dying
And some were responding and some crying
I remembered her head bent towards my head,
Her breath in mine, our fluent dipping knives –
Never closer the whole rest of our lives.

### 4

Fear of affectation made her affect
Inadequacy whenever it came to
Pronouncing words 'beyond her'. *Bertold Brek.*
She'd manage something hampered and askew
Every time, as if she might betray
The hampered and inadequate by too

Well-adjusted a vocabulary.
With more challenge than pride, she'd tell me, 'You
Know all them things.' So I governed my tongue
In front of her, a genuinely well-
adjusted adequate betrayal
Of what I knew better. I'd *naw* and *aye*
And decently relapse into the wrong
Grammar which kept us allied and at bay.

### 5

The cool that came off sheets just off the line
Made me think the damp must still be in them
But when I took my corners of the linen
And pulled against her, first straight down the hem
And then diagonally, then flapped and shook
The fabric like a sail in a cross-wind,
They made a dried-out undulating thwack.
So we'd stretch and fold and end up hand to hand
For a split second as if nothing had happened
For nothing had that had not always happened
Beforehand, day by day, just touch and go,
Coming close again by holding back
In moves where I was x and she was o
Inscribed in sheets she'd sewn from ripped-out flour sacks.

### 6

In the first flush of the Easter holidays
The ceremonies during Holy Week
Were highpoints of our *Sons and Lovers* phase.
The midnight fire. The paschal candlestick.
Elbow to elbow, glad to be kneeling next
To each other up there near the front
Of the packed church, we would follow the text
And rubrics for the blessing of the font.
*As the hind longs for the streams, so my soul . . .*
Dippings. Towellings. The water breathed on.

The water mixed with chrism and with oil.
Cruet tinkle. Formal incensation
And the psalmist's outcry taken up with pride:
*Day and night my tears have been my bread.*

### 7

In the last minutes he said more to her
Almost than in all their life together.
'You'll be in New Row on Monday night
And I'll come up for you and you'll be glad
When I walk in the door . . . Isn't that right?'
His head was bent down to her propped-up head.
She could not hear but we were overjoyed.
He called her good and girl. Then she was dead,
The searching for a pulsebeat was abandoned
And we all knew one thing by being there.
The space we stood around had been emptied
Into us to keep, it penetrated
Clearances that suddenly stood open.
High crics were felled and a pure change happened.

### 8

I thought of walking round and round a space
Utterly empty, utterly a source
Where the decked chestnut tree had lost its place
In our front hedge above the wallflowers.
The white chips jumped and jumped and skited high.
I heard the hatchet's differentiated
Accurate cut, the crack, the sigh
And collapse of what luxuriated
Through the shocked tips and wreckage of it all.
Deep planted and long gone, my coeval
Chestnut from a jam jar in a hole,
Its heft and hush become a bright nowhere,
A soul ramifying and forever
Silent, beyond silence listened for.

# The Mud Vision

Statues with exposed hearts and barbed-wire crowns
Still stood in alcoves, hares flitted beneath
The dozing bellies of jets, our menu-writers
And punks with aerosol sprays held their own
With the best of them. Satellite link-ups
Wafted over us the blessings of popes, heliports
Maintained a charmed circle for idols on tour
And casualties on their stretchers. We sleepwalked
The line between panic and formulae, screentested
Our first native models and the last of the mummers,
Watching ourselves at a distance, advantaged
And airy as a man on a springboard
Who keeps limbering up because the man cannot dive.

And then in the foggy midlands it appeared,
Our mud vision, as if a rose window of mud
Had invented itself out of the glittery damp,
A gossamer wheel, concentric with its own hub
Of nebulous dirt, sullied yet lucent.
We had heard of the sun standing still and the sun
That changed colour, but we were vouchsafed
Original clay, transfigured and spinning.
And then the sunsets ran murky, the wiper
Could never entirely clean off the windscreen,
Reservoirs tasted of silt, a light fuzz
Accrued in the hair and the eyebrows, and some
Took to wearing a smudge on their foreheads
To be prepared for whatever. Vigils
Began to be kept around puddled gaps,
On altars bulrushes ousted the lilies
And a rota of invalids came and went
On beds they could lease placed in range of the shower.

A generation who had seen a sign!
Those nights when we stood in an umber dew and smelled
Mould in the verbena, or woke to a light
Furrow-breath on the pillow, when the talk
Was all about who had seen it and our fear
Was touched with a secret pride, only ourselves
Could be adequate then to our lives. When the rainbow
Curved flood-brown and ran like a water-rat's back
So that drivers on the hard shoulder switched off to watch,
We wished it away, and yet we presumed it a test
That would prove us beyond expectation.

We lived, of course, to learn the folly of that.
One day it was gone and the east gable
Where its trembling corolla had balanced
Was starkly a ruin again, with dandelions
Blowing high up on the ledges, and moss
That slumbered on through its increase. As cameras raked
The site from every angle, experts
Began their *post factum* jabber and all of us
Crowded in tight for the big explanations.
Just like that, we forgot that the vision was ours,
Our one chance to know the incomparable
And dive to a future. What might have been origin
We dissipated in news. The clarified place
Had retrieved neither us nor itself – except
You could say we survived. So say that, and watch us
Who had our chance to be mud-men, convinced and estranged,
Figure in our own eyes for the eyes of the world.

# MICHAEL LONGLEY

## Persephone

### 1

I see as through a skylight in my brain
The mole strew its buildings in the rain,

The swallows turn above their broken home
And all my acres in delirium.

### 2

Straitjacketed by cold and numskulled
Now sleep the welladjusted and the skilled –

The bat folds its wing like a winter leaf,
The squirrel in its hollow holds aloof.

### 3

The weasel and ferret, the stoat and fox
Move hand in glove across the equinox.

I can tell how softly their footsteps go –
Their footsteps borrow silence from the snow.

# The Hebrides

*for Eavan Boland*

I

The winds' enclosure, Atlantic's premises,
      Last balconies
   Above the waves, The Hebrides –
    Too long did I postpone
Presbyterian granite and the lack of trees,
      This orphaned stone

Day in, day out colliding with the sea.
      Weather forecast,
   Compass nor ordnance survey
    Arranges my welcome
For, on my own, I have lost my way at last,
      So far from home.

In whom the city is continuing,
      I stop to look,
   To find my feet among the ling
    And bracken – over me
The bright continuum of gulls, a rook
      Occasionally.

2

My eyes, slowly accepting panorama,
      Try to include
   In my original idea
    The total effect
Of air and ocean – waterlogged all wood –
      All harbours wrecked –

My dead-lights latched by whelk and barnacle
      Till I abide

By the sea wall of the time I kill –
    My each nostalgic scheme
Jettisoned, as crises are, the further side
    Of sleep and dream.

Between wind and wave this holiday
    The cormorant,
  The oyster-catcher and osprey
    Proceed and keep in line
While I, hands in my pockets, hesitant,
    Am in two minds.

### 3

Old neighbours, though shipwreck's my decision,
    People my brain –
  Like breakwaters against the sun,
    Command in silhouette
My island circumstance – my cells retain,
    Perpetuate

Their crumpled deportment through bad weather.
    And I feel them
  Put on their raincoats for ever
    And walk out in the sea.
I am, though each one waves a phantom limb,
    The amputee,

For these are my sailors, these my drowned –
    In their heart of hearts,
  In their city I ran aground.
    Along my arteries
Sluice those homewaters petroleum hurts.
    Dry dock, gantries,

Dykes of apparatus educate my bones
    To track the buoys
  Up sea lanes love emblazons
    To streets where shall conclude

My journey back from flux to poise, from poise
    To attitude.

Here, at the edge of my experience,
    Another tide
  Along the broken shore extends
    A lifetime's wrack and ruin –
No flotsam I may beachcomb now can hide
    That water line.

### 4

Beyond the lobster pots where plankton spreads
    Porpoises turn.
  Seals slip over the cockle beds.
    Undertow dishevels
Seaweed in the shallows – and I discern
    My sea levels.

To right and left of me there intervene
    The tumbled burns –
  And these, on turf and boulder weaned,
    Confuse my calendar –
Their tilt is suicidal, their great return
    Curricular.

No matter what repose holds shore and sky
    In harmony,
  From this place in the long run I,
    Though here I might have been
Content with rivers where they meet the sea,
    Remove upstream,

Where the salmon, risking fastest waters –
    Waterfall and rock
  And the effervescent otters –
    On bridal pools insist
As with fin and generation they unlock
    The mountain's fist.

## 5

Now, buttoned up, with water in my shoes,
    Clouds around me,
  I can, through mist that misconstrues,
    Read like a palimpsest
My past – those landmarks and that scenery
    I dare resist.

Into my mind's unsympathetic trough
    They fade away –
  And to alter my perspective
    I feel in the sharp cold
Of my vantage point too high above the bay
    The sea grow old.

Granting the trawlers far below their stance,
    Their anchorage,
  I fight all the way for balance –
    In the mountain's shadow
Losing foothold, covet the privilege
    Of vertigo.

# Wounds

Here are two pictures from my father's head –
I have kept them like secrets until now:
First, the Ulster Division at the Somme
Going over the top with 'Fuck the Pope!'
'No Surrender!': a boy about to die,
Screaming 'Give 'em one for the Shankill!'
'Wilder than Gurkhas' were my father's words
Of admiration and bewilderment.
Next comes the London-Scottish padre
Resettling kilts with his swagger-stick,
With a stylish backhand and a prayer.
Over a landscape of dead buttocks
My father followed him for fifty years.
At last, a belated casualty,
He said – lead traces flaring till they hurt –
'I am dying for King and Country, slowly.'
I touched his hand, his thin head I touched.

Now, with military honours of a kind,
With his badges, his medals like rainbows,
His spinning compass, I bury beside him
Three teenage soldiers, bellies full of
Bullets and Irish beer, their flies undone.
A packet of Woodbines I throw in,
A lucifer, the Sacred Heart of Jesus
Paralysed as heavy guns put out
The night-light in a nursery for ever;
Also a bus-conductor's uniform –
He collapsed beside his carpet-slippers
Without a murmur, shot through the head
By a shivering boy who wandered in
Before they could turn the television down
Or tidy away the supper dishes.
To the children, to a bewildered wife,
I think 'Sorry Missus' was what he said.

# The West

Beneath a gas-mantel that the moths bombard,
Light that powders at a touch, dusty wings,
I listen for news through the atmospherics,
A crackle of sea-wrack, spinning driftwood,
Waves like distant traffic, news from home,

Or watch myself, as through a sandy lens,
Materializing out of the heat-shimmers
And finding my way for ever along
The path to this cottage, its windows,
Walls, sun and moon dials, home from home.

# In Memory of Gerard Dillon

### 1

You walked, all of a sudden, through
The rickety gate which opens
To a scatter of curlews,
An acre of watery light; your grave
A dip in the dunes where sand mislays
The sound of the sea, earth over you
Like a low Irish sky; the sun
An electric light bulb clouded
By the sandy tides, sunlight lost
And found, a message in a bottle.

### 2

You are a room full of self-portraits,
A face that follows us everywhere;
An ear to the ground listening for
Dead brothers in layers; an eye
Taking in the beautiful predators –
Cats on the windowsill, birds of prey
And, between the diminutive fields,
A dragonfly, wings full of light
Where the road narrows to the last farm.

### 3

Christening robes, communion dresses,
The shawls of factory workers,
A blind drawn on the Lower Falls.

# Skara Brae

*for Sheila and Denis Smyth*

A window into the ground,
The bumpy lawn in section,
An exploded view
Through middens, through lives,

The thatch of grass roots,
The gravelly roof compounding
Periwinkles, small bones,
A calendar of meals,

The thread between sepulchre
And home a broken necklace,
Knuckles, dice scattering
At the warren's core,

Pebbles the tide washes
That conceded for so long
Living room, the hard beds,
The table made of stone.

# Ash Keys

Ghosts of hedgers and ditchers,
The ash trees rattling keys
Above tangles of hawthorn
And bramble, alder and gorse,

Would keep me from pacing
Commonage, long perspectives
And conversations, a field
That touches the horizon.

I am herding cattle there
As a boy, as the old man
Following in his footsteps
Who begins the task again,

As though there'd never been
In some interim or hollow
Wives and children, milk
And buttermilk, market days.

Far from the perimeter
Of watercress and berries,
In the middle of the field
I stand talking to myself,

While the ash keys scatter
And the gates creak open
And the barbed wire rusts
To hay-ropes strung with thorns.

# Frozen Rain

I slow down the waterfall to a chandelier,
Filaments of daylight, bones fleshed out by ice
That recuperate in their bandages of glass
And, where the lake behaves like a spirit-level,
I save pockets of air for the otter to breathe.

I magnify each individual blade of grass
With frozen rain, a crop of icicles and twigs,
Fingers and thumbs that beckon towards the thaw
And melt to the marrow between lip and tongue
While the wind strikes the branches like a celeste.

# Peace

*after Tibullus*

Who was responsible for the very first arms deal –
The man of iron who thought of marketing the sword?
Or did he intend us to use it against wild animals
Rather than ourselves? Even if he's not guilty
Murder got into the bloodstream as gene or virus
So that now we give birth to wars, short cuts to death.
Blame the affluent society: no killings when
The cup on the dinner table was made of beechwood,
And no barricades or ghettos when the shepherd
Snoozed among sheep that weren't even thoroughbreds.

I would like to have been alive in the good old days
Before the horrors of modern warfare and warcries
Stepping up my pulse rate. Alas, as things turn out
I've been press-ganged into service, and for all I know
Someone's polishing a spear with my number on it.
God of my Fathers, look after me like a child!
And don't be embarrassed by this handmade statue
Carved out of bog oak by my great-great-grandfather
Before the mass-production of religious art
When a wooden god stood simply in a narrow shrine.

A man could worship there with bunches of early grapes,
A wreath of whiskery wheat-ears, and then say Thank you
With a wholemeal loaf delivered by him in person,
His daughter carrying the unbroken honeycomb.
If the good Lord keeps me out of the firing line
I'll pick a porker from the steamy sty and dress
In my Sunday best, a country cousin's sacrifice.
Someone else can slaughter enemy commanders
And, over a drink, rehearse with me his memoirs,
Mapping the camp in wine upon the table top.

It's crazy to beg black death to join the ranks
Who dogs our footsteps anyhow with silent feet –
No cornfields in Hell, nor cultivated vineyards,
Only yapping Cerberus and the unattractive
Oarsman of the Styx: there an anaemic crew
Sleepwalks with smoky hair and empty eye-sockets.
How much nicer to have a family and let
Lazy old age catch up on you in your retirement,
You keeping track of the sheep, your son of the lambs,
While the woman of the house puts on the kettle.

I want to live until the white hairs shine above
A pensioner's memories of better days. Meanwhile
I would like peace to be my partner on the farm,
Peace personified: oxen under the curved yoke;
Compost for the vines, grape-juice turning into wine,
Vintage years handed down from father to son;
Hoe and ploughshare gleaming, while in some dark corner
Rust keeps the soldier's grisly weapons in their place;
The labourer steering his wife and children home
In a hay cart from the fields, a trifle sozzled.

Then, if there are skirmishes, guerilla tactics,
It's only lovers quarrelling, the bedroom door
Wrenched off its hinges, a woman in hysterics,
Hair torn out, cheeks swollen with bruises and tears –
Until the bully-boy starts snivelling as well
In a pang of conscience for his battered wife:
Then sexual neurosis works them up again
And the row escalates into a war of words.
He's hard as nails, made of sticks and stones, the chap
Who beats his girlfriend up. A crime against nature.

Enough, surely, to rip from her skin the flimsiest
Of negligees, ruffle that elaborate hair-do,
Enough to be the involuntary cause of tears –
Though upsetting a sensitive girl when you sulk
Is a peculiar satisfaction. But punch-ups,

Physical violence, are out: you might as well
Pack your kit-bag, goose-step a thousand miles away
From the female sex. As for me, I want a woman
To come and fondle my ears of wheat and let apples
Overflow between her breasts. I shall call her Peace.

# The Linen Industry

Pulling up flax after the blue flowers have fallen
And laying our handfuls in the peaty water
To rot those grasses to the bone, or building stooks
That recall the skirts of an invisible dancer,

We become a part of the linen industry
And follow its processes to the grubby town
Where fields are compacted into window-boxes
And there is little room among the big machines.

But even in our attic under the skylight
We make love on a bleach green, the whole meadow
Draped with material turning white in the sun
As though snow reluctant to melt were our attire.

What's passion but a battering of stubborn stalks,
Then a gentle combing out of fibres like hair
And a weaving of these into christening robes,
Into garments for a marriage or funeral?

Since it's like a bereavement once the labour's done
To find ourselves last workers in a dying trade,
Let flax be our matchmaker, our undertaker,
The provider of sheets for whatever the bed –

And be shy of your breasts in the presence of death,
Say that you look more beautiful in linen
Wearing white petticoats, the bow on your bodice
A butterfly attending the embroidered flowers.

# Remembering Carrigskeewaun

A wintry night, the hearth inhales
And the chimney becomes a windpipe
Fluffy with soot and thistledown,
A voice-box recalling animals:
The leveret come of age, snipe
At an angle, then the porpoises'
Demonstration of meaningless smiles.
Home is a hollow between the waves,
A clump of nettles, feathery winds,
And memory no longer than a day
When the animals come back to me
From the townland of Carrigskeewaun,
From a page lit by the Milky Way.

# SEAMUS DEANE

## Power Cut

Any dogsbody can sit up all night
And work in a cube of electric light
With only a little spilt ink of shadow
Under the hands and feet. This is a slight
On creativity, the whiter-than-white
Hope to be in there with the black
Shadow-boxers of the past. It's too neat,
Too easy, and it can't be right.

But in candlelight, a high devil looms
On my shoulder and my hand locks on the white
Fire circle. He is so real I can smell
His bad breath of the old rooms
Where the exorcist abandoned him,
The cinemas, jukeboxes and bars
Of a dark city kicked in by winter.
Medusa-light, with yellow wing of flame,

And waxy, serpent head, you are the bright
Petrifier of this darkness, the white lady
Of these locked shadows, the diamond
In the coal-black night, and in you,
As in a lover, I recapture the slight
Moonbeams in the linens of long ago,
The afternoons moiling in the keyhole;
In you, petrified, I recapture night.

# Return

The train shot through the dark.
Hedges leapt across the window-pane.
Trees belled in foliage were stranded,
Inarticulate with rain.
A blur of lighted farm implied
The evacuated countryside.

I am appalled by its emptiness.
Every valley glows with pain
As we run like a current through;
Then the memories darken again.
In this Irish past I dwell
Like sound implicit in a bell.

The train curves round a river,
And how tenderly its gouts of steam
Contemplate the nodding moon
The waters from the clouds redeem.
Two hours from Belfast
I am snared in my past.

Crusts of light lie pulsing
Diamanté with the rain
At the track's end. Amazing!
I am in Derry once again.
Once more I turn to greet
Ground that flees from my feet.

# Fording the River

Sunday afternoon and the water
Black among the stones, the forest
Ash-grey in its permanent dusk
Of unquivering pine. That day
You unexpectedly crossed the river.

It was cold and you quickly shouted
As your feet felt the white stones
Knocking together. I had bent
To examine a strand of barbed wire
Looping up from a buried fence

When I heard you shout. And,
There you were, on the other side,
Running away. In a slow puncturing
Of anticipation I shivered
As if you had, unpermitted, gone forever.

Gone, although you were already in the middle
Coming back; I picked up
Your shoes with a sense that years
Had suddenly decided to pass.
I remembered your riddle

On the way up here. '"Brother or sister
I have none, but that man's father
Is my father's son." Who am I
Talking about?' About my son,
Who crossed cold Lethe, thought it Rubicon.

# Osip Mandelstam

'The people need poetry.' That voice
That was last heard asking for warm
Clothes and money, also knew the hunger
We all have for the gold light
The goldfinch carries into the air
Like a tang of crushed almonds.

Nine months before heart-failure
Silenced his silk-sharp whistle
That haunted the steppes as though
A small shrapnel of birds scattered,
Bukharin, his protector, was shot
Along with Yagoda, Rykov, others.

The kerosene flash of his music
Leaps from the black earth,
From the whitening dead of the War
Who burn in its flammable spirit.
The fire-crop smokes in the Kremlin's
Eyes and the scorched marl

Cinders. Son of Petropolis, tell us,
Tell us how to turn into the flash,
To lie in the lice-red shirt
On the bank of the Styx and wait
For the gossamer of Paradise
To spider in our dirt-filled eyes.

# History Lessons

*for Ronan Sheehan and Richard Kearney*

'The proud and beautiful city of Moscow
Is no more.' So wrote Napoleon to the Czar.
It was a November morning when we came
On this. I remember the football pitches
Beyond, stretched into wrinkles by the frost.
Someone was running across them, late for school,
His clothes scattered open by the wind.

Outside Moscow we had seen
A Napoleonic, then a Hitlerian dream
Aborted. The firegold city was burning
In the Kremlin domes, a sabred Wehrmacht
Lay opened to the bone, churches were ashen
Until heretics restored their colour
And their stone. Still that boy was running.

Fragrance of Christ, as in the whitethorn
Brightening through Lent, the stricken aroma
Of the Czars in ambered silence near Pavlovsk,
The smoking gold of icons at Zagorsk,
And this coal-smoke in the sunlight
Stealing over frost, houses huddled up in
Droves, deep drifts of lost

People. This was history, although the State
Exam confined Ireland to Grattan and allowed
Us roam from London to Moscow. I brought
Black gladioli bulbs from Samarkand
To flourish like omens in our cooler air;
Coals ripening in a light white as vodka.
Elections, hunger-strikes and shots

Greeted our return. Houses broke open
In the season's heat and the bulbs
Burned in the ground. Men on ladders
Climbed into roselight, a roof was a swarm of fireflies
At dusk. The city is no more. The lesson's learned.
I will remember it always as a burning
In the heart of winter and a boy running.

# Reading *Paradise Lost* in Protestant Ulster 1984

Should I give in to sleep? This fire's warm,
I know the story off by heart,
Was up so late last night and all the harm
That can be done is done. Far apart
From Milton's devils is the present crew
Of zombie soldiers and their spies,
Supergrasses in whose hiss
We hear the snake and sense the mist
Rise in dreams that crowd the new
Awaking with their demobbed cries.

In the old ground of apocalypse
I saw a broken church near where
Two lines of trees came to eclipse
The summer light. Beside the stair
A grey crow from an old estate
Gripped on the Book of Common Prayer,
A rope of mice hung on a strip
Of altar-cloth and a blurring date
Smeared the stone beneath the choir.

Awake again, I see the window take
An arc of rainbow and a fusing rain.
None should break the union of this State
Which God with Man conspired to ordain.
But the woe the long evening brings
To the mazy ambushes of streets
Marks us more deeply now than that bower
Of deepest Eden in our first parents' hour
Of sexual bliss and frail enamourings
Could ever do. Our 'sovran Planter' beats

Upon his breast, dyadic evil rules;
A syncope that stammers in our guns,
That forms and then reforms itself in schools
And in our daughters' couplings and our sons'!
We feel the fire's heat, Belial's doze;
A maiden city's burning on the plain;
Rcbcls surround us, Lord. Ah, whence arose
This dark damnation, this hot unrainbowed rain?

# EAMON GRENNAN

## Facts of Life, Ballymoney

I would like to let things be:

The rain comes down on the roof
The small birds come to the feeder
The waves come slowly up the strand.

Three sounds to measure
My hour here at the window:
The slow swish of the sea
The squeak of hungry birds
The quick ticking of rain.

Then of course there are the trees.
Bare for the most part.
The grass wide open to the rain
Clouds accumulating over the sea
The water rising and falling and rising
Herring-gulls bobbing on the water.

They are killing cuttlefish out there,
One at a time without fuss.
With a brisk little shake of the head
They rinse their lethal beaks.

Swollen by rain, the small stream
Twists between slippery rocks.
That's all there's to it, spilling
Its own sound onto the sand.

In one breath one wink all this
Melts to an element in my blood.
And still it's possible to go on
Simply living
As if nothing had happened.

Nothing has happened:
Rain inching down the window,
Me looking out at the rain.

# Sunday Morning Through Binoculars

Balmy as summer. It won't last.
The wind is idling somewhere
Out to sea, making its mind up.
No bells. Silence is a state of grace.
From here the farmers' cottages
Are barnacles, limewhite,
Jutting from the lumpy plum-blue hill.
For once the birds seem unwary, careless:
Meadow pipits foam out of the furze,
A lark plummets into dead heather,
Two twites perch on a grey shoulder
Of limestone. Their tiny mouths
Open and close. I suppose they're singing.
Four black whiteheaded cows
Roam in slow fat lazy waves
The spongy green shallows
Of their pasture. In the distance
Two boys stand knee-deep
In a platinum pond, skimming stones;
Their motions slow, deliberate as dreams.
I can't hear the stones slap water,
The water hissing, their fox-red dog's
Ecstatic barking. They step now
Gently from the water backwards.
And turn to go. The Sabbath
Winking on drenched wellingtons.

*Renvyle, February 1981*

# Wing Road

Amazing, how the young man who empties
our dustbin ascends the truck as it moves
away from him, rises up like an angel
in a china-blue check shirt and lilac
woollen cap, dirty work-gloves, rowanberry
red bandanna flapping at his throat. He plants
one foot above the mudguard, locks his
left hand to a steel bar stemming
from the dumper's loud mouth and is borne
away, light as a cat, right leg dangling,
the dazzled air snatching at that black-
bearded face. He breaks to a smile, leans
wide and takes the morning to his puffed
chest, right arm stretched far out, a checkered
china-blue wing gliding between blurred earth
and heaven, a messenger under the locust trees
that stand in silent panic at his passage. But
his mission is not among the trees: he has
flanked both sunlit rims of Wing Road
with empty dustbins, each lying on its side,
its battered lid fallen beside it, each
letting noonlight scour its emptiness
to shining. Carried off in a sudden cloud
of diesel smoke, in a woeful crying out
of brakes and gears, a roaring of monstrous
mechanical appetite, he has left this unlikely
radiance straggled behind him, where the crows,
covening in branches, will flash and haggle.

# Soul Music: The Derry Air

A strong drink, hundred-year-old
schnapps, to be sipped at, invading
the secret places that lie in wait and
lonely between bone and muscle, or
counting (Morse code for insomniacs)
the seconds round the heart
when it stutters to itself. Or to be
taken in at the eyes in small doses,
phrase by somatic phrase, a line
of laundry after dawn, air clean as
vodka, snow all over, the laundry
lightly shaking itself
from frigid sleep. Shirts, flowered sheets,
pyjamas, empty trousers, empty
socks – risen as at a last day's dawn
to pure body, light as air. Whiteness
whiter than snow, blueness bluer than
new day brightening the sky-lid
behind trees stripped of their illusions
down to a webbed geometry
subtler than speech. A fierce blue eye
farther off than God, witnessing
house-boxes huddled together
for comfort, fronting blindly
the deserted streets down which in time
come farting lorries full of soldiers.
You are a fugitive *I*, a singing
nerve: you flit from garden to garden
in your fit of silence, bits of you
flaking off in steam and sizzling
like hot fat in the snow. Listen
to the pickers and stealers, the shots,
man-shouts, women wailing, the cry of kids

who clutch stuffed dolls or teddy bears
and shiver, gripping tight as a kite
whatever hand is offered. Here
is the light glinting on top-boots, on
the barrel of an M-16 that grins, holding
its breath, beyond argument. And here is
a small room where robust winter sunlight
rummages much of the day when the day
is cloudless, making some ordinary potted plants
flower to your surprise again, again,
and again: pink, anaemic red, wax-white
their resurrection petals. Like hearts
drawn by children, like oiled arrowheads,
their unquestioning green leaves seem
alive with expectation.

# Men Roofing

### *for Seamus Heaney*

Bright burnished day, they are laying fresh roof down
on Chicago Hall. Tight cylinders of tarred felt-paper
lean against one another on the cracked black shingles
that shroud those undulant ridges. Two squat drums
of tar-mix catch the light; a fat canister of gas
gleams between a heap of old tyres and a paunchy
plastic sack, beer-bottle green. A TV dish-antenna
stands propped to one side, a harvest moon, cocked
to passing satellites and steadfast stars. Gutters
overflow with starlings, lit wings and whistling throats
going like crazy. A plume of blue smoke feathers up
out of a pitch-black cauldron, making the air fragrant
and medicinal, as my childhood's was, with tar. Overhead
against the gentian sky a sudden first flock whirls
of amber leaves and saffron, quick as breath, fine
as origami birds. Watching from a window opposite,
I see a man in a string vest glance up at the exalted
leaves, kneel to roll a roll of tar-felt flat; another
tilts a drum of tar-mix till a slow bolt of black silk
oozes, spreads. One points a silver hose and conjures
from its nozzle a fretted trembling orange lick
of fire. The fourth one dips to the wrist in the green sack
and scatters two brimming fistfuls of granite grit:
broadcast, the bright grain dazzles on black. They pause,
straighten, study one another – a segment done. I can see
the way the red-bearded one in the string vest grins and
slowly whets his two stained palms along his jeans; I see
the one who cast the grit walk to the roof-edge, look over,
then, with a little lilt of the head, spit contemplatively
down. What a sight between earth and air they are, drenched
in sweat and sunlight, relaxed masters for a moment

of all our elements! Here is my image, given, of the world
at peace: men roofing, taking pains to keep the weather
out, simmering in ripe Indian-summer light, winter
on their deadline minds. Briefly they stand balanced
between our common ground and nobody's sky, then move
again to their appointed tasks and stations, as if they
were amazing strangers come to visit for a short spell our
familiar shifty climate of blown leaves, birdspin. Odorous,
their column of lazuli smoke loops up from the dark
heart of their mystery; and they ply, they intercede.

# Conjunctions

I

In the cold dome of the college observatory
I wait my turn to lay an eye on
Halley's Comet. For a minute I'm a watcher
of the skies in total silence, my whole self
swimming the shaft of the telescope, blunt as
a big gun, out across the dark to our one and
only rendezvous. It's a faint milky bristling,
like the frizzled head of a small dandelion
gone to seed. Distinctly throbbing, sperm-like
and full of purpose in its journey, it seems as intimate
as the tick of my own pulse, though its far heart is
ice and a rage of lizard-green, sulphur, steel-blue,
its corona cloudy rose, riding into the light
of our world at biblical intervals, a hard fact, a sign
simply *out there*, meaning maybe nothing at all
or just what we make of it. But this once, at least,
I'm here to meet it, make its path cross mine, figuring
the unthinkable winter space between the lot of us –
those impossible distances and the uncanny, happy,
unrepeatable accident. This is all I see before
I step back out into our night glinting with chill
and see the sky an unreadable maze of stars, its sudden
comings and goings – brief white birds ablaze – and
under my boots the snow gleaming, hard as stone.

2

A hard bright day, late February, you tell me
you're pregnant. The dead grass is scabbed with snow
and oozing a premature, deceptive thaw. We cross
at the lights on Raymond, holding hands against
the heavy traffic. You've been sick – your system

briefly poisoned, in a fist of fever by day, night-
sweats – and we worry it will make some dangerous
difference. I imagine this circumstantial creature
taking shape inside you, our quick derivative
yet already someone separate and strange, a pulse
of difference in the dark uncharted space
you've offered up, a hurried little heartbeat
syncopate with yours, compounding hearts. It's early
days yet, but you've opened my weather eye
for signs – for a warm corner in the ice-wind
rattling last year's locust pods like maracas, a
flash of frantic amber in the stark branches
of the willow, a few lemon flecks on the goldfinch,
or a hoarse wheeze from the first redwing blackbird
to claim home ground among the mazy brush and cattails
out back. These live signs will wind around you
like planets, love, while you grow more than yourself
at the season's weathery, fragrant, unprevailing
heart. And on the outskirts I will bend to listen
to that other heart kicking its mysteries, before
our common ground and gravity, in the enlarging dark.

### 3

I'm in the dark, going home fast
along the Palisades, the night roaring and flashing
with the cars I pass, that pass me, all our lives at hazard
on the simple spin of a wheel, locked anonymously into
this meteor shower above the legal speed limit. I've
been handing over to Joan the children, as happens
every other week-end: we meet at a gas-station and
deliver our children up – lovingly, to take the sting
out of it – to one another. I'm thinking about this,
about the way my words can't catch it yet but
*about must, and about must go* – trying to be true
to the unavoidable ache in the grain of healing,
trying to boil the big words down to size – when

a fox lights out of hiding in the highway's grassy
island and arrows across the road before me, a rustgold
flash from dark to dark. In that split second I catch
the compass-point of his nose, the quilled tip
of ears *in áirde*,[1] the ruddering lift of a tail as he
streams by my sight, and I only have time to
lift my instinct's foot from the gas, clap hands, cry
'Fox!' in fright or invocation and he's gone, under
the metal fence, into the trees, home free. But all
the rest of the way home I hold him in my mind: a body
burning to its outer limits of bristle with this
moment, creature eyes alive with purpose, child
of time and impeccable timing
who has cometed across my vacant dark, a flow of
leaf-rust and foxy gold, risk-taker
shooting sure as a bird into the brush
with every hair in place, a splice
of apprehension, absolute, and pure indifference. He
is only getting on with his life, I know,
but engraved on my brain for good now
is his cave shape at full stretch, caught
in the brief blaze of my headlights
just like that . . . and still running.

[1] Up, erect, cocked.

# MICHAEL HARTNETT
·

## A Small Farm

All the perversions of the soul
I lcarnt on a small farm.
How to do the neighbours harm
by magic, how to hate.
I was abandoned to their tragedies,
minor but unhealing:
bitterness over boggy land,
casual stealing of crops,
venomous cardgames
across swearing tables,
a little music on the road,
a little peace in decrepit stables.
Here were rosarybeads,
a bleeding face,
the glinting doors
that did encase
their cutler needs,
their plates, their knives,
the cracked calendars
of their lives.

I was abandoned to their tragedies
and began to count the birds,
to deduct secrets in the kitchen cold
and to avoid among my nameless weeds
the civil war of that household.

# There will be a Talking

There will be a talking of lovely things
there will be cognizance of the seasons,
there will be men who know the flights of birds,
in new days there will be love for women:
we will walk the balance of artistry.
And things will have a middle and an end,
and be loved because being beautiful.
Who in a walk will find a lasting vase
depicting dance and hold it in his hands
and sell it then? No man on the new earth
will barter with malice nor make of stone
a hollowed riddle: for art will be art,
the freak, the rare no longer commonplace:
there will be a going back to the laws.

# For My Grandmother, Bridget Halpin

Maybe morning lightens over
the coldest time in all the day,
but not for you: a bird's hover,
seabird, blackbird, or bird of prey,
was rain, or death, or lost cattle:
the day's warning, the red plovers
so etched and small in clouded sky
was book to you, and true bible.
You died in utter loneliness,
your acres left to the childless.
You never saw the animals
of God, and the flower under
your feet: and the trees change a leaf:
and the red fur of a fox on
a quiet evening: and the long
birches falling down the hillside.

# The Person as Dreamer: We Talk about the Future

. . . it has to be a hill,
high, of course, and twilit.
There have to be some birds,
all sadly audible:
a necessary haze,
and small wristlets of rain:
yes, and a tremendous
air of satisfaction.
Both of us shall be old
and both our wives, of course,
had died, young, and tragic.
And all our children have
gone their far ways, estranged,
or else not begotten.
We have been through a war,
been hungry, and heroes:
and here we are now, calm,
fed, and reminiscent.
The hills are old, silent:
our pipe-smoke rises up.
We have come a long way . . .

# 'I saw magic on a green country road'

I saw magic on a green country road –
That old woman, a bag of sticks her load,

Blackly down to her thin feet a fringed shawl,
A rosary of bone on her horned hand,
A flight of curlews scribing by her head,
And ashtrees combing with their frills her hair.

Her eyes, wet sunken holes pierced by an awl,
Must have deciphered her adoring land:
And curlews, no longer lean birds, instead
Become ten scarlet comets in the air.

Some incantation from her canyoned mouth,
Irish, English, blew frost along the ground,
And even though the wind was from the South
The ashleaves froze without an ashleaf sound.

# A Visit to Castletown House

*for Nora Graham*

The avenue was green and long, and green
light pooled under the fernheads; a jade screen
could not let such liquid light in, a sea
at its greenest self could not pretend to be
so emerald. Men had made this landscape
from a mere secreting wood: knuckles bled
and bones broke to make this awning drape
a fitting silk upon its owner's head.

The house was lifted by two pillared wings
out of its bulk of solid chisellings
and flashed across the chestnut-marshalled lawn
a few lit windows on a bullock bawn.
The one-way windows of the empty rooms
reflected meadows, now the haunt
of waterbirds: where hawtrees were in bloom,
and belladonna, a poisonous plant.

A newer gentry in their quaint attire
looked at maps depicting alien shire
and city, town and fort: they were his seed,
that native who had taken coloured beads
disguised as chandeliers of vulgar glass
and made a room to suit a tasteless man
– a graceful art come to a sorry pass –
painted like some demented tinker's van.

But the music that was played in there –
that had grace, a nervous grace laid bare,
Tortellier unravelling sonatas
pummelling the instrument that has
the deep luxurious sensual sound,
allowing it no richness, making stars

where moons would be, choosing to expound
music as passionate as guitars.

I went into the calmer, gentler hall
in the wineglassed, chattering interval:
there was the smell of rose and woodsmoke there.
I stepped into the gentler evening air
and saw black figures dancing on the lawn,
Eviction, Droit de Seigneur, Broken Bones:
and heard the crack of ligaments being torn
and smelled the clinging blood upon the stones.

# Death of an Irishwoman

Ignorant, in the sense
she ate monotonous food
and thought the world was flat,
and pagan, in the sense
she knew the things that moved
all night were neither dogs nor cats
but púcas[1] and darkfaced men
she nevertheless had fierce pride.
But sentenced in the end
to eat thin diminishing porridge
in a stone-cold kitchen
she clenched her brittle hands
around a world
she could not understand.
I loved her from the day she died.
She was a summer dance at the crossroads.
She was a cardgame where a nose was broken.
She was a song that nobody sings.
She was a house ransacked by soldiers.
She was a language seldom spoken.
She was a child's purse, full of useless things.

[1] Hobgoblin, puck.

# Lament for Tadhg Cronin's Children

*based on a poem by Aodhagán Ó Rathaille*

That day the sails of the ship were torn
and a fog obscured the lawns.
In the whitewashed house the music stopped.
A spark jumped up at the gables
and the silk quilts on the bed caught fire.
They cry without tears –
their hearts cry –
for the three dead children.

Christ God neglect them not
nor leave them in the ground!

They were ears of corn!
They were apples!
They were three harpstrings!
And now their limbs lie underground
and the black beetle walks across their faces.
I, too, cry without tears –
my heart cries –
for the three dead children.

# The Retreat of Ita Cagney

*for Liam Brady*

### 1

Their barbarism did not assuage the grief:
their polished boots, their Sunday clothes,
the drone of hoarse melodeons.
The smoke was like the edge of blue scythes.
The downpour smell of overcoats
made the kitchen cry for air:
snuff lashed the nose like nettles
and the toothless praising of the dead
spun on like unoiled bellows.
She could not understand her grief:
the women who had washed his corpse
were now more intimate with him
than she had ever been.
She put a square of silk upon her head
and hidden in the collars of her coat
she felt her way along the whitewashed walls.
The road became a dim knife.
She had no plan
but instinct neighed around her
like a pulling horse.

### 2

Moulded to a wedge of jet
by the wet night, her black hair
showed one grey rib, like a fine
steel filing on a forge floor.
One deep line, cut by silent
days of hate in the expanse
of sallow skin above her brows,

dipped down to a tragic slant.
Her eyebrows were thin penlines
finely drawn on parchment sheets,
hair after minuscule hair
a linear masterpiece.
Triangles of minute gold
broke her open blue of eyes
that had looked on bespoke love,
seeing only to despise.

Her long nose was almost bone
making her face too severe:
the tight and rose-edged nostrils
never belled into a flare.
A fine gold down above the
upper lip did not maintain
its prettiness nor lower's swell
make it less a graph of pain.
Chin and jawline delicate,
neither weak nor skeletal:
bone in definite stern mould,
small and strong like a fox-skull.
Her throat showed no signs of age.
No sinews reinforced flesh
or gathered in clenched fistfuls
to pull skin to lined mesh.

The rest was shapeless, in black woollen dress.

### 3

Door opened halving darkness bronze
and half an outlined man
filled half the bronze.
Lamplight whipped upright into gold
the hairs along his nose,
poured coils of honey
around his head.

In the centre of his throat
clipped on his blue-striped shirt
a stud briefly pierced a thorn of light.
The male smell of the kitchen
engulfed her face,
odours of lost gristle
and grease along the wall:
her headscarf laughed a challenge
its crimson wrinkles crackling.
He knuckled up the wooden latch
and closed the door for many years.

4

Great ceremony later causes pain:
next year in hatred and in grief, the vain
white dress, the bulging priest, the frantic dance,
the vowing and the sickening wishes, land
like careful hammers on a broken hand.
But in this house no sacred text was read.
He offered her some food: they went to bed,
his arm and side a helmet for her head.
This was no furtive country coupling: this
was the ultimate hello, kiss and kiss
exchanged and bodies introduced: their sin
to choose so late a moment to begin
while shamefaced chalice, pyx, ciborium
clanged their giltwrapped anger in the room.

5

The swollen leather creaks
like lost birds
and the edges of her shawl
fringe down into the dark
while glaciers of oilskins drip around her
and musical traces and chafing of harness

and tedious drumming of hooves on the gravel
make her labour pains become
the direct rebuke and pummel of the town.
Withdrawing from her pain
to the nightmare warmth
beneath her shawl
the secret meeting in the dark
becomes a public spectacle
and baleful sextons turn their heads
and sullen shadows mutter hate
and snarl and debate
and shout vague threats of hell.

The crossroads blink their headlamp warning
and break into a rainbow on the shining tar:
the new skull turns in its warm pain,
the new skull pushes towards its morning.

## 6

O my small and warm creature
with your gold hair and your skin
that smells of milk and apples,
I must always lock you in
where nothing much can happen.
But you will hate these few rooms,
for a dove is bound to come
with leaves and outdoor perfumes:
already the talons drum
a beckoning through the slates,
bringing from the people words
and messages of hate.
Soon the wingbeats of this bird
will whisper down in their dive:
I dread the coming of this dove
for its beak will be a knife
and if you leave armed with my love

they will tell you what you lack:
they will make you wear my life
like a hump upon your back.

### 7

. . . each footprint being green in the wet grass
in search of mushrooms like white moons of lime,
each hazel ooze of cowdung through the toes,
being warm, and slipping like a floor of silk . . .
but all the windows are in mourning here:
the giant eye gleams like a mucous hill.
She pictured cowslips, then his farmer's face,
and waited in a patient discontent.
A heel of mud fell from his garden boots
embossed with nails and white-hilt shoots of grass
a hive of hayseeds in the woollen grooves
of meadow-coats fell golden on the floor,
and apples with medallions of rust
englobed a thickening cider on the shelf:
and holly on the varnished frames bent in
and curved its catsharp fingernails of green.
The rooms became resplendent with these signs.

### 8

I will put purple crêpe and crimson crêpe
and white crêpe on the shelf
and watch the candles cry
*o salutaris hostia.*
I will light the oil lamp till it burns
like a scarlet apple
and watch the candlegrease
upon the ledges interweave
to ropes of ivory.
I have not insulted God:
I have insulted
crombie coats and lace mantillas

Sunday best and church collections
and they declare my life a sinful act:
not because it hurts
the God they say they love –
but because my happiness
is not a public fact.

## 9

In rhythmic dance the neighbours move
outside the door: become dull dolls
as venom breaks in strident fragments
on the glass: broken insults clatter
on the slates: the pack retreats,
the instruments of siege withdraw
and skulk into the foothills to regroup.
The houses nudge and mutter through the night
and wait intently for the keep to fall.
She guards her sleeping citizen
and paces the exhausting floor:
on the speaking avenue of stones
she hears the infantry of eyes advance.

# An Dobharchú Gonta

Dobharchú gonta
ar charraig lom
ga ina taobh,
í ag cuimilt a féasóige
ag cuimilt scamaill a cos.

Chuala sí uair
óna sinsir
go raibh abhainn ann,
abhainn chriostail,
gan uisce inti.

Chuala fós go raibh breac ann
chomh ramhar le stoc crainn,
go raibh cruidín ann
mar gha geal gorm;
chuala fós go raibh fear ann
gan luaith ina bhróga,
go raibh fear ann
gan chúnna ar chordaí.

D'éag an domhan,
d'éag an ghrian i ngan fhios di
mar bhí sí cheana
ag snámh go sámh
in abhainn dhraíochta an chriostail.

# The Wounded Otter

A wounded otter
on a bare rock
a bolt in her side,
stroking her whiskers
stroking her webbed feet.

Her ancestors
told her once
that there was a river,
a crystal river,
a waterless bed.

They also said
there were trout there
fat as tree-trunks
and kingfishers
bright as blue spears –
men there without cinders
in their boots,
men without dogs
on leashes.

She did not notice
the world die
nor the sun expire.
She was already
swimming at ease
in the magic crystal river.

# Fís Dheireanach Eoghain Rua Uí Shúilleabháin

Do thál bó na maidine
ceo bainne ar gach gleann
is tháinig glór cos anall
ó shleasa bána na mbeann.
Chonaic mé, mar scáileanna,
mo spailpíní fánacha,
is in ionad sleán nó rámhainn acu
bhí rós ar ghualainn chách.

# The Last Vision of Eoghan Rua Ó Súilleabháin

The cow of morning spurted
milk-mist on each glen
and the noise of feet came
from the hills' white sides.
I saw like phantoms
my fellow-workers
and instead of spades and shovels
they had roses on their shoulders.

# 'Pity the man who English lacks'

*from the Irish of Daibhí Ó Bruadair*

Pity the man who English lacks
    now turncoat Ormonde's made a come-back.
As I have to live here, I now wish
    to swap my poems for squeaky English.

# DEREK MAHON

## In Carrowdore Churchyard

*at the grave of Louis MacNeice*

Your ashes will not stir, even on this high ground,
However the wind tugs, the headstones shake.
This plot is consecrated, for your sake,
To what lies in the future tense. You lie
Past tension now, and spring is coming round
Igniting flowers on the peninsula.

Your ashes will not fly, however the rough winds burst
Through the wild brambles and the reticent trees.
All we may ask of you we have. The rest
Is not for publication, will not be heard.
Maguire, I believe, suggested a blackbird
And over your grave a phrase from Euripides.

Which suits you down to the ground, like this churchyard
With its play of shadow, its humane perspective.
Locked in the winter's fist, these hills are hard
As nails, yet soft and feminine in their turn
When fingers open and the hedges burn.
This, you implied, is how we ought to live –

The ironical, loving crush of roses against snow,
Each fragile, solving ambiguity. So
From the pneumonia of the ditch, from the ague
Of the blind poet and the bombed-out town you bring
The all-clear to the empty holes of spring;
Rinsing the choked mud, keeping the colours new.

228

# Lives

*for Seamus Heaney*

First time out
I was a torc of gold
And wept tears of the sun.

That was fun
But they buried me
In the earth two thousand years

Till a labourer
Turned me up with a pick
In eighteen fifty-four

And sold me
For tea and sugar
In Newmarket-on-Fergus.

Once I was an oar
But stuck in the shore
To mark the place of a grave

When the lost ship
Sailed away. I thought
Of Ithaca, but soon decayed.

The time that I liked
Best was when
I was a bump of clay

In a Navaho rug,
Put there to mitigate
The too godlike

Perfection of that
Merely human artifact.
I served my maker well —

He lived long
To be struck down in
Tucson by an electric shock

The night the lights
Went out in Europe
Never to shine again.

So many lives,
So many things to remember!
I was a stone in Tibet,

A tongue of bark
At the heart of Africa
Growing darker and darker . . .

It all seems
A little unreal now,
Now that I am

An anthropologist
With my own
Credit card, dictaphone,

Army surplus boots
And a whole boatload
Of photographic equipment.

I know too much
To be anything any more;
And if in the distant

Future someone
Thinks he has once been me
As I am today,

Let him revise
His insolent ontology
Or teach himself to pray.

# The Snow Party

*for Louis Asekoff*

Bashō, coming
To the city of Nagoya,
Is asked to a snow party.

There is a tinkling of china
And tea into china;
There are introductions.

Then everyone
Crowds to the window
To watch the falling snow.

Snow is falling on Nagoya
And farther south
On the tiles of Kyōto.

Eastward, beyond Irago,
It is falling
Like leaves on the cold sea.

Elsewhere they are burning
Witches and heretics
In the boiling squares,

Thousands have died since dawn
In the service
Of barbarous kings;

But there is silence
In the houses of Nagoya
And the hills of Ise.

# A Disused Shed in Co. Wexford

*Let them not forget us, the weak souls among the asphodels.*
— Seferis, *Mythistorema*

### *for J. G. Farrell*

Even now there are places where a thought might grow —
Peruvian mines, worked out and abandoned
To a slow clock of condensation,
An echo trapped for ever, and a flutter
Of wildflowers in the lift-shaft,
Indian compounds where the wind dances
And a door bangs with diminished confidence,
Lime crevices behind rippling rainbarrels,
Dog corners for bone burials;
And in a disused shed in Co. Wexford,

Deep in the grounds of a burnt-out hotel,
Among the bathtubs and the washbasins
A thousand mushrooms crowd to a keyhole.
This is the one star in their firmament
Or frames a star within a star.
What should they do there but desire?
So many days beyond the rhododendrons
With the world waltzing in its bowl of cloud,
They have learnt patience and silence
Listening to the rooks querulous in the high wood.

They have been waiting for us in a foetor
Of vegetable sweat since civil war days,
Since the gravel-crunching, interminable departure
Of the expropriated mycologist.
He never came back, and light since then
Is a keyhole rusting gently after rain.
Spiders have spun, flies dusted to mildew

And once a day, perhaps, they have heard something –
A trickle of masonry, a shout from the blue
Or a lorry changing gear at the end of the lane.

There have been deaths, the pale flesh flaking
Into the earth that nourished it;
And nightmares, born of these and the grim
Dominion of stale air and rank moisture.
Those nearest the door grow strong –
'Elbow room! Elbow room!'
The rest, dim in a twilight of crumbling
Utensils and broken pitchers, groaning
For their deliverance, have been so long
Expectant that there is left only the posture.

A half century, without visitors, in the dark –
Poor preparation for the cracking lock
And creak of hinges. Magi, moonmen,
Powdery prisoners of the old regime,
Web-throated, stalked like triffids, racked by drought
And insomnia, only the ghost of a scream
At the flash-bulb firing squad we wake them with
Shows there is life yet in their feverish forms.
Grown beyond nature now, soft food for worms,
They lift frail heads in gravity and good faith.

They are begging us, you see, in their wordless way,
To do something, to speak on their behalf
Or at least not to close the door again.
Lost people of Treblinka and Pompeii!
'Save us, save us,' they seem to say,
'Let the god not abandon us
Who have come so far in darkness and in pain.
We too had our lives to live.
You with your light meter and relaxed itinerary,
Let not our naive labours have been in vain!'

# Ford Manor

*Non sapei tu che qui è l'uom felice?*

Even on the quietest days the distant
Growl of cars remains persistent,
Reaching us in this airy box
We share with the field-mouse and the fox;
But she drifts in maternity blouses
Among crack-paned greenhouses –
A smiling Muse come back to life,
Part child, part mother, and part wife.

Even on the calmest nights the fitful
Prowl of planes is seldom still
Where Gatwick tilts to guide them home
From Tokyo, New York or Rome;
Yet even today the earth disposes
Bluebells, roses and primroses,
The dawn throat-whistle of a thrush
Deep in the dripping lilac bush.

DEREK MAHON

# Everything is Going to be All Right

How should I not be glad to contemplate
the clouds clearing beyond the dormer window
and a high tide reflected on the ceiling?
There will be dying, there will be dying,
but there is no need to go into that.
The poems flow from the hand unbidden
and the hidden source is the watchful heart.
The sun rises in spite of everything
and the far cities are beautiful and bright.
I lie here in a riot of sunlight
watching the day break and the clouds flying.
Everything is going to be all right.

# Courtyards in Delft
*– Pieter de Hooch, 1659*

*for Gordon Woods*

Oblique light on the trite, on brick and tile –
Immaculate masonry, and everywhere that
Water tap, that broom and wooden pail
To keep it so. House-proud, the wives
Of artisans pursue their thrifty lives
Among scrubbed yards, modest but adequate.
Foliage is sparse, and clings. No breeze
Ruffles the trim composure of those trees.

No spinet-playing emblematic of
The harmonies and disharmonies of love;
No lewd fish, no fruit, no wide-eyed bird
About to fly its cage while a virgin
Listens to her seducer, mars the chaste
Precision of the thing and the thing made.
Nothing is random, nothing goes to waste:
We miss the dirty dog, the fiery gin.

That girl with her back to us who waits
For her man to come home for his tea
Will wait till the paint disintegrates
And ruined dykes admit the esurient sea;
Yet this is life too, and the cracked
Out-house door a verifiable fact
As vividly mnemonic as the sunlit
Railings that front the houses opposite.

I lived there as a boy and know the coal
Glittering in its shed, late-afternoon
Lambency informing the deal table,
The ceiling cradled in a radiant spoon.
I must be lying low in a room there,

A strange child with a taste for verse,
While my hard-nosed companions dream of war
On parched veldt and fields of rain-swept gorse;

For the pale light of that provincial town
Will spread itself, like ink or oil,
Over the not yet accurate linen
Map of the world which occupies one wall
And punish nature in the name of God.
If only, now, the Maenads, as of right,
Came smashing crockery, with fire and sword,
We could sleep easier in our beds at night.

# The Woods

Two years we spent
down there, in a quaint
outbuilding bright with recent paint.

A green retreat,
secluded and sedate,
part of a once great estate,

it watched our old
banger as it growled
with guests and groceries through heat and cold,

and heard you tocsin
meal-times with a spoon
while I sat working in the sun.

Above the yard
an old clock had expired
the night Lenin arrived in Petrograd.

Bourbons and Romanovs
had removed their gloves
in the drawing-rooms and alcoves

of the manor house;
but these illustrious
ghosts never imposed on us.

Enough that the pond
steamed, the apples ripened,
the chestnuts on the gravel opened.

Ragwort and hemlock,
cinquefoil and ladysmock
throve in the shadows at the back;

beneath the trees
foxgloves and wood-anemones
looked up with tearful metamorphic eyes.

We woke the rooks
on narrow, winding walks
familiar from the story books,

or visited
a disused garden shed
where gas-masks from the war decayed;

and we knew peace
splintering the thin ice
on the bath-tub drinking-trough for cows.

But how could we
survive indefinitely
so far from the city and the sea?

Finding, at last,
too creamy for our taste
the fat profusion of that feast,

we travelled on
to chaos and confusion,
our birthright and our proper portion.

Another light
than ours convenes the mute
attention of those woods tonight –

while we, released
from that pale paradise,
confront the darkness in another place.

# A Garage in Co. Cork

Surely you paused at this roadside oasis
In your nomadic youth, and saw the mound
Of never-used cement, the curious faces,
The soft-drink ads and the uneven ground
Rainbowed with oily puddles, where a snail
Had scrawled its slimy, phosphorescent trail.

Like a frontier store-front in an old western
It might have nothing behind it but thin air,
Building materials, fruit boxes, scrap iron,
Dust-laden shrubs and coils of rusty wire,
A cabbage-white fluttering in the sodden
Silence of an untended kitchen garden.

Nirvana! But the cracked panes reveal a dark
Interior echoing with the cries of children.
Here in this quiet corner of Co. Cork
A family ate, slept, and watched the rain
Dance clean and cobalt the exhausted grit
So that the mind shrank from the glare of it.

Where did they go? South Boston? Cricklewood?
Somebody somewhere thinks of this as home,
Remembering the old pumps where they stood,
Antique now, squirting juice into a chrome
Lagonda or a dung-caked tractor while
A cloud swam on a cloud-reflecting tile.

Surely a whitewashed sun-trap at the back
Gave way to hens, wild thyme, and the first few
Shadowy yards of an overgrown cart-track,
Tyres in the branches such as Noah knew –
Beyond, a swoop of mountain where you heard,
Disconsolate in the haze, a single blackbird.

Left to itself, the functional will cast
A death-bed glow of picturesque abandon.
The intact antiquities of the recent past,
Dropped from the retail catalogues, return
To the materials that gave rise to them
And shine with a late sacramental gleam.

A god who spent the night here once rewarded
Natural courtesy with eternal life –
Changing to petrol pumps, that they be spared
For ever there, an old man and his wife.
The virgin who escaped his dark design
Sanctions the townland from her prickly shrine.

We might be anywhere – in the Dordogne,
Iquitos, Bethlehem – wherever the force
Of gravity secures houses and the sun
Selects this fan-blade of the universe
Decelerating while the fates devise
What outcome for the dawdling galaxies?

But we are in one place and one place only,
One of the milestones of earth-residence
Unique in each particular, the thinly
Peopled hinterland serenely tense –
Not in the hope of a resplendent future
But with a sure sense of its intrinsic nature.

DEREK MAHON

# The Globe in North Carolina

*There are no religions, no revelations; there are women.*
— Voznesensky, *Antiworlds*

The earth spins to my finger-tips and
Pauses beneath my outstretched hand;
White water seethes against the green
Capes where the continents begin.
Warm breezes move the pines and stir
The hot dust of the piedmont where
Night glides inland from town to town.
I love to see that sun go down.

It sets in a coniferous haze
Beyond Tennessee: the anglepoise
Rears like a moon to shed its savage
Radiance on the desolate page,
On Dvořák sleeves and Audubon
Bird-prints. An electronic brain
Records the concrete music of
Our hardware in the heavens above.

From Hatteras to the Blue Ridge
Night spreads like ink on the unhedged
Tobacco fields and clucking lakes,
Bringing the lights on in the rocks
And swamps, the farms and motor courts,
Substantial cities, kitsch resorts —
Until, to the mild theoptic eye,
America is its own night-sky,

Its own celestial fruit, on which
Sidereal forms appear, their rich
Clusters and vague attenuations
Miming galactic dispositions.
Hesperus is a lighthouse, Mars

An air-force base; molecular cars
Arrowing the turnpikes become
Lost meteorites in search of home.

No doubt we could go on like this
For decades yet; but nemesis
Awaits our furious make-believe,
Our harsh refusal to conceive
A world so different from our own
We wouldn't know it were we shown.
Who, in its halcyon days, imagined
Carthage a ballroom for the wind?

And what will the new night be like?
Why, as before, a partial dark
Stage-lit by a mysterious glow
As in the *Night Hunt* of Uccello.
Era-provincial self-regard
Finds us, as ever, unprepared
For the odd shifts of emphasis
Time regularly throws up to us.

Here, as elsewhere, I recognize
A wood invisible for its trees
Where everything must change except
The fact of change; our scepticism
And irony, grown trite, be dumb
Before the new thing that must come
Out of the scrunched Budweiser can
To make us sadder, wiser men.

Out in the void and staring hard
At the dim stone where we were reared,
Great mother, now the gods have gone
We place our faith in you alone,
Inverting the procedures which
Knelt us to things beyond our reach.
Drop of the oceans, may your salt
Astringency redeem our fault!

Veined marble, if we only knew,
In practice as in theory, true
Salvation lies not in the thrust
Of action only, but the trust
We place in our peripheral
Night garden in the glory-hole
Of space, a home from home, and what
Devotion we can bring to it!

. . . You lie, an ocean to the east,
Your limbs composed, your mind at rest,
Asleep in a sunrise which will be
Your mid-day when it reaches me;
And what misgivings I might have
About the true importance of
The merely human pale before
The mere fact of your being there.

Five miles away a south-bound freight
Shrieks its euphoria to the state
And passes on; unfinished work
Awaits me in the scented dark.
The halved globe, slowly turning, hugs
Its silence, and the lightning bugs
Are quiet beneath the open window
Listening to that lonesome whistle blow . . .

# Achill

*im chaonaí uaigneach nach mór go bhfeicim an lá*[1]

I lie and imagine a first light gleam in the bay
   After one more night of erosion and nearer the grave,
Then stand and gaze from a window at break of day
   As a shearwater skims the ridge of an incoming wave;
And I think of my son a dolphin in the Aegean,
   A sprite among sails knife-bright in a seasonal wind,
And wish he were here where currachs walk on the ocean
   To ease with his talk the solitude locked in my mind.

I sit on a stone after lunch and consider the glow
   Of the sun through mist, a pearl bulb containèdly fierce;
A rain-shower darkens the schist for a minute or so
   Then it drifts away and the sloe-black patches disperse.
Croagh Patrick towers like Naxos over the water
   And I think of my daughter at work on her difficult art
And wish she were with me now between thrush and plover,
   Wild thyme and sea-thrift, to lift the weight from my heart.

The young sit smoking and laughing on the bridge at evening
   Like birds on a telephone pole or notes on a score.
A tin whistle squeals in the parlour, once more it is raining,
   Turfsmoke inclines and a wind whines under the door;
And I lie and imagine the lights going on in the harbour
   Of white-housed Náousa, your clear definition at night,
And wish you were here to upstage my disconsolate labour
   As I glance through a few thin pages and switch off the light.

---

[1] A desolate waif scarce seeing the light of day (from a poem by Piaras Feiritéar, 1600–1653, as translated by Thomas Kinsella).

# Dejection

Bone-idle, I lie listening to the rain,
Not tragic now nor yet to frenzy bold.
Must I stand out in thunderstorms again
Who have twice come in from the cold?

# Antarctica

'I am just going outside and may be some time.'
The others nod, pretending not to know.
At the heart of the ridiculous, the sublime.

He leaves them reading and begins to climb,
Goading his ghost into the howling snow;
He is just going outside and may be some time.

The tent recedes beneath its crust of rime
And frostbite is replaced by vertigo:
At the heart of the ridiculous, the sublime.

Need we consider it some sort of crime,
This numb self-sacrifice of the weakest? No,
He is just going outside and may be some time –

In fact, for ever. Solitary enzyme,
Though the night yield no glimmer there will glow,
At the heart of the ridiculous, the sublime.

He takes leave of the earthly pantomime
Quietly, knowing it is time to go:
'I am just going outside and may be some time.'
At the heart of the ridiculous, the sublime.

# MICHAEL SMITH

## City

Too soon put up for the wind that blew it down,
     Hope became despair
And despair was the sea on which my ship had sailed.

The rain became the city, the city became the rain,
And the unnested fledgling that ancient playful dog.

Barbara, Barbara, my canal-bank pinkeen girl.
Your curls are in the water with the barge,

And I am sailing down a purple Nile
Across the mill's aluminium-silver dome

From where the knacker's leans against the sky
And a solitary lilac weeps in its concrete yard.

# Asleep in the City

The church steeple fingers the sky,
The cold air glints like frost against the stars
And the moon's casual indifferent face
Simply there in the broken sky,
Bird-high above the small terraced houses
Where people dream in the hard night
Of their own private suns:
Red things beating still beneath the packed snow.

MICHAEL SMITH

# Chimes

*for John Jordan*

Small things, like the turning of a key,
open, as light does a knot of petals,
the mind locked lost in a dead routine.

Things small enough to have seeped through the pores,
the nerves, the blood, into the brain,
till they are forgotten, if ever remembered.

You smile. You clutch my hand.
Lovingly and sadly I feel the hard skin of the palm,
and its warmth touches me like a whole body.

Such incredible foliage outside the window.
The sun blazing on its myriad greens.
And the woman sitting at the bed beside,
a stupid lump of her neck, big as a fist,
tensely counting the puffs of her cigarette –
one – two – three –
and the white blue smoke fading
                gently across the glass partition.

Teatime. I go outside into the sunlight
and wait. I remark the lawn's green,
the empty pond and the heat
falling in thick waves from the brilliant sky.

A steeple clock chimed.
Its leisured sounds lifted ponderously
like great birds,
rising beyond the height of trees,
above the bell-tower and into the sky's blueness.

# Stopping to Take Notes

It is winter again
We are no nearer home
Outside, the wind lashes
the rocks and rusty gorse

\*

Voices that know no intimacy
trouble the air
whispering of death
in the bleak company of crows

\*

Once there was home
We know only that
But memory is a broken net
in a stormy sea

\*

We dream of spirits
Over the bare hills
they rise in their majesty
to eliminate differences

\*

Before the high altar
we watch dumbly
the stained glass
gloss the vacant air

\*

We have come sadly
from the streets of the city
to receive no solace
from the cold sea and the islands

\*

The wind rises
The small black cows
huddle in vain
against the granite walls

\*

In the ceaseless pour of rain
the miserable earth
seeps a black ooze
into ditch and pool

\*

As much as the living
the dead make their exactions
Someone we have not met
sent us on this journey

*Connemara, Christmas, 1976*

# A Visit to the Village

No ancestral bones of ours
roll like ivory dice
in that black sea

No father of ours
drew his boat
across these barren fields
out under that sky
bulging with grey rain

We have no roots here
are not recorded
in parochial lore
of fairdays and fights
and reciprocated help

We are strangers here
come from the impersonal city
where rain hits concrete
with the shatter of glass

We have come here
to observe local rites
learn new words for things
and once again take note
of human sameness

Such roots as we have
we carry with us
in suitcases

*Connemara, Christmas, 1976*

# From the Chinese

*for Trevor Joyce*

It is not cosy to live
in an outpost
on the crumbling edge
of an empire
on the verge of collapse,
longing for old securities,
regular mail,
certain supplies,
immediate & effective
relief in emergencies.

The desire to escape the present
increases daily.
The world of one's childhood,
of one's youth and manhood,
is coming to an end.

All around
regrets are plentiful
and totally useless.

My dreams are more real to me now
than these daily routines
of habitual survival,
And to think I was once a man of action,
considered myself so
and was so judged by others.

The Emperor's envoys
have been regularly informed
of our appraisals.
Nothing, of course, is done.
Nothing can be done.

This is neither the time nor place
for writing poems.

Gamblers and prophets
are having a field day.

# EAVAN BOLAND

## From the Painting 'Back from Market' by Chardin

Dressed in the colours of a country day –
Grey-blue, blue-grey, the white of seagulls' bodies –
Chardin's peasant woman
Is to be found at all times in her short delay
Of dreams, her eyes mixed
Between love and market, empty flagons of wine
At her feet, bread under her arm. He has fixed
Her limbs in colour, and her heart in line.

In her right hand, the hindlegs of a hare
Peep from a cloth sack; through the door
Another woman moves
In painted daylight; nothing in this bare
Closet has been lost
Or changed. I think of what great art removes:
Hazard and death, the future and the past,
This woman's secret history and her loves –

And even the dawn market, from whose bargaining
She has just come back, where men and women
Congregate and go
Among the produce, learning to live from morning
To next day, linked
By a common impulse to survive, although
In surging light they are single and distinct,
Like birds in the accumulating snow.

# After the Irish of Egan O'Rahilly

Without flocks or cattle or the curved horns
Of cattle, in a drenching night without sleep,
My five wits on the famous uproar
Of the wave toss like ships,
And I cry for boyhood, long before
Winkle and dogfish had defiled my lips.

O if he lived, the prince who sheltered me,
And his company who gave me entry
On the river of the Laune,
Whose royalty stood sentry
Over intricate harbours, I and my own
Would not be desolate in Dermot's country.

Fierce McCarthy Mor whose friends were welcome.
McCarthy of the Lee, a slave of late,
McCarthy of Kanturk whose blood
Has dried underfoot:
Of all my princes not a single word –
Irrevocable silence ails my heart,

My heart shrinks in me, my heart ails
That every hawk and royal hawk is lost;
From Cashel to the far sea
Their birthright is dispersed
Far and near, night and day, by robbery
And ransack, every town oppressed.

Take warning wave, take warning crown of the sea,
I, O'Rahilly – witless from your discords –
Were Spanish sails again afloat
And rescue on your tides,
Would force this outcry down your wild throat,
Would make you swallow these Atlantic words.

# The War Horse

This dry night, nothing unusual
About the clip, clop, casual

Iron of his shoes as he stamps death
Like a mint on the innocent coinage of earth.

I lift the window, watch the ambling feather
Of hock and fetlock, loosed from its daily tether

In the tinker camp on the Enniskerry Road,
Pass, his breath hissing, his snuffling head

Down. He is gone. No great harm is done.
Only a leaf of our laurel hedge is torn

Of distant interest like a maimed limb,
Only a rose which now will never climb

The stone of our house, expendable, a mere
Line of defence against him, a volunteer

You might say, only a crocus its bulbous head
Blown from growth, one of the screamless dead.

But we, we are safe, our unformed fear
Of fierce commitment gone; why should we care

If a rose, a hedge, a crocus are uprooted
Like corpses, remote, crushed, mutilated?

He stumbles on like a rumour of war, huge,
Threatening; neighbours use the subterfuge

Of curtains; he stumbles down our short street
Thankfully passing us. I pause, wait,

Then to breathe relief lean on the sill
And for a second only my blood is still

With atavism. That rose he smashed frays
Ribboned across our hedge, recalling days

Of burned countryside, illicit braid:
A cause ruined before, a world betrayed.

# Ode to Suburbia

Six o'clock: the kitchen bulbs which blister
Your dark, your housewives starting to nose
Out each other's day, the claustrophobia
Of your back gardens varicose
With shrubs make an ugly sister
Of you suburbia.

How long ago did the glass in your windows subtly
Silver into mirrors which again
And again show the same woman
Shriek at a child, which multiply
A dish, a brush, ash,
The gape of a fish

In the kitchen, the gape of a child in the cot?
You swelled so that when you tried
The silver slipper on your foot
It pinched your instep and the common
Hurt which touched you made
You human.

No creatures of your streets will feel the touch
Of a wand turning the wet sinews
Of fruit suddenly to a coach,
While this rat without leather reins
Or a whip or britches continues
Sliming your drains.

No magic here. Yet you encroach until
The shy countryside, fooled
By your plainness falls, then rises
From your bed changed, schooled
Forever by your skill,
Your compromises.

Midnight and your metamorphosis
Is now complete, although the mind
Which spinstered you might still miss
Your mystery now, might still fail
To see your powers defined
By this detail,

By this creature drowsing now in every house,
The same lion who tore stripes
Once off zebras, who now sleeps
Small beside the coals and may
On a red letter day
Catch a mouse.

# In Her Own Image

It is her eyes:
the irises are gold
and round they go
like the ring on my wedding finger,
round and round

and I can't touch
their histories or tears.
To think they were once my satellites!
They shut me out now.
Such light years!

She is not myself
anymore, she is not
even in my sky
anymore and I
am not myself.

I will not disfigure
her pretty face.
Let her wear amethyst thumbprints,
a family heirloom,
a sort of burial necklace

and I know just the place:
Where the wall glooms,
where the lettuce seeds,
where the jasmine springs
no surprises

I will bed her.
She will bloom there,
second nature to me,
the one perfection
among compromises.

# I Remember

I remember the way the big windows washed
out the room and the winter darks tinted
it and how, in the brute quiet and aftermath,
an eyebrow waited helplessly to be composed

from the palette with its scarabs of oil
colours gleaming through a dusk leaking from
the iron railings and the ruined evenings of
bombed-out, post-war London; how the easel was

mulberry wood and, porcupining in a jar,
the spines of my mother's portrait brushes
spiked from the dirty turpentine and the face
on the canvas was the scattered fractions

of the face which had come up the stairs
that morning and had taken up position in
the big drawing-room and had been still
and was now gone; and I remember, I remember

I was the interloper who knows both love and fear,
who comes near and draws back, who feels nothing
beyond the need to touch, to handle, to dismantle it,
the mystery; and how in the morning when I came down –

a nine-year-old in high, fawn socks –
the room had been shocked into a glacier
of cotton sheets thrown over the almond
and vanilla silk of the French Empire chairs.

# The Oral Tradition

I was standing there
at the end of a reading
or a workshop or whatever,
watching people heading
out into the weather,

only half-wondering
what becomes of words,
the brisk herbs of language,
the fragrances we think we sing,
if anything.

We were left behind
in a firelit room
in which the colour scheme
crouched well down –
golds, a sort of dun

a distressed ochre –
and the sole richness was
in the suggestion of a texture
like the low flax gleam
that comes off polished leather.

Two women
were standing in shadow,
one with her back turned.
Their talk was a gesture,
an outstretched hand.

They talked to each other
and words like 'summer'
'birth' 'great-grandmother'
kept pleading with me,
urging me to follow.

'She could feel it coming' –
one of them was saying –
'all the way there,
across the fields at evening
and no one there, God help her

'and she had on a skirt
of cross-woven linen
and the little one
kept pulling at it.
It was nearly night . . .'

(Wood hissed and split
in the open grate,
broke apart in sparks,
a windfall of light
in the room's darkness)

'. . . when she lay down
and gave birth to him
in an open meadow.
What a child that was
to be born without a blemish!'

It had started raining,
the windows dripping, misted.
One moment I was standing
not seeing out,
only half-listening

staring at the night; the next
without warning
I was caught by it:
the bruised summer light,
the musical sub-text

of mauve eaves on lilac
and the laburnum past
and shadow where the lime
tree dropped its bracts
in frills of contrast

where she lay down
in vetch and linen
and lifted up her son
to the archive
they would shelter in:

the oral song
avid as superstition,
layered like an amber in
the wreck of language
and the remnants of a nation.

I was getting out
my coat, buttoning it,
shrugging up the collar.
It was bitter outside,
a real winter's night

and I had distances
ahead of me: iron miles
in trains, iron rails
repeating instances
and reasons; the wheels

singing innuendoes, hints,
outlines underneath
the surface, a sense
suddenly of truth,
its resonance.

# PAUL DURCAN

## La Terre des Hommes

Fancy meeting *you* out here in the desert:
Hallo Clockface.

PAUL DURCAN

# Ireland 1972

Next to the fresh grave of my beloved grandmother
The grave of my firstlove murdered by my brother.

# She Mends an Ancient Wireless

You never claimed to be someone special;
Sometimes you said you had no special talent;
Yet I have seen you rear two dancing daughters
With care and patience and love unstinted;
Reading or telling stories, knitting gansies
And all the while holding down a job
In the teeming city, morning until dusk.
And in the house when anything went wrong
You were the one who fixed it without fuss;
The electricity switch which was neither on nor off,
The tv aerial forever falling out;
And now as I watch you mend an ancient wireless
From my tiny perch I cry once more your praises
And call out your name across the great divide – Nessa.

PAUL DURCAN

# The Weeping Headstones of the Isaac Becketts

The Protestant graveyard was a forbidden place
So naturally as children we explored its precincts:
Clambered over drystone walls under elms and chestnuts,
Parted long grasses and weeds, poked about under yews,
Reconnoitred the chapel whose oak doors were always closed,
Stared at the schist headstones of the Isaac Becketts.
And then we would depart with mortal sins in our bones
As ineradicable as an arthritis;
But we had seen enough to know what the old folks meant
When we would overhear them whisperingly at night refer to
'The headstones of the Becketts – they would make you weep.'
These arthritises of sin:
But although we had only six years each on our backs
We could decipher
Brand-new roads open up through heaven's fields
And upon them – like thousands upon thousands
Of pilgrims kneeling in the desert –
The weeping headstones of the Isaac Becketts.

# The Kilfenora Teaboy

I'm the Kilfenora teaboy
And I'm not so very young,
But though the land is going to pieces
I will not take up the gun;
I am happy making tea,
I make lots of it when I can,
And when I can't – I just make do;
And I do a small bit of sheepfarming on the side.

*Oh but it's the small bit of furze between two towns*
*Is what makes the Kilfenora teaboy really run.*

I have nine healthy daughters
And please God I will have more,
Sometimes my dear wife beats me
But on the whole she's a gentle soul;
When I'm not making her some tea
I sit out and watch them all
Ring-a-rosying in the street;
And I do a small bit of sheepfarming on the side.

*Oh but it's the small bit of furze between two towns*
*Is what makes the Kilfenora teaboy really run.*

Oh indeed my wife is handsome,
She has a fire lighting in each eye,
You can pluck laughter from her elbows
And from her knees pour money's tears;
I make all my tea for her,
I'm her teaboy on the hill,
And I also thatch her roof;
And I do a small bit of sheepfarming on the side.

*Oh but it's the small bit of furze between two towns*
*Is what makes the Kilfenora teaboy really run.*

And I'm not only a famous teaboy,
I'm a famous caveman too;
I paint pictures by the hundred
But you can't sell walls;
Although the people praise my pictures
As well as my turf-perfumed blend
They rarely fling a fiver in my face;
Oh don't we do an awful lot of dying on the side?

*But Oh it's the small bit of furze between two towns*
*Is what makes the Kilfenora teaboy really run.*

# Going Home to Mayo, Winter, 1949

Leaving behind us the alien, foreign city of Dublin
My father drove through the night in an old Ford Anglia,
His five-year-old son in the seat beside him,
The rexine seat of red leatherette,
And a yellow moon peered in through the windscreen.
'Daddy, Daddy,' I cried, 'Pass out the moon,'
But no matter how hard he drove he could not pass out the moon.
Each town we passed through was another milestone
And their names were magic passwords into eternity:
Kilcock, Kinnegad, Strokestown, Elphin,
Tarmonbarry, Tulsk, Ballaghaderreen, Ballavarry;
Now we were in Mayo and the next stop was Turlough,
The village of Turlough in the heartland of Mayo,
And my father's mother's house, all oil-lamps and women,
And my bedroom over the public bar below,
And in the morning cattle-cries and cock-crows:
Life's seemingly seamless garment gorgeously rent
By their screeches and bellowings. And in the evenings
I walked with my father in the high grass down by the river
Talking with him – an unheard-of thing in the city.

But home was not home and the moon could be no more outflanked
Than the daylight nightmare of Dublin city:
Back down along the canal we chugged into the city
And each lock-gate tolled our mutual doom;
And railings and palings and asphalt and traffic-lights,
And blocks after blocks of so-called 'new' tenements –
Thousands of crosses of loneliness planted
In the narrowing grave of the life of the father;
In the wide, wide cemetery of the boy's childhood.

# Backside to the Wind

A fourteen-year-old boy is out rambling alone
By the scimitar shores of Killala Bay
And he is dreaming of a French Ireland,
Backside to the wind.

What kind of village would I now be living in?
French vocabularies intertwined with Gaelic
And Irish women with French fathers,
Backsides to the wind.

The Ballina Road would become the Rue de Humbert
And wine would be the staple drink of the people;
A staple diet of potatoes and wine,
Backsides to the wind.

Monsieur O'Duffy might be the harbour-master
And Madame Duffy the mother of thirteen
Tiny philosophers to overthrow Maynooth,
Backsides to the wind.

Father Molloy might be a worker-priest
Up to his knees in manure at the cattle-mart;
And dancing and loving on the streets at evening
Backsides to the wind.

Jean Arthur Rimbaud might have grown up here
In a hillside terrace under the round tower;
Would he, like me, have dreamed of an Arabian Dublin,
Backside to the wind?

Garda Ned MacHale might now be a gendarme
Having hysterics at the crossroads;
Excommunicating male motorists, ogling females,
Backside to the wind.

I walk on, facing the village ahead of me,
A small concrete oasis in the wild countryside;
Not the embodiment of the dream of a boy,
Backside to the wind.

Seagulls and crows, priests and nuns,
Perch on the rooftops and steeples,
And their Anglo-American mores asphyxiate me,
Backside to the wind.

Not to mention the Japanese invasion:
Blunt people as serious as ourselves
And as humourless; money is our God,
Backsides to the wind.

The medieval Franciscan Friary of Moyne
Stands house-high, roofless, by;
Past it rolls a vast asphalt pipe,
Backside to the wind,

Ferrying chemical waste out to sea
From the Asahi synthetic-fibre plant;
Where once monks sang, wage-earners slave,
Backsides to the wind.

Run on, sweet River Moy,
Although I end my song; you are
The scales of a salmon of a boy,
Backside to the wind.

Yet I have no choice but to leave, to leave,
And yet there is nowhere I more yearn to live
Than in my own wild countryside,
Backside to the wind.

# Birth of a Coachman

His father and grandfather before him were coachmen:
How strange, then, to think that this small, bloody, lump of flesh,
This tiny moneybags of brains, veins, and intestines,
This zipped-up purse of most peculiar coin,
Will one day be coachman of the Cork to Dublin route,
In a great black greatcoat and white gauntlets,
In full command of one of our famous coaches
– *Wonder, Perseverance, Diligence,* or *Lightning* –
In charge of all our lives on foul winter nights,
Crackling his whip, whirling it, lashing it,
Driving on the hapless horses across the moors
Of the Kilworth hills, beating them on
Across rivers in spate, rounding sharp bends
On only two wheels, shriekings of axle-trees,
Rock-scrapes, rut-squeals, quagmire-squelches,
For ever in dread of the pitiless highwayman
Lurking in ambush with a brace of pistols;
Then cantering carefully in the lee of the Galtees,
Bowing his head to the stone gods of Cashel;
Then again thrusting through Urlingford;
Doing his bit, and his nut, past the Devilsbit;
Praising the breasts of the hills round Port Laoise;
Sailing full furrow through the Curragh of Kildare,
Through the thousand sea-daisies of a thousand white sheep;
Thrashing gaily the air at first glimpse of the Liffey;
Until stepping down from his high perch in Dublin
Into the sanctuary of a cobbled courtyard,
Into the arms of a crowd like a triumphant toreador
All sweat and tears: the man of the moment
Who now is but a small body of but some fleeting seconds old.

# Irish Hierarchy Bans Colour Photography

After a Spring meeting in their nineteenth-century fastness at
   Maynooth
The Irish Hierarchy has issued a total ban on the practice of colour
   photography:
A spokesman added that while in accordance with tradition
No logical explanation would be provided
There were a number of illogical explanations which he would
   discuss;
He stated that it was not true that the ban was the result
Of the Hierarchy's tacit endorsement of racial discrimination;
(And, here, the spokesman, Fr Marksman, smiled to himself
But when asked to elaborate on his smile, he would not elaborate
Except to growl some categorical expletives which included the
   word 'liberal')
He stated that if the Press corps would countenance an unhappy
   pun
He would say that negative thinking lay at the root of the ban;
Colour pictures produced in the minds of people,
Especially in the minds (if any) of young people,
A serious distortion of reality;
Colour pictures showed reality to be rich and various
Whereas reality in point of fact was the opposite;
The innate black and white nature of reality would have to be
   safeguarded
At all costs and, talking of costs, said Fr Marksman,
It ought to be borne in mind, as indeed the Hierarchy had borne in
   its collective mind,
That colour photography was far costlier than black and white
   photography
And, as a consequence, more immoral;
The Hierarchy, stated Fr Marksman, was once again smiting two
   birds with one boulder;

And the joint-hegemony of Morality and Economics was being
upheld.

The total ban came as a total surprise to the accumulated Press
corps
And Irish Roman Catholic pressmen and presswomen present
Had to be helped away as they wept copiously in their cups:
'No more oranges and lemons in Maynooth' sobbed one
cameraboy.
The general public, however, is expected to pay no heed to the ban;
Only politicians and time-servers are likely to pay the required
lip-service;
But the operative noun is lip: there will be no hand or foot service.
And next year Ireland is expected to become
The EEC's largest money-spender in colour photography:

*This is Claudia Conway RTE News (Colour) Maynooth.*

# Micheál Mac Liammóir

'Dear Boy, What a superlative day for a funeral:
It seems St Stephen's Green put on the appareil
Of early Spring-time especially for me.
That is no vanity: but – dare I say it – humility
In the fell face of those nay-neighers who say we die
At dying-time. Die? Why, I must needs cry
No, no, no, no,
Now I am living whereas before – no –
'Twas but breathing, choking, croaking, singing,
Superb sometimes but nevertheless but breathing:
You should have seen the scene in University Church:
Packed to the hammer-beams with me left in the lurch
All on my ownio up-front centre-stage;
People of every nationality in Ireland and of every age;
Old age and youth – Oh, everpresent, oldest, wished-for youth;
And old Dublin ladies telling their beads for old me; forsooth.
'Twould have fired the cockles of John Henry's heart
And his mussels too: only Sarah Bernhardt
Was missing but I was so glad to see Marie Conmee
Fresh, as always, as the morning sea.
We paid a last farewell to dear Harcourt Terrace,
Dear old, bedraggled, doomed Harcourt Terrace
Where I enjoyed, amongst the crocuses, a Continual Glimpse of
    Heaven
By having, for a living partner, Hilton.
Around the corner the canal-waters from Athy gleamed
Engaged in their never-ending courtship of Ringsend.
Then onward to the Gate – and to the rose-cheeked ghost of Lord
    Edward Longford;
I could not bear to look at Patrick Bedford.
Oh tears there were, there and everywhere,
But especially there; there outside the Gate where
For fifty years we wooed the goddess of our art;

How many, many nights she pierced my heart.
*Ach, níl aon tinteán mar do thinteán féin:*[1]
The Gate and the *Taibhdhearc* – each was our name;
I dreamed a dream of Jean Cocteau
Leaning against a wall in Killnamoe;
And so I voyaged through all the nations of Ireland with McMaster
And played in Cinderella an ugly, but oh so ugly, sister.
Ah but we could not tarry for ever outside the Gate;
Life, as always, must go on or we'd be late
For my rendezvous with my brave grave-diggers
Who were as shy but snappy as my best of dressers.
We sped past the vast suburb of Clontarf – all those lives
Full of hard-working Brian Borús with their busy wives.
In St Fintan's Cemetery there was spray from the sea
As well as from the noonday sun, and clay on me:
And a green carnation on my lonely oaken coffin.
Lonely in heaven? Yes, I must not soften
The deep pain I feel at even a momentary separation
From my dear, sweet friends. A green carnation
For you all, dear boy; If you must weep, ba(w)ll;
*Slán agus Beannacht:*[2] Micheál.'

*March 1978*

---

[1] But there's no place like home.

[2] Farewell.

# The Pietà's Over

The Pietà's Over – and, now, my dear, droll, husband,
As middle age tolls its bell along the via dolorosa of life,
It is time for you to get down off my knees
And learn to walk on your own two feet.
I will admit it is difficult for a man of forty
Who has spent all his life reclining in his wife's lap,
Being given birth to by her again and again, year in, year out,
To stand on his own two feet, but it has to be done –
Even if at the end of the day he commits harikari.
A man cannot be a messiah for ever,
Messiahing about in his wife's lap,
Suffering fluently in her arms,
Flowing up and down in the lee of her bosom,
Forever being mourned for by the eternal feminine,
Being keened over every night of the week for sixty mortal years.

The Pietà's Over – it is Easter over all our lives:
The revelation of our broken marriage, and its resurrection;
The breaking open of the tomb, and the setting free.
Painful as it was for me, I put you down off my knee
And I showed you the door.
Although you pleaded with me to keep you on my knee
And to mollycoddle you, humour you, within the family circle
('Don't put me out into the cold world' you cried),
I did not take the easy way out and yield to you –
Instead I took down the door off its hinges
So that the sunlight shone all the more squarely
Upon the pure, original brokenness of our marriage;
I whispered to you, quietly, yet audibly,
For all the diaspora of your soul to hear:
The Pietà's Over.

Yet even now, one year later, you keep looking back
From one side of Europe to the other,

Gaping at my knees as if my knees
Were the source of all that you have been, are, or will be.
By all means look around you, but stop looking back.
I would not give you shelter if you were homeless in the streets
For you must make your home in yourself, and not in a woman.
Keep going out the road for it is only out there –
Out there where the river achieves its riverlessness –
That you and I can become at last strangers to one another,
Ready to join up again on Resurrection Day.
Therefore, I must keep whispering to you, over and over:
My dear loved one, I have to tell you
You have run the gamut of piety –
The Pietà's Over.

# The Divorce Referendum, Ireland, 1986

By the time the priest started into his sermon
I was adrift on a leaf of tranquillity,
Feeling only the need and desire to praise,
To feed praise to the tiger of life.
Hosanna, Hosanna, Hosanna.
He was a gentle-voiced, middle-aged man,
Slightly stooped under a gulf of grey hair,
Slightly tormented by an excess of humility.
He talked felicitously of the Holy Spirit –
As if he really believed in what he was preaching –
Not as if he was aiming to annotate a diagram
Or to sub-edit the gospel,
But as if the Holy Spirit was real as rainwater.
Then his voice changed colour –
You could see it change from pink into white.
He remarked icily: 'It is the wish of the Hierarchy
That today the clergy of Ireland put before you
Christ's teaching on the indissolubility of marriage
And to remind you that when you vote in the Divorce Referendum
The Church's teaching and Christ's teaching are one and the
   same.'
Stunned, I stared up at him from my pew
As he stood there supported by candles and gladioli,
Vestments, and altarboys at his feet;
I could feel my breastplate tighten and my shoulderblades quiver;
I knew the anger that Jesus Christ felt
When he drove from the temple the traders and stockbrokers.
I have come into this temple today to pray
And be healed by, and joined with, the Spirit of Life;
Not to be invaded by ideology.
I say unto you, preacher, and orators of the Hierarchy,
Do not bring ideology into my house of prayer.
I closed my eyes

And I did not open them again until I could hear
The priest murmuring the prayers of the Consecration.
At Holy Communion I kept my eyes on a small girl
To whom the priest had to bend low to give her the host.
Curtseying, she smiled eagerly, and flew back down the aisle,
Carrying in her breast the Eucharist of her innocence:
May she have children of her own
And as many husbands as will praise her –
For what are husbands for, but to praise their wives?

# JOHN ENNIS

## Alice of Daphne, 1799

I am Alice of Daphne, and my heart clogs for John Pounden.
As the stag cornered by pitch-forks, so antlered his thought
  against the Croppies.
As the Jonathan amongst scented trees of the orchard, so rose my
  sweet back in Daphne. I knew a tender spot down under his
  branches, basked long among his juicy apples.
He rushed me the road to Enniscorthy. I was far gone, awkward
  with our loving:
Bed me with slovens, madden me with fiddles, I grow big now,
  sick for Daphne.
His trunk leant gently onto mine, for I was fourteen years of age.

*

And I said, Never, Never shall we be torn asunder or cut off from
  petalled Daphne, though our green hills crawl black with
  Croppies like flies, for I will not unloose that daft chase
  wreathing our laurels up the sloped white blossoms.
I grafted and shall graft, Jonathan, my virgin bones to yours.
McGuire, good tenant, coffined you when we stank Enniscorthy
  where Croppies piked the brave Orange.

John was twenty-one under the fruiting tree. I played the skittery
  dove after his apples.
Look, my lovelies, the mason plumbs our Wall! You can walk by
  the Slaney!
Crocus open on the Spring Lawn. On Vinegar Hill Providence
  stooped and smiled and picked but a few of the Croppies.
The Black Prince plum blooms early this March for my dears,
  Mary, John Colley, Jane, Patrick, Fanny.
But poor baby Joshua is down with the fits.

285

# Coyne's

### I

I think of that meadow off down in Coyne's
And you walking in the gap at the cherries
With a hayfork as I turned the cut swathes.
Over a generation was making between us.

The sun rising in the prodigal sub-tropic sky
Squandered its windfall gold. My swathe-turner
Prongs whirled like manic spider crabs into the hay.
Those summers were a green cleg-bitten paradise.

The south was fluent with cloudlets, the breeze, woodbine.
Slieve Bloom were dossing dull blue on the horizon.
My horse's black croup glistered with sweat.
His collar and harness were flecked with froth.

Coyne's hayfield willed us in the distant twenties
Fell to the bar with the first flush of June.
We feared the storms of Biscay. At times, indigo
Burst bitterly on the day's azure palate.

Sloe more than damson dyed the surging clouds.
Rage reined in. Beech trees swung dipsomaniac.
Dark with anger, our eyes savoured the built-up south.
The break came quiffing the soft flaxen waves about our feet.

Mostly our arms forked into good hay that was fit,
Lapped swathe on scented swathe on gold cocks
Conical as hives. The sky burned a natural sulphur
Blue, or showery and cool forecasted a change.

### 2

Coyne, a new breed of farmer looks across your hedges.
Who will cut meadow in these acres in the year two thousand?
The vices of the country grow mean, its close-knit virtues meaner.
No state commission can satisfy the hunger for land.

Greed rages in the full gut fanned by the Production God
And the EEC. Already the green ants are sharpening their jaws.
For even the all-fathering upstart in the sky must have his day.
The future becomes the mourned-for by a rag-bag of immutable
    laws.

I pit myself forever against the break-up of farms.
More than fields are carved up. The hopes of sons
Scattered across the world whose loves are pencilled on Coyne's
    walls.
Lots are cast for the bones of the living at auctions.

# A Drink of Spring

After the sweat of swathes and the sinking madder sun
The clean-raked fields of a polychrome twilight
With cloudlets of indigo nomadic on the sky,
'A drink of spring' was my father's preface to the night.

As the youngest, I made fast the dairy-window reins,
Sent the galvanized bucket plummeting to sink first
Time, weighted with steel washers at one frost-patterned side.
His request was as habitual as a creaking kitchen joist.

The rope tautened for the upward pull under the damson
Tree and back-biting thorns of a never-pruned rose.
The water, laced with lime, was glacial to the dusty throat.
Mirage of the dying, it brings relief to the lips of the comatose.

Cups furred with cold I handed round the open-door fireless
Kitchen. The taste on my lips was lingering like a first kiss.

# The Road to Patmos

There are things best not set down in books.

I knew his heart-beat better than most,
 Closer even than the Magdalen woman,
And the individual human scent that was his.
His days consumed me like a lover.
Me, the youngest, whom he loved.

He lifted the cup, the cup of accretions,
With a simple gesture, and I adored him.

We all did in a manner of speaking,
Then ran like sheep through the cowardly gap.

I see him now, my God,
In his long-benched shed of a carpenter,
Delicate with strewn wood-shavings.
Flower of the dunghill of Nazareth,
Sheepfolds and smells and the yelling hovels,
The son of a carpenter quoting for jobs,
Contracts that never materialized.
Acting out a part. Sharpening his tongue
For the viper and the poisonous grass-snake,
He nurtured visions beyond the chisel and the adze.

Casual, he looked at the seed of Zebedee, James and me,
Laughed nicknaming us 'The Sons of Thunder'
As we fished and plotted the New Jerusalem!
Love, that was his dominant face: breathing
Curse on temple priest, too, and spent tree
Craving, ahead of us, the juiciest figs!
He testily surveyed the empty casks for Mary at Cana.
I remember the mild flush wine left on his cheeks
And the way he rubbed the breadcrumbs from his fingers.

It fell to me to scribble down his words
After the débâcle at Calvary.
And when it became obvious he was risen
Among us, I began the road to Patmos,
Preaching, laying on of hands in his shadow.
And then the fiery pen became my sword,
All chaff in the wind now, eagles and congregations,
Serpents, dragons and Christ knows
What besotted creatures of indiscipline.
I outdid the hydra-headed villain!
But the lamb in him is born eternal
Desolate and begging for Peter's affection.
Peter the rock, who asked at supper,
Asked in vain for him to name the informer.

So, goodbye Jerusalem! Our laughter at the Fish Gate!
Peter swearing of a morning, haggling with women.
Wine with James by the placid pool of Siloam,
Round the Fountain Gate or the harp-lingering haunts
Of David. Here in Patmos, the young make love.
Pity they will not know him as I knew,
For soon the frosty elders will nail him down.
And I'm an old man fishing again for my supper.
I remember the jolt of his cross into the ground.
I still feel the shudder like an earthquake.
When I looked up into his eyes
I cried and knew my burning at Patmos.
For, as I have written, I was the one he loved.
And I loved him.

# RICHARD RYAN

## Father of Famine

*for Liam O'Flaherty*

Shadow boxer, fighting
Man, old locust
Eater, bruised waxwing
Of the nest of dust;
O feeder of honey to the dead –
Mon père,
I would be led:
Must I neglect food to know hunger?

# Deafness

*for my sister*

It is when I hear Mozart,
some birds, the scraping
of wind through pine and
she is there; sounds crowd
round her silence like clay.

It is then I hear the note –
an inkling of the sound
of death: not the mere being
without, but the not knowing,
at all . . .

# Winter in Minneapolis

*for Eoin McKiernan*

From my high window I can watch
the freeways coiling on their strange
stilts to where the city glows
through rain like a new planet.

Tonight the radio speaks
of snow and in the waste plots
below trees stiffen,
frost wrinkles the pools.

Through high dark air
the apartment buildings,
like computer panels, begin
again to transmit their faint signals –

for they are there now, freed one and all
from the far windy towns, the thin
bright girls compounded of heat,
movement, and a few portable needs.

But I have no calls to make tonight,
for we are all strangers here
who have only the night to share –
stereos, soft lights, and small alarm clocks:

of our photograph albums, our far
towns, and our silences we do not speak;
wisely we have learned to respect
the locked door and unanswered telephone.

I turn from my window and pause a moment
in darkness. My bed and desk
barely visible, clean paper
waits in its neat circle of light . . .

I wait; and slowly they appear, singly,
like apparitions. They stand all round me,
on metal bridges and in the wet streets,
their long hair blowing, and they will not go.

# The Lake of the Woods

*for Chester Anderson*

Winter began with
The birches turning to glass
And the wild geese

Over the lake nightly,
Evacuating in their loud squadrons.
For weeks still there

Were roads, light
And the repeating moons; but
Slowly, through the sunk woods

Snow is climbing toward
The cabins now and
Twice already our cemetery

Has opened its
Mouth and closed it again.
Nothing lives in the woods

Any longer, only
A crumbling moon and the stars
Above the lake

Collapsing, one by one.
It is getting worse, and
We will survive

As we are able: out
On the lake a man has chopped
A hole in the ice

To fish through; his
Son is snapping twigs from
The pines, it

Sounds like pistols,
But suddenly there is a fish on the ice.
Daily it worsens

But somehow they know,
The fish and the trees
And the men, that it is temporary,

That some bright
Morning the geese will return
Singing down the

Runways of sunlight and lake water.
We are sure.
Or we have no memory,

Any of us, of the ice
Like an iron giant
Stalking the earth, that

Deep beneath the
Snow, the buried bottles
And the wrecked boots, beyond

All further thaw
A lost world of lizards
And leaves lies frozen in stone.

RICHARD RYAN

# At the End

*from the Japanese of Matsuo Bashō (1644–94)*

My spirit and flesh, parting now –
trails of mist here, there,
dwindling in the bone forest.

# HUGH MAXTON

## An Urgent Letter

So this is, Jimmy, where we live;
And Ulster is the name you give
To home as to Belfast and Bogside,
All the streets where men have died.
Here in our corner of the cave
The beasts are quiet who are alive.
We both agree on this – to ditch
All who call the place a bitch
For easy money in magazines
And with their cheque-books fan the flames.
Blood banks never had our trade,
Our tribal credits are unpaid.

But pardon me, I find these parts
Too anxious for the passive arts.
Your boat's at bay, your kids at home;
You write of summers yet to come
In *Marital Sonnets by One of the Boys*
Celebrating secular joys.
Yet girls I meet with you are wide
In the tail and bushy-eyed.
And lads stand rigid in their slacks,
Muscles bunching on their backs,
While poets in pubs sit on wishing
Instead of up-and-fishing.

The room is bright, the window open,
Again I hear your warm voice ripen

In songs that laugh at mad disasters.
(I dully think of wounds and plasters.)
The wind blows sweet with condiments
And harps Aeolian commonsense
When you strum your gay guitar
And sing of pleasures near and far;
I hanker for a tauter line,
For salt instead of saccharin,
And train an eye that will not miss
Things your humour can dismiss
— HEDLEY MURPHY GOSPELPREACHER
On tea-bags in the local grocer's.
Such absurdity, you argue,
Can never be poetic cargo.
Yet are the huckster-priests of Bethel
Wholly removed from all that's lethal?
What of the guns that we have seen
In the shop windows of Coleraine
For sale between the hooks and bait,
Tackle for no soul-redeeming
Or anything so pious seeming,
Bullets coiled in a figure of eight,
Bandoliers and long-range sights?
Discord in the political spectrum
Rarely disturbs your steady plectrum.

Yet Hell lies round us. Look and see
The gods are changed to infantry.
The ancient saracens now lurch
Protectively around your church;
The sacred blood-and-water gash
Is swaddled under an orange sash.
And all the state may do through terror
Rhymed aside as regrettable error!

Were I to spice your song with wit,
A little angry thought admit

Of governmental violence
And undercover killing agents
Who make it cosy for the poet
To sing of death and still not know it –
Were I to add this pinch of salt
I suspect that you would fault
My sophistry that puts one name
On two things that are the same,
Murder of men who dress in blue,
Murder by men who dress in blue.

I too deplore the patent Muse
Would make our every line a fuse,
Agree that wilful propaganda
Has no place on the poet's agenda.
If silence is the form he uses
To echo uniform excuses
For 'springing traps' and 'shoot to kill'
And headlines mindless, callous, shrill
Where only language only dies,
Then musical notes tell political lies.
And winters will follow when the papers
Ignore the pleas of legislators
Acknowledged or not, poets in gaol,
Painters reduced to learning braille,
Pianists fingered out of work
Banned by council, court or kirk.
When monstrous regiments and banks
Approach new customers in tanks,
Men better than we are surely sink
Riddled with something worse than drink.

We both approve of bridge and sex,
Prefer this world to the next.
We'd live in peace if peace were easy,
Enjoy a summer warm and breezy,
Walk with the girls we never knew,

Sing anthems to our own home brew.
We snap because we care, we quarrel
To make less solemn some little moral
In bitter words we may have said,
In better words we left unsaid.

# Ode

To read our few poets
you'd think there had been
a recent withdrawal
from our land of the stoat
and the yellow-scarf mouse.

A land in which nothing
twitches in the woodlands
but our nerves;
and every swan
is someone else's daughter.

Their lives are mashed
in the engine of politics
or, high on dynamite,
they industrialize the old dreads.
Yet truth is

ours is still a rural country
in which we never need
the stoat for savagery
or the yellow-scarf
for extinction.

# Elegies

*after the Russian of Joseph Brodsky*

I

When John Donne dropped to sleep all around him slept.
Pictures were drowsy on the wall, the floor
was deep in rugs and tables; furniture
whose certain essence was a sleep that kept
the clocks as motionless as lumber.
At rest in cupboards as in dormitories
the linen slept as though it were bodies
draped in animal slumber.
Night was not idly here and there
turning the key or coiled in locks
but paused in heat exhaling human shocks
to be at once impenetrable as air.
All slept: the window in its envelope
of snow might never have been written;
the words it might have read remained unseen
when John Donne unwakened and took his sleep.

The iron weights in the butcher's shop are prone
in care of watchdogs shrunken from the chains.
Mice are asleep and cats stiffened; the Thames
nods its way towards a salted dawn
shaking the reflected tower and arch.
Ships are anchorless by the wharf safely.
The sea lies down beside a promontory,
the land her bolster, intent and white as starch.
The walls of the gaol loosen in this rest
and prisoners lie still in their freedom
heedless of a momentary calm
before light draws its finger from the east.

The angels also sleep above the globe,
a world forgotten by the sleeping saints.
In holy shame fair paradise faints
under the waves of the Lord's deepest robe.
Gehenna sleeps and man must fail to be;
John Donne fails tonight his last disaster;
his breath and kiss and manly lines are lost.
Satan sleeps, and with him all enmity.
The prophets sleep. Good rests on Evil's arm.
The paling snow completes its last full stop
as his stressed and weary syllables drop
in place, to his drift of words' alarm.
Everybody sleeps: the saints, devils, God,
friends, deceitful servants, lovers in bed
lie dormant on this night John Donne is dead.
And the snow shuffles its feet on the road.

2

In the darkness of the white snowroad
I hear a cry, I hear a frightened call
as if a man were left to carry all
the bitter climate with his own painful load.
He is weeping. Yes, somebody is there,
his voice flaking at the brink of silence
like nervous hands, thin as a needle's
eye and blind of thread. Somebody is near.
Whose tears are these that I hear in darkness?
An angel, waiting in a cape of snow
for re-birth of my last-year's love below?
Oh, seraph, do I recognize your voice?

I have often heard them in sombre course.
Have you absconded from my sleeping church
to troop in silence under this dark birch,
or have your vain trumpetings made you hoarse?

Then, Paul, this silence canvasses your name,
the darkness surely being pure as glass.
And yet your voice was distinctly harsh
from straight talk, driving the pegs of Christ's claim.
Or, is our Father here, whose mighty hand
has loomed over this place time out of mind?
'Speak, Lord, thy servant heareth.' Oh I find
the impress of Thy silence stuns the land.
Was I alone to keep my open eyes
when guardsmen gathered in impassive gloom?
Gabriel! announce your presence, whom
I knew to summon myriads in the skies.

'No, it is I your soul, John Donne, complains;
alone on heaven's pinnacle I weep
for things my labour, even at its neap,
had set afloat, thoughts heavy as chains.
You were aloft, and from the heights you saw
a people whole. Despite your load you could
fly again through sin and passion to God;
Hell having seen, first as image, then raw.
Seeing life, your *Island* was its twin.
And soaring past your lord, in pride fell
content with burdens in the abysmal
tide of the roaring ocean.
From then the Lord seemed but a light that gleams
and all His Radiant Country was to you
a fitful image moving to and fro –
marsh-fire, a credal squint, or just a dream.
His fields persist unbroken by a plough;
the years lie fallow and the eras;
rain dances hugely in the formal grass;
a perfect tense preserves your broken vow.
But here I stand and weep; the road is gone.
I cannot fly with my spirit's temple
before death brings to me his ample
deductions and certainty of tone.

I languish in a passion of desire
stitching the last remnant of my spirit,
the needle passing through my soul in merit
of the empty snow so uselessly pure.

'But listen! while my weeping now disturbs
your rest, the busy snow shuttles through the dark
unmelting but sewing up our hurt.
Endlessly to and fro the needle works.
It is not I who weep but you, John Donne;
who lies alone. Your poems in presses sleep
while snow assumes your house into the deep
and snow is drifting down from darkest Heaven.'

### 3

All things are sunk in sleep. The final verse
awaits its cue baring its teeth to snarl
that earthly love is just a joker's role
and heavenly love becomes a friar's flesh.
We find in life companions of such pith
that life is shared and ground to common salt;
but there's no lover under Heaven's vault
can intimate our soul and share our death.
Man's coat is tattered. And it may be torn
by all who want to tear it more.
It frays and is redeemed to soar
briefly, the wearer's shroud. Once more it's worn.
Sleep soundly, Donne, and let your soul not mope
in such dejected rags as darkness gives.
The convex sky is glowing like a sieve
and holy stars invest your world with Hope.

# Deutschland

*The minority always guilty*
　　　－ Louis MacNeice

The thing not done,
thing considered slowly
as a word and chosen
as itself the act
of notcommitting
the atrocity.

It was eleven years ago.
Admonished now
by the one body among them
whom I love.
To have been there
at the back of the crowd
an adequate memory.

Clarity's no
*aide-mémoire:*
the cold field
lay between the houses
like a natural misunderstanding.
The club that night
sound dead.

These nights are endless,
remembering and retelling
we forge ourselves and sorrows,
a thousand
recitations of identity.
How we become
our culled inheritors,

divided between shrill
unspoken research

granite emotion,
between these –
containment of hysteria
retaliation's exile.

Eleven years now,
these nights are endless,
an adequate memory.
We forget ourselves and sorrows.
And start at the thing not done,
the atrocity.

*Sunday, 30 January 1983*

# FRANK ORMSBY

## Landscape with Figures

What haunts me is a farmhouse among trees
Seen from a bus window, a girl
With a suitcase climbing a long hill
And a woman waiting.
The time the bus took to reach and pass
The lane's entrance nothing was settled,
The girl still climbing and the woman still
On the long hill's summit.

Men were not present. Neither in the fields
That sloped from hedges, nor beyond the wall
That marked the yard's limits
Was there sign of hens, or hands working.
No sight that might have softened
On the eye the scene's
Relentlessness.

Nothing had happened, yet the minute spoke
And the scene spoke and the silence,
And oppressed as air does, loading
For a storm's release.

All lanes and houses
Secretive in trees and gaunt hills' jawlines
Turn my thoughts again
To that day's journey and the thing I saw
And could not fathom. Struck with the same dread
I seem to share in sense, not detail,

What was heavy there:
Sadness of dim places, obscure lives,
Ends and beginnings,
Such extremities.

# Spot the Ball

Once, with a certain pride, we kept attempts
To the minimum. Reason was all:
To trace invisibly the upraised eyes
Of backs and forwards; where the lines converged
To plant our crosses.

Later we combed the stand advertisements
For smudged lettering, or held the thin page
Up to the light to test for shadow.
Those paler patches, blotches near the goal
Could well be erasions.

And, later still, the joking nonchalance,
The stray marks in all the wrong places,
Floodlights and flags and corners that the teams
Had turned their backs on. Even the goalie's crotch
Was not immune.

Four years now and never on the right end
Of a Snowball. Thursday's edition tells
Of prizes bound for places elsewhere.
The 'Belfast man who requests no publicity'
Is always another.

We persevere from habit. When we try
These days our hope's mechanical, we trust
To accident. We are selective
No longer, the full hundred crosses
Filling the sky.

FRANK ORMSBY

# A Day in August

And still no stronger. Swathed in rugs he lingered
  Near to the windows, gauging distant hills.
Balked by the panes that promised light and flowers,
  The wasps were dying furiously on sills.

A doctor called. She walked him to the doorstep,
  Then sent the children out to gather cones
Under the trees beside the ruined churchyard.
  They romped, unheeding, in the tilted stones.

And now the wheels are turning. They impress
  Tracks that will not outlast the winter's rain.
The siren leaves a wash of emptiness.
  He is lost to the small farms, lane by lane.

# Under the Stairs

Look in the dark alcove under the stairs:
a paintbrush steeped in turpentine, its hairs

softening for use; rat-poison in a jar;
bent spoons for prising lids; a spare fire-bar;

the shaft of a broom; a tyre; assorted nails;
a store of candles for when the light fails.

# My Careful Life

My careful life says: 'No surrender.
Not an inch.' Sometimes I wonder

what thrills the darkness as I pass
the scented gardens of excess

or pause in the twilight to condemn
the parked cars rocking in the lane.

But still my life cries: 'Work and save.
Rise early. Stay home after five

and pull the curtains. They are blessed
– prudent, abstemious – who resist.

All things in moderation. Share
nothing. Be seemly and austere.'

My careful life sighs: 'Love? Forget it!
Avoid what is sexually transmitted.

The "wasteful virtues", I'm afraid,
earn nothing. They put you in the red.

Samaritans get mugged. Be wise.
Pass watchfully on the other side.

Your youth was stainless. Now your joy'll
be the middle years full of self-denial,

and an old age as ripe and warm
as is commensurate with decorum.'

# Home

Once, in the Giant's Ring, I closed my eyes
and thought of Ireland,
the air-wide, skin-tight, multiple meaning of here.

When I opened them I was little the wiser,
in that, perhaps, one
with the first settlers in the Lagan Valley
and the Vietnamese boat-people of Portadown.

# CIARAN CARSON

## Céilí

If there was a house with three girls in it,
It only took three boys to make a dance.
You'd see a glimmer where McKeown's once was
And follow it till it became a house.
But maybe they'd have gone on, up the hill
To Loughran's, or made across the grazing,
Somewhere else. All those twistings and turnings,
Crossroads and dirt roads and skittery lanes:
You'd be glad to get in from the dark.

And when you did get in, there'd be a power
Of poteen. A big tin creamery churn,
A ladle, those mugs with blue and white bars.
Oh, good and clear like the best of water.
The music would start up. This one ould boy
Would sit by the fire and rosin away,
Sawing and sawing till it fell like snow.
That poteen was quare stuff. At the end of
The night you might be fiddling with no bow.

When everyone was ready, out would come
The tin of Tate and Lyle's *Golden Syrup*,
A spoon or a knife, a big farl of bread.
Some of those same boys wouldn't bother with
The way you were supposed to screw it up.
There might be courting going on outside,
Whisperings and cacklings in the barnyard;
A spider thread of gold-thin syrup
Trailed out across the glowing kitchen tiles
Into the night of promises, or broken promises.

# Dresden

Horse Boyle was called Horse Boyle because of his brother Mule;
Though why Mule was called Mule is anybody's guess. I stayed
there once,
Or rather, I nearly stayed there once. But that's another story.
At any rate they lived in this decrepit caravan, not two miles out of
Carrick,
Encroached upon by baroque pyramids of empty baked bean tins,
rusts
And ochres, hints of autumn merging into twilight. Horse believed
They were as good as a watchdog, and to tell you the truth
You couldn't go near the place without something falling over:
A minor avalanche would ensue – more like a shop bell, really,

The old-fashioned ones on string, connected to the latch, I think,
And as you entered in, the bell would tinkle in the empty shop, a
musk
Of soap and turf and sweets would hit you from the gloom.
Tobacco.
Baling wire. Twine. And, of course, shelves and pyramids of tins.
An old woman would appear from the back – there was a sizzling
pan in there,
Somewhere, a whiff of eggs and bacon – and ask you what you
wanted;
Or rather, she wouldn't ask; she would talk about the weather. It
had rained
That day, but it was looking better. They had just put in the spuds.
I had only come to pass the time of day, so I bought a token packet
of Gold Leaf.
All this time the fry was frying away. Maybe she'd a daughter in
there
Somewhere, though I hadn't heard the neighbours talk of it; if
anybody knew,
It would be Horse. Horse kept his ears to the ground.

And he was a great man for current affairs; he owned the only TV
　　in the place.
Come dusk he'd set off on his rounds, to tell the whole townland
　　the latest
Situation in the Middle East, a mortar bomb attack in
　　Mullaghbawn –
The damn things never worked, of course – and so he'd tell the
　　story
How in his young day it was very different. Take young Flynn, for
　　instance,
Who was ordered to take this bus and smuggle some sticks of
　　gelignite

Across the border, into Derry, when the RUC – or was it the
　　RIC? –
Got wind of it. The bus was stopped, the peeler stepped on. Young
　　Flynn
Took it like a man, of course: he owned up right away. He opened
　　the bag
And produced the bomb, his rank and serial number. For all the
　　world
Like a pound of sausages. Of course, the thing was, the peeler's
　　bike
Had got a puncture, and he didn't know young Flynn from Adam.
　　All he wanted
Was to get home for his tea. Flynn was in for seven years and
　　learned to speak
The best of Irish. He had thirteen words for a cow in heat;
A word for the third thwart in a boat, the wake of a boat on the ebb
　　tide.

He knew the extinct names of insects, flowers, why this place was
　　called
Whatever: *Carrick*, for example, was *a rock*. He was damn right
　　there –
As the man said, *When you buy meat you buy bones, when you buy land
you buy stones.*

You'd be hard put to find a square foot in the whole bloody parish
That wasn't thick with flints and pebbles. To this day he could hear
   the grate
And scrape as the spade struck home, for it reminded him of broken
   bones:
Digging a graveyard, maybe – or better still, trying to dig a
   reclaimed tip
Of broken delph and crockery ware – you know that sound that sets
   your teeth on edge
When the chalk squeaks on the blackboard, or you shovel ashes
   from the stove?

Master McGinty – he'd be on about McGinty then, and discipline,
   the capitals
Of South America, Moore's *Melodies*, the Battle of Clontarf, and
*Tell me this, an educated man like you: What goes on four legs when it's*
   *young,*
*Two legs when it's grown up, and three legs when it's old?* I'd pretend
I didn't know. McGinty's leather strap would come up then, stuffed
With threepenny bits to give it weight and sting. Of course, it never
   did him
Any harm: *You could take a horse to water but you couldn't make him*
   *drink.*
He himself was nearly going on to be a priest.
*And many's the young cub left the school, as wise as when he came.*

Carrowkeel was where McGinty came from – *Narrow Quarter*,
   Flynn explained –
Back before the Troubles, a place that was so mean and crabbed,
Horse would have it, men were known to eat their dinner from a
   drawer.
Which they'd slide shut the minute you'd walk in.
He'd demonstrate this at the kitchen table, hunched and furtive,
   squinting
Out the window – past the teetering minarets of rust, down the
   hedge-dark aisle –

To where a stranger might appear, a passer-by, or what was maybe
worse,
Someone he knew. Someone who wanted something. Someone
who was hungry.
Of course who should come tottering up the lane that instant but his
brother

Mule. I forgot to mention they were twins. They were as like two –
No, not peas in a pod, for this is not the time nor the place to go into
Comparisons, and this is really Horse's story, Horse who – now I'm
getting
Round to it – flew over Dresden in the war. He'd emigrated first, to
Manchester. Something to do with scrap – redundant mill
machinery,
Giant flywheels, broken looms that would, eventually, be ships, or
aeroplanes.
He said he wore his fingers to the bone.
And so, on impulse, he had joined the RAF. He became a rear
gunner.
Of all the missions, Dresden broke his heart. It reminded him of
china.

As he remembered it, long afterwards, he could hear, or almost
hear
Between the rapid desultory thunderclaps, a thousand tinkling
echoes –
All across the map of Dresden, store-rooms full of china shivered,
teetered
And collapsed, an avalanche of porcelain, slushing and cascading:
cherubs,
Shepherdesses, figurines of Hope and Peace and Victory, delicate
bone fragments.
He recalled in particular a figure from his childhood, a milkmaid
Standing on the mantelpiece. Each night as they knelt down for the
rosary,
His eyes would wander up to where she seemed to beckon to him,
smiling,

Offering him, eternally, her pitcher of milk, her mouth of rose and
    cream.

One day, reaching up to hold her yet again, his fingers stumbled,
    and she fell.
He lifted down a biscuit tin, and opened it.
It breathed an antique incense: things like pencils, snuff, tobacco.
His war medals. A broken rosary. And there, the milkmaid's creamy
    hand, the outstretched
Pitcher of milk, all that survived. Outside, there was a scraping
And a tittering; I knew Mule's step by now, his careful drunken
    weaving
Through the tin-stacks. I might have stayed the night, but there's
    no time
To go back to that now; I could hardly, at any rate, pick up the
    thread.
I wandered out through the steeples of rust, the gate that was a
    broken bed.

# Judgement

*The tarred road simmered in a blue haze. The reservoir was dry.*
*The railway sleepers oozed with creosote. Not a cloud to be seen in the sky*

We were sitting at the Camlough halt – Johnny Mickey and myself –
    waiting
For a train that never seemed to come. He was telling me this story
Of a Father Clarke, who wanted to do in his dog. A black and
    white terrier.
He says to the servant boy, *Take out that old bitch*, he says, *and drown
    her*.
Johnny Mickey said the servant boy was Quigley, and now that he
    remembered it,
He'd been arrested by a Sergeant Flynn, for having no bell on his
    bike.
Hardly a hanging crime, you might say. But he was fined fifteen
    shillings.

*The prisoner left the court-room and his step was long and slow*
*By day and night he did contrive to fill this sergeant's heart with woe*

So there was this auction one day, and Quigley sneaks in the back.
A lot of crockery ware came up. Delph bowls. Willow-pattern.
    Chamberpots.
The bidding started at a shilling. Quigley lifts his finger.
    One-and-six.
Everyone pretending not to look at one another. Or to know each
    other.
Nods and winks. A folded *Dundalk Democrat*. Spectacles put on and
    off.
And so on, till he won the bid at fifteen shillings. *Name, please,*
Says the auctioneer. *Sergeant Flynn*, says Quigley, *Forkhill Barracks*.

*For to uphold the letter of the law this sergeant was too willing*
*I took the law upon myself and fined him back his fifteen shillings*

He rambled on a bit – how this Flynn's people on his mother's side

Were McErleans from County Derry, how you could never trust
A McErlean. When they hanged young McCorley on the bridge of
  Toome
It was a McErlean who set the whole thing up. That was in '98,
But some things never changed. You could trust a dog but not a cat.
It was something in their nature, and nature, as they say, will out.
The pot would always call the kettle black. He hummed a few lines.

*Come tender-hearted Christians all attention pay to me*
*Till I relate and communicate these verses two or three*
*Concerning of a gallant youth was cut off in his bloom*
*And died upon the gallows tree near to the town of Toome*

Which brought Johnny Mickey back to the priest and the terrier
  bitch.
Quigley, it transpired, had walked the country – Ballinliss and
  Aughaduff,
Slievenacapall, Carnavaddy – looking for a place to drown her.
It was the hottest summer in living memory. Not a cloud to be seen
  in the sky.
The Cully Water was a trickle. The Tullyallen and the
  Ummeracam were dry.
Not a breath of wind. Not so much water as would drown a rat.
  After three days
Quigley and the bitch came back. They were both half-dead with
  thirst.

*He looked her up he looked her down in his heart was ne'er a pang*
*I'll tell you what says Father Clarke if she won't be drowned she'll hang*

Johnny Mickey said that priests had a great way with ropes and
  knots.
It was one of the tricks that they learned in the seminary. Something
  to do
With chasubles and albs. In less time than it takes to tell, Father
  Flynn
Had rigged up a noose. They brought the bitch out to the orchard

323

And strung her up from the crook of an apple tree. And who was
    passing by
But the poet McCooey. He peeped through a hole in the hedge.
He spotted the two boys at their trade, and this is what he said:

*A man with no bell on his bike a man with a single bed*
*It's hardly any wonder that you'd go off your head*
*Poor old bitch poor old friend you died without a bark*
*Sentenced by Johnny Quigley and hung by Father Clarke*

Of course, said Johnny Mickey, your man McCooey's long since
    dead.
A white plume of steam appeared around the bend. A long
    lonesome blast.
The tracks began to shimmer and to hum. Our train was coming in
And not a minute late. It shivered to a halt. We both got on.
We would pass the crazy map of a dried-up reservoir. A
    water-tower.
We would watch the telegraph lines float up and down, till we
    arrived
At the other end; I would hand Mickey Quigley over to the two
    attendants.

*Farewell unto you sweet Drumaul if in you I had stayed*
*Among the Presbyterians I ne'er would have been betrayed*
*The gallows tree I ne'er would have seen had I remained there*
*For Dufferin you betrayed me McErlean you set the snare*

# Army

The duck patrol is waddling down the odd-number side of Raglan
  Street,
The bass-ackwards private at the rear trying not to think of a third
  eye
Being drilled in the back of his head. Fifty-five. They stop. The
  head
Peers round, then leaps the gap of Balaclava Street. He waves the
  body over
One by one. Forty-nine. Cape Street. A gable wall. Garnet Street.
  A gable wall.

Frere Street. Forty-seven. Forty-five-and-a-half. Milan Street. A
  grocer's shop.
They stop. They check their guns. Thirteen. Milton Street. An iron
  lamp-post.
Number one. Ormond Street. *Two ducks in front of a duck and two
  ducks*
*Behind a duck, how many ducks?* Five? *No. Three.* This is not the end.

# Cocktails

Bombing at about ninety miles an hour with the exhaust skittering
The skid-marked pitted tarmac of Kennedy Way, they hit the ramp
and sailed
Clean over the red-and-white guillotine of the check-point and
landed
On the M1 flyover, then disappeared before the Brits knew what hit
them. So
The story went: we were in the Whip and Saddle bar of the Europa.

There was talk of someone who was shot nine times and lived, and
someone else
Had the inside info. on the Romper Room. We were trying to
remember the facts
Behind the Black & Decker case, when someone ordered another
drink and we entered
The realm of Jabberwocks and Angels' Wings, Widows' Kisses,
Corpse Revivers.

# Bloody Hand

*Your man*, says the Man, *will walk into the bar like this* – here his
  fingers
Mimic a pair of legs, one stiff at the knee – *so you'll know exactly*
*What to do*. He sticks a finger to his head. Pretend it's child's play –
The hand might be a horse's mouth, a rabbit or a dog. Five
  handclaps.
Walls have ears: the shadows you throw are the shadows you try to
  throw off.

I snuffed out the candle between finger and thumb. Was it the left
  hand
Hacked off at the wrist and thrown to the shores of Ulster? Did
  Ulster
Exist? Or the Right Hand of God, saying *Stop* to this and *No* to that?
My thumb is the hammer of a gun. The thumb goes up. The thumb
  goes down.

# TOM PAULIN

## In the Lost Province

As it comes back, brick by smoky brick,
I say to myself – strange I lived there
And walked those streets. It is the Ormeau Road
On a summer's evening, a haze of absence
Over the caked city, that slumped smell
From the blackened gasworks. Ah, those brick canyons
Where Brookeborough unsheathes a sabre,
Shouting 'No Surrender' from the back of a lorry.

And the sky is a dry purple, and men
Are talking politics in a back room.
Is it too early or too late for change?
Certainly the province is most peaceful.
Who would dream of necessity, the angers
Of Leviathan, or the years of judgement?

# Anastasia McLaughlin

Her father is sick. He dozes most afternoons.
The nurse makes tea then and scans *The Newsletter*.
She has little to say to his grey daughter
Whose name began a strangeness the years took over.
His trade was flax and yarns, he brought her name
With an ikon and *matrioshka* – gifts for his wife
Who died the year that Carson's statue was unveiled.

McLaughlin is dreaming of a sermon he once heard
From a righteous preacher in a wooden pulpit
Who frowned upon a sinful brotherhood and shouted
The Word of deserts and rainy places where the Just
Are stretched to do the work a hard God sent them for.
His text was taken from the land of Uz
Where men are upright and their farms are walled.

'Though we may make sand to melt in a furnace
And make a mirror of it, we are as shadows
Thrown by a weaver's shuttle: and though we hide ourselves
In desolate cities and in empty houses,
His anger will seek us out till we shall hear
The accent of the destroyer, the sly champing
Of moths busy with the linen in our chests.'

He wakes to a dull afternoon like any other –
The musty dampness of his study, the window panes
That flaw his view of the lawn and settled trees.
The logs in the grate have turned to a soft ash.
The dour gardener who cut them is smoking
In the warm greenhouse, wondering did his nephew
Break in the week before and thieve McLaughlin's silver?

Constables came to the Mill House with alsatians,
And the wet spring was filled with uniforms and statements.
When they found nothing, they suspected everyone.

Even the plain woman who served them tea.
'Father, I am the lost daughter whose name you stole.
Your visions slide across these walls: dry lavender,
Old memories of all that wronged us. I am unkind.'

He sees his son below the bruised Atlantic,
And on a summer's morning in Great Victoria Street
He talks with Thomas Ferguson outside the Iceworks.
He sees the north stretched out upon the mountains,
Its dream of fair weather rubbing a bloom on rinsed slates;
He watches the mills prosper and grow derelict,
As he starts his journey to the Finland Station.

# Desertmartin

At noon, in the dead centre of a faith,
Between Draperstown and Magherafelt,
This bitter village shows the flag
In a baked absolute September light.
Here the Word has withered to a few
Parched certainties, and the charred stubble
Tightens like a black belt, a crop of Bibles.

Because this is the territory of the Law
I drive across it with a powerless knowledge –
The owl of Minerva in a hired car.
A Jock squaddy glances down the street
And grins, happy and expendable,
Like a brass cartridge. He is a useful thing,
Almost at home, and yet not quite, not quite.

It's a limed nest, this place. I see a plain
Presbyterian grace sour, then harden,
As a free strenuous spirit changes
To a servile defiance that whines and shrieks
For the bondage of the letter: it shouts
For the Big Man to lead his wee people
To a clean white prison, their scorched tomorrow.

Masculine Islam, the rule of the Just,
Egyptian sand dunes and geometry,
A theology of rifle-butts and executions:
These are the places where the spirit dies.
And now, in Desertmartin's sandy light,
I see a culture of twigs and bird-shit
Waving a gaudy flag it loves and curses.

# Off the Back of a Lorry

A zippo lighter
and a quilted jacket,
two rednecks troughing
in a gleamy diner,
the flinty chipmarks
on a white enamel pail,
Paisley putting pen to paper
in Crumlin jail,
a jumbo double
fried peanut butter
sandwich Elvis scoffed
during the last
diapered days –
they're more than tacky,
these pured fictions,
and like the small ads
in a country paper
they build a gritty
sort of prod baroque
I must return to
like my own boke.

# Last Statement

*Vladimir Mayakovsky*

It's after one,
you're in the sack, I guess.
The stars are echoed
in the Volga's darkness
and I'm not fussed
or urgent anymore.
I won't be wiring you
my slogans and my kisses
in daft capitals:
we bit green chillies
and we're through.
We were like lovers
leaning from a ferry
on the White Canal –
our arguments, statistics,
our fucks and cries
notched on the calculus.
Ack, the night has jammed
each signal from the stars,
and this, this is my last
stittering, grief-splintered
call-sign to the future.
Christ, I want to wow
both history and technology . . .
I could tell it to the world right now.

# Presbyterian Study

A lantern-ceiling and quiet.
I climb here often and stare
At the scoured desk by the window,
The journal open
At a date and conscience.

It is a room without song
That believes in flint, salt,
And new bread rising
Like a people who share
A dream of grace and reason.

A bit starchy perhaps.
A shade chill, like a draper's shop.
But choosing the free way,
Not the formal,
And warming the walls with its knowing.

Memory is a moist seed
And a praise here, for they live,
Those linen saints, lithe radicals,
In the bottled light
Of this limewashed shrine.

Hardly a schoolroom remembers
Their obstinate rebellion;
Provincial historians
Scratch circles on the sand,
And still, with dingy smiles,

We wait on nature,
Our jackets a dungy pattern
Of mud and snapped leaves,
Our state a jacked corpse
Committed to the deep.

# MICHAEL DAVITT

## An Scáthán

*i gcuimhne m'athar*

### 1

Níorbh é m'athair níos mó é
ach ba mise a mhacsan;
paradacsa fuar a d'fháisceas,
dealbh i gculaith Dhomhnaigh
a cuireadh an lá dár gcionn.

Dhein sé an-lá deora, seirí,
fuiscí, ceapairí feola is tae.
Bhí seanchara leis ag eachtraí
faoi sciurd lae a thugadar
ar Eochaill sna triochaidí
is gurbh é a chéad pháirtí é
i seirbhís Chorcaí/An Sciobairín
amach sna daicheadaí.
Bhí dornán cártaí Aifrinn
ar mhatal an tseomra suí
ina gcorrán thart ar vás gloine,
a bhronntanas scoir ó CIE.

### 2

Níorbh eol dom go gceann dhá lá
gurbh é an scáthán a mharaigh é . . .

An seanscáthán ollmhór Victeoiriach

335

leis an bhfráma ornáideach bréagórga
a bhí romhainn sa tigh trí stór
nuair a bhogamar isteach ón tuath.
Bhínn scanraithe roimhe: go sciorrfadh
anuas den bhfalla is go slogfadh mé
d'aon tromanáil i lár na hoíche . . .

Ag maisiú an tseomra chodlata dó
d'ardaigh sé an scáthán anuas
gan lámh chúnta a iarraidh;
ar ball d'iompaigh dath na cré air,
an oíche sin phléasc a chroí.

### 3

Mar a chuirfí de gheasa orm
thugas faoin jab a chríochnú:
an folús macallach a pháipéarú,
an fhuinneog ard a phéinteáil,
an doras marbhlainne
a scríobadh. Nuair a rugas ar an scáthán
sceimhlíos. Bhraitheas é ag análú tríd.
Chuala é ag rá i gcogar téiglí:
*I'll give you a hand, here.*

Is d'ardaíomar an scáthán thar n-ais in airde
os cionn an tinteáin,
m'athair á choinneáil
fad a dheineas-sa é a dhaingniú
le dhá thairne.

MICHAEL DAVITT

# The Mirror

*in memory of my father*

### 1

He was no longer my father
but I was still his son;
I would get to grips with that cold paradox,
the remote figure in his Sunday best
who was buried the next day.

A great day for tears, snifters of sherry,
whiskey, beef sandwiches, tea.
An old mate of his was recounting
their day excursion
to Youghal in the Thirties,
how he was his first partner
on the Cork/Skibbereen route
in the late Forties.
There was a splay of Mass cards
on the sitting-room mantelpiece
which formed a crescent round a glass vase,
his retirement present from CIE.

### 2

I didn't realize till two days later
it was the mirror took his breath away . . .

The monstrous old Victorian mirror
with the ornate gilt frame
we had found in the three-storey house
when we moved in from the country.
I was afraid that it would sneak
down from the wall and swallow me up
in one gulp in the middle of the night . . .

While he was decorating the bedroom
he had taken down the mirror
without asking for help;
soon he turned the colour of terracotta
and his heart broke that night.

### 3

There was nothing for it
but to set about finishing the job,
papering over the cracks,
painting the high window,
stripping the door of the crypt.
When I took hold of the mirror
I had a fright. I imagined him breathing through it.
I heard him say in a reassuring whisper:
*I'll give you a hand, here.*

And we lifted the mirror back in position
above the fireplace,
my father holding it steady
while I drove home
the two nails.

*translated by Paul Muldoon*

# Ciorrú Bóthair

Dúirt sé liom gur dhuine é
A bhí ag plé le diantalmhaíocht,
A d'oibrigh riamh faoin spéir;
Bhí an chuma sin ar an stróinséir
Ó dhubh a iongan is ó bholadh an fhéir ghearrtha
Ar a Bhéarla deisceartach.

Cith eile flichshneachta;
Ansin do las an ghrian
An bóthar romhainn tríd an Uarán Mór
Soir go Béal Átha na Sluaighe
Is bhí an carr ina tigín gloine
Ar tinneall lena scéalta garraíodóireachta.

Bhí roinnt laethanta caite aige
Le gaolta taobh thiar den Spidéal:
'Tá Gaeilge agat, mar sin?'
'Níl ná Gacilgc ach Gaolainn . . .'
Múscraíoch siúrálta, mheasas; ach níorbh ea,
'Corcaíoch ó lár Chorcaí amach.'

Ghin san splanc; phléasc comhrá Gaeilge
Gur chíoramar dúchas
Is tabhairt suas a chéile,
Is a Dhia nach cúng í Éire
Go raibh na bóithríní céanna canúna
Curtha dínn araon:

Coláiste Samhraidh i mBéal Átha an Ghaorthaigh,
Graiméar na mBráithre Críostaí,
Tithe tábhairne Chorca Dhuibhne,
Is an caolú, ansin, an géilleadh,
Toradh cúig nó sé de bhlianta
I gcathair Bhaile Átha Cliath.

'Caithfidh gur breá an jab sa tsamhradh é?'
'Sea mhuis ach b'fhearr liom féin an tEarrach,
Tráth fáis, tá misniú ann,
Agus tá míorúiltí datha sa bhFómhar
A choimeádfadh duine ón ól . . .'
D'éalaigh an splanc as a ghlór.

Ach bhí an ghráin aige ar an Nollaig,
Mar a bhí ag gach deoraí singil
Trí bliana is dhá scór ag déanamh
A bhuilín i bparthas cleasach an tí óil.
'A bhfuil de thithe gloine á ndúnadh síos . . .
Táim bliain go leith díomhaoin . . .'

Níor chodail sé néal le seachtain,
Bhí sruthán truaillithe ag caismirneach
Trína cheann, ba dhóbair dó bá.
Bhí air teitheadh arís ón bpéin
Is filleadh ar Chamden Town,
Bhí *pub* beag ag baintreach uaigneach ann.

Thar Sionainn soir trí scrabhanna
Faoi áirsí na gcrann méarach,
Dár gcaidreamh comhchuimhní
Dhein faoistin alcólaigh:
Mise im choinfeasóir drogallach
Faoi gheasa na gcuimleoirí.

Stopas ag droichead Shráid Bhagóid.
Dúirt sé gur thugas uchtach dó,
Go lorgódh sé jab i dtuaisceart an chontae,
Go mba bhreá leis a bheith
Chomh socair liom féin,
Go bhfeicfeadh sé arís mé, le cúnamh Dé.

Ar imeacht uaim sa cheobhrán dó
Taibhríodh dom athchaidreamh leis an stróinséir
Ar imeall mórbhealaigh san imigéin:

Ach go mba mise fear na hordóige
Is go mb'eisean an coinfeasóir –
É chomh socair liom féin,
Chomh socair liom féin.

# Shortening the Road

He told me he had spent
His life in horticulture,
Had always worked in the open air;
That was clear about the stranger
From his black nails and the smell of cut grass
Off his southern English.

Another sleet-shower;
Then the sun lit up
The road before us through Oranmore
East to Ballinasloe
And the car was a glasshouse
Warming to his gardening lore.

He had been spending a few days
With relatives west of Spiddal:
'You have Irish then, I suppose?'
'Not Irish, but Munster Irish . . . !'
A Muskerry man definitely, I thought; but no:
'A Corkman out of the heart of Cork.'

That lit a spark, exploding into Irish
And we combed through our backgrounds
And upbringings,
And God it's a small world
That we both could have travelled
The same backroads of dialect:

A Summer College in Ballingeary,
The Christian Brothers' Grammar,
The pubs of the Dingle Peninsula,
Then the compromise and watering down
Of five or six years
In the city of Dublin.

'It must be a great job in the summertime?'
'Yes indeed, but I prefer the Spring,
A time of growth, it's reassuring,
And there are miracles of colour in Autumn
That would keep a man off the booze . . .'
The spark had left his voice.

But he hated Christmas,
As would any single exile
Reaching forty-three
Loafing in the deluded paradise of the pub.
'They're closing the glasshouses down . . .
I'm a year and a half on the dole . . .'

He hadn't slept for a week,
A polluted stream was meandering
Through his brain, he had nearly drowned,
He was running from the pain again
Going back to Camden Town
Where a lonely widow had a small pub of her own.

East across the Shannon through squally showers
Under the arches of fingery trees,
What had been an exchange of memories
Had become an alcoholic's confession:
I the reluctant confessor
Under the spell of the windscreen wipers.

I stopped at Baggot Street bridge.
He said I'd given him hope,
That he would look for a job

In the north of the county,
That he'd love to be as steady as me,
That he'd see me again, please God, someday.

As he walked away into the fog
I imagined meeting the stranger again
On the verge of a foreign motorway
But I was the hitch-hiker
And he the confessor –
As steady as me,
As steady as me.

*translated by Philip Casey*

# Seandaoine

Chuimil sí a teanga dem shrón ghoirt
is dem spéaclaí a bhí sioctha
ag an sáile cáite is d'iarr sí orm
na luibheanna a ainmniú. A ainmniú?
(ní aithneoinnse an chopóg ón neantóg
an dtuigeann tú.)
Bhuel stathamar an crobh préacháin
is an méaracán dearg (An Dálach
a d'ainmnigh ar ball iad
á choiscreacan féin faoi thrí)
is dúrtsa gur sheandaoine iad
a léimeadh isteach sa chlaí
chun beannú do na gluaisteáin
is go rabhadar ag beannú dúinne
anois ar dhá thaobh an chasáin.
Leagamar síos ar thinteán an Dálaigh iad
gur eachtraigh sé dúinn mar a bhris
Peig Sayers a cromán lá dár thug
bean leighis lán a croibh
de mhéiríní sí isteach sa tigh chuici.
Nuair a d'fhilleamar abhaile
chuireamar ár bpiseoga faoi uisce
is chuireamar ar salann ár gcuimhne
tráthnóna lusach.

# Old People

She licked my salty nose
and my glasses which were frosted
by the sea spray and she asked me
to name the plants. Me name plants?

(I couldn't tell a dock from a nettle
you know.)
Well, we pulled the crowsfoot
and foxglove (Daly
named them for us later
crossing himself three times)
and I said these were old people
who had jumped into the hedge
to salute the motorcars
and were saluting us now
from both sides of the pathway.
We laid them down on Daly's fireplace
and he related to us
that Peig Sayers broke her hip one day
after a healing woman had brought her
a handful of foxgloves unannounced.
When we got home
we put our superstitions in water
and preserved in salt the memory
of a herbal afternoon.

*translated by Michael Hartnett*

# An Góchumadóir

B'fhearr liom
don chéad uair le stáir
luí anseo ag stánadh
aníos ón gcruinne
isteach i spéir chlúmh lachan
atá ag teitheadh roimh an rud alltarach fuiníoch
a rug greim ar an ngrian,

ná bheith im dhuine gan fód
ar fán is mo phócaí lán
de phinginí a bhfuil cloigeann
ar chaon taobh díobh
is béal air siar go cluasa
i ngáire uafar
bithcheimiceach.

B'fhearr liom luí anseo
is mo chumha a chaitheamh
gan scáth
mar aibíd bhán othair
in áit nach gá an dubh
a chur ina gheal
ná cuirtín a tharrac.

# The Counterfeiter

I would prefer
for the first time in a long time
to lie here and stare
up from the earth
into a duck's down sky
which flies before the Western beast
that smothered the sun,

than be rootless
wandering with pockets full
of pennies with heads
on both sides
with a mouth drawn back to the ears
in a grotesque
biochemical laugh.

I'd prefer to lie here
wearing my parting sorrow
without fear
like an invalid's white gown
in a place where there is no need
for black to be white
or for curtains to be drawn.

*translated by Philip Casey*

# Medbh McGuckian

## Gateposts

A man will keep a horse for prestige,
But a woman ripens best underground.
He settles where the wind
Brings his whirling hat to rest,
And the wind decides which door is to be used.

Under the hip-roofed thatch,
The bed-wing is warmed by the chimney breast;
On either side the keeping-holes
For his belongings, hers.

He says it's unlucky to widen the house,
And leaves the gateposts holding up the fairies.
He lays his lazy-beds and burns the river,
He builds turf-castles,
And sprigs the corn with apple-mint.

She spreads heather on the floor
And sifts the oatmeal ark for thin-bread farls:
All through the blue month
She tosses stones in basins to the sun,
And watches for the trout in the holy well.

# Lychees

You wonder at that Georgian terrace
Miles out of town where the motorway begins.
My great-grandfather was a coachman,
And knew how far away he was in the dark
By mysteries of the Rosary. My grandmother said
You could tell a good husband
By the thumbed leaves of his prayer-book.

A dead loss, my mother counts you,
Setting my teeth on edge at all hours,
Getting me to break the lychee's skin.
She underestimates the taste of sacrifice,
The irrelevance of distances,
Cat's-eyes, the cleanness of hands.

# The Sofa

Do not be angry if I tell you
Your letter stayed unopened on my table
For several days. If you were friend enough
To believe me, I was about to start writing
At any moment; my mind was savagely made up,
Like a serious sofa moved
Under a north window. My heart, alas,

Is not the calmest of places.
Still it is not my heart that needs replacing:
And my books seem real enough to me,
My disasters, my surrenders, all my loss . . .
Since I was child enough to forget
That you loathe poetry, you ask for some –
About nature, greenery, insects, and of course,

The sun – surely that would be to open
An already open window? Celebrating
The impudence of flowers? If I could
Interest you instead in his large, gentle stares,
How his soft shirt is the inside of pleasure
To me, why I must wear white for him,
Imagine he no longer trembles

When I approach, no longer buys me
Flowers for my name day . . . But I spread
On like a house, I begin to scatter
To a tiny to-and-fro at odds
With the wear on my threshold. Somewhere
A curtain rising wonders where I am,
My books sleep, pretending to forget me.

# The Aphrodisiac

She gave it out as if it were
A marriage or a birth, some other
Interesting family event, that she
Had finished sleeping with him, that
Her lover was her friend. It was his heart
She wanted, the bright key to his study,
Not the menacings of love. So he is
Banished to his estates, to live
Like a man in a glasshouse; she has taken to
A little cap of fine white lace
In the mornings, feeds her baby
In a garden you could visit blindfold
For its scent alone:
$\qquad\qquad$ But though a ray of grace
Has fallen, all her books seem as frumpish
As the last year's gambling game, when she
Would dress in pink taffeta, and drive
A blue phaeton, or in blue, and drive
A pink one, with her black hair supported
By a diamond comb, floating about
Without panniers. How his most
Caressing look, his husky whisper suffocates her,
This almost perfect power of knowing
More than a kept woman. The between-maid
Tells me this is not the only secret staircase.
Rumour has it she's taken to rouge again.

# The Flitting

'You wouldn't believe all this house has cost me –
In body-language terms, it has turned me upside down.'
I've been carried from one structure to the other
On a chair of human arms, and liked the feel
Of being weightless, that fraternity of clothes . . .
Now my own life hits me in the throat, the bumps
And cuts of the walls as telling
As the poreholes in strawberries, tomato seeds.
I cover them for safety with these Dutch girls
Making lace, or leaning their almond faces
On their fingers with a mandolin, a dreamy
Chapelled ease abreast this other turquoise-turbanned,
Glancing over her shoulder with parted mouth.

She seems a garden escape in her unconscious
Solidarity with darkness, clove-scented
As an orchid taking fifteen years to bloom,
And turning clockwise as the honeysuckle.
Who knows what importance
She attaches to the hours?
Her narrative secretes its own values, as mine might
If I painted the half of me that welcomes death
In a faggoted dress, in a peacock chair,
No falser biography than our casual talk
Of losing a virginity, or taking a life, and
No less poignant if dying
Should consist in more than waiting.

I postpone my immortality for my children,
Little rock-roses, cushioned
In long-flowering sea-thrift and metrics,
Lacking elemental memories:
I am well-earthed here as the digital clock,
Its numbers flicking into place like overgrown farthings

On a bank where once a train
Ploughed like an emperor living out a myth
Through the cambered flesh of clover and wild carrot.

# On Not Being Your Lover

Your eyes were ever brown, the colour
Of time's submissiveness. Love nerves
Or a heart, beat in their world of
Privilege, I had not yet kissed you
On the mouth.

But I would not say, in my un-freedom
I had weakly drifted there, like the
Bone-deep blue that visits and decants
The eyes of our children:

How warm and well-spaced their dreams
You can tell from the sleep-late mornings
Taken out of my face! Each lighted
Window shows me cardiganed, more desolate
Than the garden, and more hallowed
Than the hinge of the brass-studded
Door that we close, and no one opens,
That we open and no one closes.

In a far-flung, too young part,
I remembered all your slender but
Persistent volume said, friendly, complex
As the needs of your new and childfree girl.

# To a Cuckoo at Coolanlough

Driving the perfect length of Ireland,
Like a worn fold in a newspaper,
All my deep, country feelings
Wished I could have hypnotized myself
Into going back for the cherry-market
At Borris-in-Ossory.

But all I could think of was the fountain
Where Shelley wrote his 'Ode to the West Wind'
Nesting like a train-fever or combing jacket
Over the town.

A child will only
Sleep so long, and I wonder
If he is an artist, or have the six
Muscles around his eye forgotten colour,
And look it up, that Saturn-red, wild smudging,
In a dream-book?

And I wonder, after the three-minute
News, if you remember
The bits of road that I do?

# Sea or Sky?

Small doses, effleurage will do,
Because I never garden. Wednesday comes
Out of the rim of bones with a port-wine
Stain on its face, a day of possible
Excitements, no sky, yet you know immediately
The colour it should be. I play it down,
The agitated sky of my choice, I assume
That echo of light over there is the sun
Improperly burning. In a sea of like mood
A wave is trying to break, to give a reason
For water striking something else, and the grey
Below the wave is a darker version
Of the moisture-laden sky I should be working in.
(Not the clear water of your sleep where you
Seem lighter, and the garden's voice has gone inside.)

The athletic anatomy of waves, in their
Reflectiveness, rebirth, means my new, especially
Dense breasts can be touched, can be
Uplifted from the island of burned skin
Where my heart used to be, now I'm
Seeing eyes that, sea or sky, have seen you.

# On Ballycastle Beach

If I found you wandering round the edge
Of a French-born sea, when children
Should be taken in by their parents,
I would read these words to you,
Like a ship coming in to harbour,
As meaningless and full of meaning
As the homeless flow of life
From room to homesick room.

The words and you would fall asleep,
Sheltering just beyond my reach
In a city that has vanished to regain
Its language. My words are traps
Through which you pick your way
From a damp March to an April date,
Or a mid-August misstep; until enough winter
Makes you throw your watch, the heartbeat
Of everyone present, out into the snow.

My forbidden squares and your small circles
Were a book that formed within you
In some pocket, so permanently distended,
That what does not face north, faces east.
Your hand, dark as a cedar lane by nature,
Grows more and more tired of the skidding light,
The hunched-up waves, and all the wet clothing,
Toys and treasures of a late summer house.

Even the Atlantic has begun its breakdown
Like a heavy mask thinned out scene after scene
In a more protected time – like one who has
Gradually, unnoticed, lengthened her pre-wedding
Dress. But, staring at the old escape and release
Of the water's speech, faithless to the end,
Your voice was the longest I heard in my mind,
Although I had forgotten there could be such light.

# PETER FALLON

## Winter Work

Friends are unhappy; their long night
finds no day, their lane no turn. They wait
for things to change, as if history
happens to others, elsewhere. They hibernate

in dreams and fear. And Cathryn writes from Dublin:
she lies awake at night and hears
the noise of cars on Rathgar Road,
far from where her life coheres.

I warm to winter work, its rituals
and routines, and find – indoors
and out – a deal of pleasure, alone
or going out to work with neighbours,

a *meitheal*[1] still. All I approve persists,
is here, at home. I think it exquisite
to stand in the yard, my feet on the ground,
in cowshit and horseshit and sheepshit.

[1] A co-operative workforce.

# Spring Song

It was as if
someone only had to say
*Abracadabra*
to set alight
the chestnut
candelabra.

Bloom and blossom
everywhere, on furze,
on Queen Anne's Lace.
A breeze blew
cherry snows
on the common place.

Weeds on walls;
the long grass
of the long acre:
the elderberry bushes
blazing thanks
to their maker.

Loud leaves of
southside trees,
the reticent buds of ash,
the reach of undergrowth
were voices, voices,
woods' panache.

Cub foxes.
Pheasants galvanized
themselves to sing.
The white thorn flowers
were the light infantry
of Spring

marching down the headlands.
A new flock flowed
through a breach,
a makeshift gate.
And this is heaven:
sunrise through a copper beech.

# The Herd

I studied in the hedge school
and learned religions are a cod.
They're all the one.
Ask any fool.
Every lamb's a lamb of God.

# Airs and Graces

Nine times out of ten
he'd be complaining
and the tenth
condemning neighbours' stock
or the way they kept their fences.
Or he'd be crowing about
something of his own.
Cock of the walk,
a cut above buttermilk –
his geese were swans apparently.
The harvest moon perched
in his *Pendula* pear tree.

He went astray one winter.
They started soon to say
he's not the full shilling.
And someone said he'd take
so much in his stride
he hadn't feet on the ground
at all. A head in the clouds,
from which advantage he could see
no more nor the next man,
a world throughother.
When pressed he'd say
if it's not one thing, it's another.

The night he struck
the woman of the house
and shut her in the meal shed
they had it from the daughters.
He'd taken them to bed
once and again
and one conceived.
The doctor came and called the guards.

A cousin came to help
start the milking machine
and stayed to finish foddering. There was
no moon. The stars were few and far between.

PETER FALLON

# The Meadow

We have welded the towbar
and turned the mower's eighteen blades –
the mower, the meadow reiver.
We'll work all night, by the last
and first light and, in between, by the minutes
of moonlight. This is hay fever.

For weeks we've watched smudged fields
weighed down by mean July.
We've heard them broadcast
brightness and woken to wet weather.
We'd be better off watching Billy McNamee
than paying heed to the radio forecast.

When meadows grow he finds a way.
We say we'll trust our own translation
of the sky and start to mow
this evening. We'll be racing the rain.
Tomorrow we'll turn and turn again.
Midweek we'll set the bob to row.

Then we'll bale. We did that then,
headed the stacks with loose hay
from the headlands. We thought we'd won
until we heard of loss that rotted in rows
and stopped aftergrass. Insult to injury.
Talk everywhere of fusty fodder, self-combustion.

Ten years ago we built ten thousand bales,
two of us, and climbed the mountain
afterwards to rest in forestry that mearns
sheep pasture, a famine field
of lazy beds. We gazed down from
a cemetery of thirty cairns

across a stonewalled country.
Stacks of bales in circles – our work
stood out like harvest monoliths.
A thousand stones, standing,
speaking, leaning, lying stones,
the key- and cornerstones of myths . . .

Our farms began in those.
It was as if we tried to read the signs
of Newgrange from the moon. A thistle splinter
brought us back to earth
knowing that we'd gathered of its plenty
enough to fortify our care against the winter.

# Himself

Long before the father died
there was something the matter
with your man
but that's when he took to the fields.
He slept the latter

dozen years sheltered
near sheughs, in winter sheds.
He'd hoosh the heifers
from their lying
and settle down in their grass beds.

A woman left him dinner
in a dish.
Sometimes he'd take it,
more he wouldn't.
They'd a wish

that he'd come home
but not a hope.
He was wed to the four winds.
You might as well be rowing
with a rope

as ask. He kept within
a hen's race
of the place, seldom seen
but sometimes heard,
the base

sound that he made
all laugh
and no laughter.
His beard a bush,
he was chaff

of the whole world's threshing.
Wodwo. Sweeney. Troll,
who did no wrong.
They took him handcuffed
to the hospital

and clipped his nails.
He stirs early
still, a child of fields and gripes,
the intimacy of open air,
and whispers near an orderly

about himself as someone else:
He's not the sort who dares
the devil in his den.
He wouldn't try to teach
the priest his prayers

but they, they know
it all, that crowd.
Let them sing loudly
when they've harrowed
all he's ploughed.

# PAUL MULDOON

## Hedgehog

The snail moves like a
Hovercraft, held up by a
Rubber cushion of itself,
Sharing its secret

With the hedgehog. The hedgehog
Shares its secret with no one.
We say, *Hedgehog, come out
Of yourself and we will love you.*

*We mean no harm. We want
Only to listen to what
You have to say. We want
Your answers to our questions.*

The hedgehog gives nothing
Away, keeping itself to itself.
We wonder what a hedgehog
Has to hide, why it so distrusts.

We forget the god
Under this crown of thorns.
We forget that never again
Will a god trust in the world.

PAUL MULDOON

# Our Lady of Ardboe

### 1

Just there, in a corner of the whin-field,
Just where the thistles bloom.
She stood there as in Bethlehem
One night in nineteen fifty-three or four.

The girl leaning over the half-door
Saw the cattle kneel, and herself knelt.

### 2

I suppose that a farmer's youngest daughter
Might, as well as the next, unravel
The winding road to Christ's navel.

Who's to know what's knowable?
Milk from the Virgin Mother's breast,
A feather off the Holy Ghost?
The fairy thorn? The holy well?

Our simple wish for there being more to life
Than a job, a car, a house, a wife –
The fixity of running water.

For I like to think, as I step these acres,
That a holy well is no more shallow
Nor plummetless than the pools of Shiloh,
The fairy thorn no less true than the Cross.

### 3

Mother of our Creator, Mother of our Saviour,
Mother most amiable, Mother most admirable.
Virgin most prudent, Virgin most venerable,
Mother inviolate, Mother undefiled.

And I walk waist-deep among purples and golds
With one arm as long as the other.

# Ireland

The Volkswagen parked in the gap,
But gently ticking over.
You wonder if it's lovers
And not men hurrying back
Across two fields and a river.

# The Avenue

Now that we've come to the end
I've been trying to piece it together,
Not that distance makes anything clearer.
It began in the half-light
While we walked through the dawn chorus
After a party that lasted all night,
With the blackbird, the wood-pigeon,
The song-thrush taking a bludgeon
To a snail, our taking each other's hand
As if the whole world lay before us.

# Something of a Departure

Would you be an angel
And let me rest,
This one last time,
Near that plum-coloured beauty spot
Just below your right buttock?

Elizabeth, Elizabeth,
Had words not escaped us both
I would have liked to hear you sing
*Farewell to Tarwathie*
Or *Ramble Away*.

Your thigh, your breast,
Your wrist, the ankle
That might yet sprout a wing –
You're altogether as slim
As the chance of our meeting again.

So put your best foot forward
And steady, steady on.
Show me the plum-coloured beauty spot
Just below your right buttock,
And take it like a man.

# Why Brownlee Left

Why Brownlee left, and where he went,
Is a mystery even now.
For if a man should have been content
It was him; two acres of barley,
One of potatoes, four bullocks,
A milker, a slated farmhouse.
He was last seen going out to plough
On a March morning, bright and early.

By noon Brownlee was famous;
They had found all abandoned, with
The last rig unbroken, his pair of black
Horses, like man and wife,
Shifting their weight from foot to
Foot, and gazing into the future.

# Truce

It begins with one or two soldiers
And one or two following
With hampers over their shoulders.
They might be off wildfowling

As they would another Christmas Day,
So gingerly they pick their steps.
No one seems sure of what to do.
All stop when one stops.

A fire gets lit. Some spread
Their greatcoats on the frozen ground.
Polish vodka, fruit and bread
Are broken out and passed round.

The air of an old German song,
The rules of Patience, are the secrets
They'll share before long.
They draw on their last cigarettes

As Friday-night lovers, when it's over,
Might get up from their mattresses
To congratulate each other
And exchange names and addresses.

# Gathering Mushrooms

The rain comes flapping through the yard
like a tablecloth that she hand-embroidered.
My mother has left it on the line.
It is sodden with rain.
The mushroom shed is windowless, wide,
its high-stacked wooden trays
hosed down with formaldehyde.
And my father has opened the Gates of Troy
to that first load of horse manure.
Barley straw. Gypsum. Dried blood. Ammonia.
Wagon after wagon
blusters in, a self-renewing gold-black dragon
we push to the back of the mind.
We have taken our pitchforks to the wind.

All brought back to me that September evening
fifteen years on. The pair of us
tripping through Barnett's fair demesne
like girls in long dresses
after a hail-storm.
We might have been thinking of the fire-bomb
that sent Malone House sky-high
and its priceless collection of linen
sky-high.
We might have wept with Elizabeth McCrum.
We were thinking only of psilocybin.
You sang of the maid you met on the dewy grass –
*And she stooped so low gave me to know*
*it was mushrooms she was gathering O.*

He'll be wearing that same old donkey-jacket
and the sawn-off waders.
He carries a knife, two punnets, a bucket.
He reaches far into his own shadow.

We'll have taken him unawares
and stand behind him, slightly to one side.
He is one of those ancient warriors
before the rising tide.
He'll glance back from under his peaked cap
without breaking rhythm:
his coaxing a mushroom – a flat or a cup –
the nick against his right thumb;
the bucket then, the punnet to left or right,
and so on and so forth till kingdom come.

We followed the overgrown tow-path by the Lagan.
The sunset would deepen through cinnamon
to aubergine,
the wood-pigeon's concerto for oboe and strings,
allegro, blowing your mind.
And you were suddenly out of my ken, hurtling
towards the ever-receding ground,
into the maw
of a shimmering green-gold dragon.
You discovered yourself in some outbuilding
with your long-lost companion, me,
though my head had grown into the head of a horse
that shook its dirty-fair mane
and spoke this verse:

*Come back to us. However cold and raw, your feet*
*were always meant*
*to negotiate terms with bare cement.*
*Beyond this concrete wall is a wall of concrete*
*and barbed wire. Your only hope*
*is to come back. If sing you must, let your song*
*tell of treading your own dung,*
*let straw and dung give a spring to your step.*
*If we never live to see the day we leap*
*into our true domain,*

*lie down with us now and wrap*
*yourself in the soiled grey blanket of Irish rain*
*that will, one day, bleach itself white.*
*Lie down with us and wait.*

# Quoof

How often have I carried our family word
for the hot water bottle
to a strange bed,
as my father would juggle a red-hot half-brick
in an old sock
to his childhood settle.
I have taken it into so many lovely heads
or laid it between us like a sword.

An hotel room in New York City
with a girl who spoke hardly any English,
my hand on her breast
like the smouldering one-off spoor of the yeti
or some other shy beast
that has yet to enter the language.

# Yggdrasill

From below, the waist-thick pine
seemed to arch
its back. It is a birch,
perhaps. At any rate, I could discern
a slight curvature of the spine.

They were gathered in knots
to watch me go.
A pony fouled the hard-packed snow
with her glib cairn,
someone opened a can of apricots.

As I climb
my nose is pressed to the bark.
The mark
of a cigarette burn
from your last night with him.

A snapshot of you and your sister
walking straight
through 1958,
*The Works of Laurence Sterne*
your only aid to posture.

The air is aerosol-
blue and chill. I have notched
up your pitch-
pine scent and the maidenhair fern's
spry arousal.

And it would be just swell and dandy
to answer
them with my tonsure,
to return
with the black page from *Tristram Shandy*.

Yet the lichened
tree trunk will taper
to a point where one scrap of paper
is spiked, and my people yearn
for a legend:

*It may not be today*
*or tomorrow, but sooner or later*
*the Russians will water*
*their horses on the shores of Lough Erne*
*and Lough Neagh.*

# The Wishbone

Maureen in England, Joseph in Guelph,
my mother in her grave.

\*

At three o'clock in the afternoon
we watch the Queen's
message to the Commonwealth
with the sound turned off.

\*

He seems to favour *Camelot*
over *To Have and Have Not.*

\*

Yet we agree, my father and myself,
that here is more than enough
for two; a frozen chicken,
spuds, sprouts, *Paxo* sage and onion.

\*

The wishbone like a rowelled spur
on the fibula of Sir— or Sir— .

# The Lass of Aughrim

On a tributary of the Amazon
an Indian boy
steps out of the forest
and strikes up on a flute.

Imagine my delight
when we cut the outboard motor
and I recognize the strains
of *The Lass of Aughrim*.

'He hopes,' Jesus explains,
'to charm
fish from the water

on what was the tibia
of a priest
from a long-abandoned Mission.'

# The Soap-Pig

I must have been dozing in the tub
when the telephone
rang and a small, white grub
crawled along the line
and into my head:
Michael Heffernan was dead.

All I could think of
was his Christmas present
from what must have been 1975.
It squatted there on the wash-stand,
an amber, pig-shaped
bar of soap.

He had breezed into Belfast
in a three-quarter length coney-fur
to take up the post
of Drama Producer
with the still-reputable Beeb,
where I had somehow wangled a jòb.

Together we learned from Denys
Hawthorne and Allan McClelland
to float, like Saint Gennys,
on our own hands
through airwaves mostly jammed by cub-
reporters and poisoned pups.

He liked to listen at full tilt
to bootleg tapes
of Ian Paisley's assaults
on Papes,
regretful only that they weren't in quad.
His favourite word was *quidditas*.

I could just see the Jesuitical,
kitsch-camp slip-
knot in the tail
of even that bar of soap.
For this was Heffernan
saying, 'You stink to high heaven.'

Which I well knew. Many's an Arts Club
night with Barfield and Mason
ended with me throwing up
at the basin.
Anne-Marie looked on, her unspoken,
'That's to wash, not boke in.'

This, or any, form of self-regard
cut no ice
with Michael, who'd undergone heart-
surgery at least twice
while I knew him. On a trip
once to the Wexford slobs

he and I had shared
a hotel room. When he slipped
off his shirt
there were two unfashionably-broad lap-
els where the surgeons had sawn
through the xylophone

on which he liked to play
Chopin or *Chop-*
*sticks* until he was blue
in the face; be-bop, doo-wop:
they'd given him a tiny, plastic valve
that would, it seemed, no more dissolve

than the soap-pig I carried
on successive flits
from Marlborough Park (and Anne-Marie)
to the Malone Avenue flat

(*Chez Moy*, it was later dubbed)
to the rented house in Dub (as in *Dub-*

lin) Lane,
until, at last, in Landseer Street
Mary unpeeled its cellophane
and it landed on its feet
among porcelain, glass and heliotrope
pigs from all parts of the globe.

When we went on holiday to France
our house-sitter was troub-
led by an unearthly fragrance
at one particular step
on the landing. It was no pooka,
of course, but the camomile soap-pig

that Mary, in a fit of pique,
would later fling into the back yard.
As I unpicked
the anthracite-shards
from its body, I glimpsed the scrab-
nosed, condemned slab

of our sow that dropped
dead from a chill in 1966,
its uneven litter individually wrapped
in a banana box
with polystyrene and wood-shavings;
this time Mary was leaving,

taking with her the gold
and silver pigs, the ivory.
For Michael Heffernan, the common cold
was an uncommon worry
that might as easily have stopped
him in his tracks. He'd long since escaped

Belfast for London's dog-eat-dog
back-stab
and leap-frog.
More than once he collap-
sed at his desk. But Margaret
would steady him through the Secretariat

towards their favourite restaurant
where, given my natural funk
I think of as restraint,
I might have avoided that Irish drunk
whose slow jibes
Michael parried, but whose quick jab

left him forever at a loss for words.
For how he would delib-
erate on whether two six-foot boards
sealed with ship's
varnish and two tea-chests
(another move) on which all this rests

is a table; or this merely a token
of some ur-chair,
or – being broken –
a chair at all: the mind's a razor
on the body's strop.
And the soap-pig? It's a bar of soap,

now the soap-sliver
in a flowered dish
that I work each morning into a lather
with my father's wobbling-brush,
then reconcile to its pool of glop
on my mother's wash-stand's marble top.

# HARRY CLIFTON

## Monsoon Girl

In the airconditioned drone
Of a room we rent by the hour,
You go to the telephone
Lovely and naked, to put through a call
For drinks, or hire a car
To take us home.

Your nudity dapples the walls
With shadows, and splashes the mirrors
Like a vision, in the blue light
That bathes you, a pleasure-girl
On a lost planet, sincere
But only at night.

Outside, it will rain
For weeks, months on end . . .
We'll come here again
As we did before, where Chinese women,
Blank and inscrutable, attend
Nightly to our linen.

We'll come again
In drunkenness, for the child's play
Of lovemaking, or to part the rain
Like curtains of jet beads,
And dream the rainy months away
On pampered beds

Where forgetfulness lies down
With executive power
After hours, in a tangle of legs
And juices, a world turned upside down,
And I feed on the lotus-flower
Of your delicate sex.

At three, we'll be driven back
Through depths of Bangkok
Already tomorrow. There will be roads
Closed, and a dope squad
Flashing its query through windowglass,
Letting us pass . . .

There will be lights
In Chinatown, sampans on the river –
The poor starting early. Elsewhere the night
Will separate us, having seeded within you
Miscarriage of justice forever,
And the rain will continue.

# Death of Thomas Merton

Losing altitude, you can see below you the flames
Of the Tet Offensive, giving the lie to your visions
Of eastern mystics, like uncensored newsreel
In which the slaves of history are spreading the blame –
And so your mind records it, a sin of omission
In a mystic journal. Meanwhile the wheels
Descend for Bangkok, with one of the Catholic great,
In late October, Nineteen Sixty Eight.

A clean declaration. One a.m. and you're through
The bulletproof glass of security, like a conscience
Filtered through judgement, leaving behind
Temptations you were dead to, years ago –
Hippies frisked for heroin, women and incense
For the American soldiers. Only the life of the mind
You hide on your person – all the rest you can shed
Like a stale narcotic. Shortly, you'll be dead.

So wake before daylight, breakfast alone,
Remembering what you came for. Below you a river
Seeps out of Buddhist heartlands, not in meditation
But in commerce, irrigating zones
Of military fleshpots, where the barges deliver
Rice and Thai girls, and a drifting vegetation
Drags at the chains of destroyers, moored in Bangkok –
And you wait to be chauffeured, at nine o'clock,

To the other side of the city . . .
                              Spiritual masters
Shrunken to skin and bone, await you in silence
On a neutral ground of Buddhas, golden and hollow,
Smiling from inner space, beyond disaster
To an old complacency. Starving for nonviolence
In saffron robes, their shavenheaded followers

Beg on the streets. From an airconditioned car
You can see them in passing, as cut off as you are –

Cut off from each other, disconnected by history
In Paris and Calcutta, linked alone by the airspace
Of a temporal pilgrimage. Diplomatic immunity,
This is your saving grace – to restore mystery
To a common weal, and resurrect from disgrace
The nonpolitical, kneeling in the unity
Of a moment's prayer, with the Dalai Lama and wife –
For the flash-photographers of *Time* and *Life*.

Judas has other betrayals. At your last supper
In a Hungarian restaurant, among friends in Bangkok,
It's left to the Chinese waiter to overprice you –
So unworldly. You can switch from corruption
Suddenly into wisdom, through an electric shock
Turning your hair white, resolving your crisis
Into anticlimax. But it leaves you dead,
With a powerline shortcircuited through your head . . .

A small embarrassment, for the United States –
Your motherhouse at Gethsemani awaits
Its anti-hero. A gaggle of monks are released
To New Haven for the day, to identify and separate
Among the Vietnam dead, the maimed in crates
From an Air Force plane, this body of a priest
And holy fool – from beyond the international
Dateline, and the jungle war with the irrational.

# The Distaff Side

Elopement and civil wedding . . . the sham squire
Looks back on it all, remembering Guadeloupe
Where they lived on nothing, cooked and sang for the troops –
Himself and this runaway daughter. God knows why
They ever came back, to dampen the fires
Of passion in Ireland, to put down roots and die.

Because *she* wanted to. Because it made sense.
Because, as she keeps repeating, nothing intense
Goes on forever . . . Restless, he hears from bed
The brokenhearted weeping of a daughter
And wishes he was somewhere else instead
Like back in the army, ladling stew before slaughter

From an old field-kitchen, safe in the middle of war –
But no such luck. The pillowtalk of a spouse
So down to earth she makes even sex a chore
Admonishes, chides, 'The day you become breadwinner
I'll pacify children . . .' sends him out through the house
As nude as a ghost. Already, tomorrow's dinner

Bleeds on the flagstones, waiting to be skinned
From a day of boyish hunting.
                              How did the years
Imprison him here, in an Irish house and grounds,
With a redhaired wife, who sees him when she can –
Divorced from history, stalking Wicklow deer,
A jealous minder of children, a kept man?

'Tomorrow I'll take you fishing . . .' he quiets his daughter
While out on the Eastern Marches, wholesale slaughter
Drains the silos . . . Nobody knows him, his rages
Are all domestic, tantrums at bad little girls
Upsetting the basket of eels he gathered for ages
And starting their passionate journeys back to the world.

# Id

What if, with my life half over,
I was to go back again
On abandoned ways, and instead of taking a lover,
Instead of taking a wife,
I shook off my status, a man among men,
And disappeared back into life –

Would they still be there
To absolve me, the professional liars
With telephones unlisted and whereabouts hid
In a maze of cities, the women on hire
The desk clerk knows, and the bellhop shows upstairs?
The heroines of the id,

They came to me once, when I lived alone
In African hotels –
And when we had finished, they whispered to me,
As they whisper, now, to somebody else,
'Young man, by the time you are thirty
Everything will be known . . .'

And so it was, on Sandal Street,
One night in old Calcutta
Of rain and cooking fires, along roof and gutter,
And families camped under plastic sheets
Among the imperial ruins the viceroys created
And rickshaw coolies waited –

I saw myself, as I washed in the copper bowl
And let cold water, a strip of towel
Restore the world to me, by slow degrees –
The girl I was with, the room I was in,
And somewhere about me, a jangle of keys
And the voices of middlemen.

'Oh, marry us,' they said to me,
The girls sold into slavery
So long ago, and the wards of court
Escaping from love, in need of a foreign address,
'If not for ourselves, at least for the chance of a passport
To the Europe of consciousness . . .'

And far away, under Western time,
Again I lie down, in the home from home
Of a democratic city,
Whose lights I can reconstruct from, whose darkness I cannot
    defend,
Though the woman lying beside me, now,
Is conscious, and a friend.

# Euclid Avenue

*after Hart Crane*

The blazing stanchions and the corporate lights –
Manhattan over the bridge, from Brooklyn Heights –
Were energies like yours, without a home,
That would not be condensed inside a poem

But endlessly dispersed, and went to work
For time and money, hovering over the masses
Like terrible angels . . . Now, I stand in New York
And watch those energies sweat themselves out, like gases

Through a subway grille, to keep the derelicts warm
In a new depression. Or, at station bookstalls,
Calm at the eye of the electric storm
I drink your words, like prohibition alcohol

Capital hides from itself. On soundless trains
Through Middle America, citizens fishing in creeks
That rise and flow nowhere, disappear again
In a private wilderness you were born to seek

And lose yourself in. But none of them will thank you –
They, nor the desolate children that they raised
On a thousand streets called Euclid Avenue
For travelling inwards, damning with faint praise

The forces that they freed, to blast through gravity
Into a loveless, extraterrestrial space
Like night bus stations, galaxies of strays –
The sons and daughters of the human race.

# Eccles Street, Bloomsday, 1982

Onesided, stripped of its ghosts,
The half that was left of Eccles Street
Stood empty, on that day of days
My own unconscious feet
Would carry me through
To a blind date, or a rendezvous.

Invisible pressure, invisible heat
Laid down the blue coordinates
Of a Hellenic city
From Phoenix Park to the Merrion Gates,
Where disconnected, at one remove
From wisdom, or eternal love,

A million citizens worked, ate meals,
Or dreamt a moment of Joyce,
And felt themselves wholly real,
The equals of fate, the masters of choice,
As I did too, on Eccles Street,
Before ever you and I could meet

In the larger scheme . . . Coincidence
Ruled invisibly, the casual date
Upstaged by Greek infinities
Moving among us like common sense,
Imprisoning, setting me free
To dream and circumambulate

In a myth too young to be formed.
I would build it myself, from the ruined door
Of Bella Cohen's bawdyhouse,
From other basements, other whores
Unbuttoning their blouses
Forever, while traffic swarmed

And the lights outside turned green and red
On shifting planes of reality –
And you, a final student, read
Of Joyce in the National Library,
Or stood in the crowd, my love unseen,
At the unveiling in Stephen's Green.

An hour went by, on Eccles Street –
Two drunks, at ease in the Mater portals,
Swigged, and sang Republican songs.
I watched a line of taxis wait
And saw where real grass had sprung
Through mythic pavements, already immortal,

Green as life, and unresearched.
I had come, only that morning,
From Ringsend docks, and Sandymount Church,
Along the arc of odyssey,
With my invisible yearning
To break the circle, set myself free,

As you had yours, until one day
In the prefigured city,
Where every step is a step of fate
And recognition comes only later,
We would meet, you and I,
Weigh anchor at last, and go away.

# Nuala Ní Dhomhnaill

## Féar Suaithinseach

Nuair a bhís i do shagart naofa
i lár an Aifrinn, faoi do róbaí corcra
t'fhallaing lín, do stól, do chasal,
do chonnaicís m'aghaidh-se ins an slua
a bhí ag teacht chun comaoineach chughat
is thit uait an abhlainn bheannaithe.

Mise, ní dúrt aon ní ina thaobh.
Bhí náire orm.
Bhí glas ar mo bhéal.
Ach fós do luigh sé ar mo chroí
mar dhealg láibe, gur dhein sé slí
dó fhéin istigh im ae is im lár
gur dhóbair go bhfaighinn bás dá bharr.

Ní fada nó gur thiteas 'on leabaidh;
oideasaí leighis do triaileadh ina gcéadtaibh,
do tháinig chugham dochtúirí, sagairt is bráithre
is n'fhéadadar mé a thabhairt chun sláinte
ach thugadar suas i seilbh bháis mé.

Is téigí amach, a fheara,
tugaíg libh rámhainn is speala
corráin, grafáin is sluaiste.
Réabaíg an seanafhothrach,
bearraíg na seacha, glanaíg an luifearnach,
an slámas fáis, an brus, an ainnise
a fhás ar thalamh bán mo thubaiste.

Is ins an ionad inar thit
an chomaoine naofa féach go mbeidh
i lár an bhiorlamais istigh
toirtín d'fhéar suaithinseach.

Tagadh an sagart is lena mhéireanna
beireadh sé go haiclí ar an gcomaoine naofa
is tugtar chugham í, ar mo theanga
leáfaidh sí, is éireod aniar sa leaba
chomh slán folláin is a bhíos is mé i mo leanbh.

## Marvellous Grass

When you were a holy priest
in the middle of Mass in your purple robes
your linen mantle, your stole, your chasuble,
you saw my face in the crowd
approaching you for communion
and you dropped the blessed host.

I – I said nothing.
I was ashamed.
My lips were locked.
But still it lay on my heart
like a mud-thorn until
it penetrated my insides.
From it I nearly died.

Not long till I took to my bed:
medical experts came in hundreds
doctors, priests and friars –
not one could cure me
they abandoned me for death.

Go out, men:
take with you spades and scythes
sickles, hoes and shovels.

Ransack the ruins
cut the bushes, clear the rubble,
the rank growth, the dust, the misery
that grows on my tragic grassland.

And in the place where fell
the sacred host you will see
among the useless plants
a patch of marvellous grass.

Let the priest come and with his fingers
take dexterously the sacred host.
And it's given to me: on my tongue
it will melt and I will sit up in the bed
as healthy as I was when young.

*translated by Michael Hartnett*

# Geasa

Má chuirim aon lámh ar an dtearmann beannaithe,
má thógaim droichead thar an abhainn,
gach a mbíonn tógtha isló ages na ceardaithe
bíonn sé leagtha ar maidin romham.

Tagann aníos an abhainn istoíche bád
is bean ina seasamh inti.
Tá coinneal ar lasadh ina súil is ina lámha.
Tá dhá mhaide rámha aici.

Tarraigíonn sí amach paca cártaí
'An imréofá breith?' a deireann sí.
Imrímid is buann sí orm de shíor
is cuireann sí de cheist, de bhreith is de mhórualach orm

gan an tarna béile a ithe in aon tigh,
ná an tarna oíche a chaitheamh faoi aon díon,
gan dhá shraic chodlata a dhéanamh ar aon leaba
go bhfaighead í. Nuair a fhiafraím di cá mbíonn sí

'Dá mba siar é soir,' a deireann sí, 'dá mba soir é siar.'
Imíonn sí léi agus splancacha tintrí léi
is fágtar ansan mé ar an bport.
Tá an dá choinneal fós ar lasadh le mo thaobh.

D'fhág sí na maidí rámha agam.


# The Bond

If I use my forbidden hand
To raise a bridge across the river,
All the work of the builders
Has been blown up by sunrise.

A boat comes up the river by night
With a woman standing in it,
Twin candles lit in her eyes
And two oars in her hands.

She unsheathes a pack of cards:
'Will you play forfeits?' she says.
We play and she beats me hands down,
And she puts three banns upon me:

Not to have two meals in one house,
Not to pass two nights under one roof,
Not to sleep twice with the same man
Until I find her. When I ask her address

'If it were north I'd tell you south,
If it were east, west.' She hooks
Off in a flash of lightning, leaving me
Stranded on the bank,

My eyes full of candles,
And the two dead oars.

*translated by Medbh McGuckian*

# Aubade

Is cuma leis an mhaidin cad air a ngealann sí; –
ar na cáganna ag bruíon is ag achrann ins na crainn
dhuilleogacha; ar an mbardal glas ag snámh go tóstalach
i measc na ngiolcach ins na curraithe; ar thóinín bán
an chircín uisce ag gobadh aníos as an bpoll portaigh;
ar roilleoga ag siúl go cúramach ar thránna móra.

Is cuma leis an ghrian cad air a éiríonn sí: –
ar na tithe bríce, ar fhuinneoga de ghloine snoite
is gearrtha i gcearnóga Seoirseacha: ar na saithí beach
ag ullmhú chun creach a dhéanamh ar ghairdíní bruachbhailte;
ar lánúine óga fós ag méanfach i gcoimhthiúin is fonn
a gcúplála ag éirí aníos iontu; ar dhrúcht ag glioscarnach
ina dheora móra ar lilí is ar róiseanna; ar do ghuaille.

Ach ní cuma linn go bhfuil an oíche aréir
thart, is go gcaithfear glacadh le pé rud a sheolfaidh
an lá inniu an tslí; go gcaithfear imeacht is cromadh síos
arís is píosaí beaga brealsúnta ár saoil a dhlúthú
le chéile ar chuma éigin, chun gur féidir
lenár leanaí uisce a ól as babhlaí briste
in ionad as a mbosa, ní cuma linne é.

# Aubade

It's all the same to morning what it dawns on –
On the bickering of jackdaws in leafy trees;
On that dandy from the wetlands, the green mallard's
Stylish glissando among reeds; on the moorhen
Whose white petticoat flickers around the boghole;
On the oystercatcher on tiptoe at low tide.

It's all the same to the sun what it rises on –
On the windows in houses in Georgian squares;
On bees swarming to blitz suburban gardens;
On young couples yawning in unison before
They do it again; on dew like sweat or tears
On lilies and roses; on your bare shoulders.

But it isn't all the same to us that night-time
Runs out; that we must make do with today's
Happenings, and stoop and somehow glue together
The silly little shards of our lives, so that
Our children can drink water from broken bowls,
Not from cupped hands. It isn't the same at all.

*translated by Michael Longley*

# An Crann

Do tháinig bean an leasa
le Black & Decker,
do ghearr sí anuas mo chrann.
D'fhanas im óinseach ag féachaint uirthi
faid a bhearraigh sí na brainsí
ceann ar cheann.

Tháinig m'fhear céile abhaile tráthnóna.
Chonaic sé an crann.
Bhí an gomh dearg air,
ní nach ionadh. Dúirt sé
'Canathaobh nár stopais í?
nó cad is dóigh léi?
cad a cheapfadh sí
dá bhfaighinnse Black & Decker
is dul chun a tí
agus crann ansúd a bhaineas léi
a ghearradh anuas sa ghairdín?'

Tháinig bean an leasa thar n-ais ar maidin.
Bhíos fós ag ithe mo bhricfeasta.
D'iarr sí orm cad dúirt m'fhear céile.
Dúrtsa léi cad dúirt sé,
go ndúirt sé cad is dóigh léi,
is cad a cheapfadh sí
dá bhfaigheadh sé siúd Black & Decker
is dul chun a tí
is crann ansúd a bhaineas léi
a ghearradh anuas sa ghairdín.

'Ó,' ar sise, '*that's very interesting.*'
Bhí béim ar an *very*.
Bhí cling leis an *-ing.*
Do labhair sí ana-chiúin.
Bhuel, b'shin mo lá-sa,

pé ar bith sa tsaol é,
iontaithe bunoscionn.

Thit an tóin as mo bholg
is faoi mar a gheobhainn lascadh chic
nó leacadar sna baotháin
líon taom anbhainne isteach orm
a dhein chomh lag san mé
gurb ar éigin a bhí ardú na méire ionam
as san go ceann trí lá.

Murab ionann is an crann
a dh'fhan ann, slán.

## As for the Quince

There came this bright young thing
with a Black & Decker
and cut down my quince-tree.
I stood with my mouth hanging open
while one by one
she trimmed off the branches.

When my husband got home that evening
and saw what had happened
he lost the rag,
as you might imagine.
'Why didn't you stop her?
What would she think
if I took the Black & Decker
round to her place
and cut down a quince-tree
belonging to her?
What would she make of that?'

Her ladyship came back next morning
while I was at breakfast.

She enquired about his reaction.
I told her straight
that he was wondering how she'd feel
if he took a Black & Decker
round to her house
and cut down a quince-tree of hers,
etcetera etcetera.

'O,' says she, 'that's very interesting.'
There was a stress on the 'very'.
She lingered over the 'ing'.
She was remarkably calm and collected.

These are the times that are in it, so,
all a bit topsy-turvy.
The bottom falling out of my belly
as if I had got a kick up the arse
or a punch in the kidneys.
A fainting-fit coming over me
that took the legs from under me
and left me so zonked
I could barely lift a finger
till Wednesday.

As for the quince, it was safe and sound
and still somehow holding its ground.

*translated by Paul Muldoon*

# An Rás

Faoi mar a bheadh leon cuthaigh, nó tarbh fásaigh,
nó ceann de mhuca allta na Fiannaíochta,
nó an gaiscíoch ag léimt faoi dhéin an fhathaigh
faoina chírín singilíneach síoda,
tiomáinim an chairt ar dalladh
trí bhailte beaga lár na hÉireann.
Beirim ar an ghaoth romham
is ní bheireann an ghaoth atá i mo dhiaidh orm.

Mar a bheadh saighead as bogha, piléar as gunna
nó seabhac rua trí scata mionéan lá Márta
scaipim na mílte slí taobh thiar dom.
Tá uimhreacha ar na fógraí bóthair
is ní thuigim an mílte iad nó kiloméadair.
Aonach, Ros Cré, Móinteach Mílic,
n'fheadar ar ghaibheas nó nár ghaibheas tríothu.
Níl iontu faoin am seo ach teorainní luais
is moill ar an mbóthar go dtí tú.

Trí ghleannta sléibhte móinte bogaithe
scinnim ar séirse ón iarthar,
d'aon seáp amháin reatha i do threo
de fháscadh ruthaig i do chuibhreann.
Deinim ardáin des na hísleáin, ísleáin de na hardáin
talamh bog de thalamh cruaidh is talamh cruaidh de thalamh bog, –
imíonn gnéithe uile seo na léarscáile as mo chuimhne,
ní fhanann ann ach gíoscán coscán is drithle soilse.

Chím sa scáthán an ghrian ag buíú is ag deargadh
taobh thiar díom ag íor na spéire.
Tá sí ina meall mór craorac lasrach amháin
croí an Ghlas Gaibhneach á chrú trí chriathar.
Braonta fola ag sileadh ón stráinín
mar a bheadh pictiúr den Chroí Ró-Naofa.

Tá gile na trí deirgeacht inti,
is pian ghéar í, is giorrosnaíl.

Deinim iontas des na braonta fola.
Tá uamhan i mo chroí, ach fós táim neafaiseach
faoi mar a fhéach, ní foláir, Codladh Céad Bliain
ar a méir nuair a phrioc fearsaid an turainn í.
Casann sí timpeall is timpeall arís í,
faoi mar a bheadh sí ag siúl i dtaibhreamh.
Nuair a fhéach Deirdre ar fhuil dhearg an laoi sa tsneachta
n'fheadar ar thuig sí cérbh é an fiach dubh?

Is nuair is dóigh liom gur chughat a thiomáinim,
a fhir álainn, a chumann na n-árann
is ná coinneoidh ó do leaba an oíche seo mé
ach mílte bóthair is soilse tráchta,
tá do chuid mífhoighne mar chloch mhór
ag titim anuas ón spéir orainn
is cuir leis ár ndrochghiúmar,
ciotarúntacht is meall mór mo chuid uabhair.

Is tá meall mór eile ag teacht anuas orainn
má thagann an tuar faoin tairngre
agus is mó go mór é ná meall na gréine
a fhuiligh i mo scáthán anois ó chianaibhín.
Is a mháthair abhalmhór, a phluais na n-iontas
ós chughatsa ar deireadh atá an spin siúil fúinn
an fíor a ndeir siad gur fearr aon bhlaise amháin de do phóigín
ná fíon Spáinneach, ná mil Ghréagach, ná beoir bhuí Lochlannach?

# The Race

> Like a mad lion, like a wild bull,
> a wild boar from a Fenian tale,
> a hero bounding towards a giant
> with a single silken crest,

I blindly drive the car
through the small towns of the west:
I drive the wind before me
and leave the wind behind.

Arrow from bow, bullet from gun.
Sparrow-hawk through flock of small March birds
I scatter miles of road behind.
Figures flash on signposts –
but in kilometres or miles?
Nenagh, Roscrea, Mountmellick
(but have I travelled through these towns?)
mere things that limit speed
mere things that slow me down.

Through geographic barricades
I rush and dart from the west
I gallop towards where you wait
I speed to where you stand.
Heights are hollows, hollows heights
dry land is marsh, marshland is dry,
all contours from the map are gone:
nothing but shriek of brakes and sparks of light.

Sun's in the mirror, red and gold
in the sky behind me,
one huge crimson blazing globe –
Glas Gaibhneach's heart milk through a sieve
her drops of blood strained out
like a picture of the Sacred Heart.
Three scarlet brightnesses are there
and pain so sharp, and sob so short.

I stared at the drops of blood
afraid but almost unaware –
like Sleeping Beauty when she gazed
at her thumb pricked by the wheel,
she turned it over, and over once more

as if her actions were unreal.
When Deirdre saw blood on the snow
did she know the raven's name?

Then I realize I drive towards you
my dearest friend and lovely man
(may nothing keep me from your bed tonight
but miles of road and traffic lights)
and your impatience like a stone
falls upon us from the sky
and adds to our uneasiness
the awkward weight of my hurt pride.

And more great loads will fall on us
if the omen comes to pass
much greater than the great sun's globe
that lately bled into the glass.
And so, Great Mother, cave of awe –
since it's towards you we race –
is it the truth? Is your embrace
and kiss more fine
than honey, beer, or Spanish wine?

*translated by Michael Hartnett*

# THOMAS McCARTHY

## The Wisdom of AE

Some days he would wander around his attic-room
in search of a recent letter or a new poem
that might have hitched from a rural Co-op,
or an unfinished painting that had desolately
hid between newspapers and a month of bills;
his life was full of things fresh or unmade

like the new country or a spring homestead.
He kept to his own chaos in the land of hot
views; opinion like a dagger couldn't disturb
his ways or alter his deepest occult reference.
(While the land was busy with war he was perturbed
by an incomplete vision of a future President.)

Visions came and went like shafts of sunlight
at the woods near Coole; nymphs playing on the shore
were part of a permanent familiar insight;
a familiar world of rocks, woods and water.
He was the first to live by the eternal Feminine,
to spill water and woodland over violent politics.

And his deepest vision was that feminine thought,
the lack of a killing view. His thoughts altered
the deepest enmities. Like a woman who gathers
her husband's arrogance into a basket of love,
he took our wars into the palm of his thought
and stroked the poisons from where we had fought.

# The Phenomenology of Stones

*for Catherine*

These summer days I carry images of stone,
Small pebbles from a photographer's shelf
Made smooth by a million years of sea and salt.
Sunlight shines roundly into their small room,
Twisting black grains into crystals and gems:
Lights call like young birds from their surfaces,
Sparrows of light flying from graves, from places
Where the dead had grown; the sorrow-gardens.

But the silence of stone quietens the mind
And calms the eye. Like their girl-collector –
In her deep solitude the stones are moved.
She is their dream-collector, pouring her kind-
ness into their sleeping form. They gather
Fables about themselves to entertain such love.

# Claud Cockburn

A flourish of sunlight in the room where
You live now, cigarette smoke in the air.
Your clothes move as if to meet your body
When you bend to watch sunlight on the sea.
Fishermen haul their lobster-pots below
Us, one or two signal to your window.
To be king of inlets and fuchsia bushes
After years of bitterness, an excessive
Dialectic of dreams and writing, is
One sweet reward for having fought alone –

Though words are never left alone. Unlike
Brickwork or well-vaulted art, words are
Dislodged from their makers. Think of the soldiers
Who bedded down with Hölderlin's irenic
Poems, or the way Fascism disfigured Goethe.
You Claud, *dear raconteur*, your toughest words
Came down on those who murdered print, absurd
Kings and magnates who kept Fascism afloat:
The wisdom of your life exposes both,
As well as war, which comes a deadly third.

*Whose submarine lingers in our harbour then,*
*Its metal eyes bobbing in the water,*
*October sunshine bouncing from its nose?*
The racing Ardmore tide tries to expose
Its menace. The brown heather lies asleep
While war and neutrality play hide and seek
Among the ruins of the harbour castle;
A breeze shaking its brass and ivied bell –
That breeze the most enlightened of us all;
Our politics as brainless as birdcall

And as colourful. What good is colour
If the navigators are blind? You Claud,

Only you have kept the millennial cause
While others settled for a luxury acre.
Now you weep for others barely employed
In the second Great Depression of our time.
*Worry* is training your neighbour and his kind
For war. You know how greatly they enjoyed
Our last Emergency, with high prices and
Good money from the most barren of land.

Go tell them about the latest nuclear device
And how the world is hanging from a precipice
That only journalists like you can cure.
Teach us what good politics may be for –
Social jobs and social good, clean rivers,
Guns into ploughshares, etc. An end to fear.
No doubt, dear author, you'd teach if you could
Simple politics for our common good.
Your ageing throat deserves some rest, and yet
You warn others to check for trouble in their nets.

THOMAS McCARTHY

# Quatrain without Sparrows, Helpful Bells or Hope

*from the Irish*

My world has been laid low, and the wind blows
Alexander's ashes and all who killed for us.
Troy is gone. And Ulster's wild sorrow,
It too, like Troy, like the English, it too will pass.

# Toast

No lovelier city than all of this,
Cork city, your early morning kiss;
peeled oranges and white porcelain,
midsummer Sunday mists
that scatter before breakfast.

Mass bells are pealing in every district,
in the Latin quarter of St Lukes,
the butter *quartier* of Blackpool.
Each brass appeal calls to prayer
our scattered books and utensils,

the newly blessed who've put on clothes.
*Why have I been as lucky as this?*
to have found one so meticulous
in love, so diffident yet close
that the house is charged with kinetic peace.

Like a secret lover, I should bring
you bowls of fresh roses, knowing
that you would show them how to thrive.
Lucky it's Sunday, or I'd have
to raid the meter for spare shillings!

Or, maybe I should wash my filthy socks,
fret at the curtains, iron clothes,
like you after Sunday breakfast.
Normal things run deep, God knows,
like love in flat-land, eggs on toast.

# The Emigration Trains

A pound-note was the best kind of passport
In those days, so I held my pound tightly
After my mother turned away. Idlers
Waved farewell from Ferrybank corners.
There was nothing heroic about my
Going, nothing like a political destiny –
I'd just wasted a summer standing round
Until a job came up on the Underground.

I felt like a vagrant, destitute, until
At Waterford Station I realized
My good luck: I owned a suitcase of card
While others carried mere bundles of cloth.
At Kilkenny every carriage was filled
To the door. One mother's last grip held fast
Despite the moving train, the rising glass.
For some it was the last touch of a child.

There was nothing pathetic about this;
Even the suffering Jews had kept a brave face.
We had our own State; a place to leave from –
Now the emigrant ship was like a big town:
That night it was Clonmel or Cappoquin,
With bars open, arguments outdoors
And politics racing through bleak corridors.

We were heading for England and the world
At war. Neutrality we couldn't afford.
I thought I would spend two years away
But in the end the two became twenty.
Within hours we'd reach the junction at Crewe
And sample powdered eggs from the menu,
As well as doodlebugs falling nearby;
All that fatal traffic of an alien sky.

I was so raw and Irish at the time
They said that shamrocks grew out of my ears.
I wasn't alone with my homesick mind:
When we sailed into Holyhead our tears
Made a pathetic sea. One labourer's voice
Rose out of the ship, like a skylark's,
Singing *Kevin Barry, Kevin Barry*.
His song became our night-cry at the dock.

# AIDAN CARL MATHEWS

## Minding Ruth

*for Seamus Deane*

She wreaks such havoc in my library,
It will take ages to set it right –
A Visigoth in a pinafore

Who, weakening, plonks herself
On the works of Friedrich Nietzsche,
And pines for her mother.

She's been at it all morning,
Duck-arsed in my History Section
Like a refugee among rubble,

Or, fled to the toilet, calling
In a panic that the seat is cold.
But now she relents under biscuits

To extemporize grace notes,
And sketch with a blue crayon
Arrow after arrow leading nowhere.

My small surprise of language,
I cherish you like an injury
And would swear by you at this moment

For your brisk chatter brings me
Chapter and verse, you restore
The city itself, novel and humming,

Which I enter as a civilian
Who plants his landscape with place-names.
They stand an instant, and fade.

Her hands sip at my cuff. She cranes,
Perturbedly, with a book held open
At plates from Warsaw in the last war.

*Why is the man with the long beard*
*Eating his booboos?* And I stare
At the old rabbi squatting in turds

Among happy soldiers who die laughing,
The young one clapping: you can see
A wedding band flash on his finger.

# Letter Following

We promise letters and send postcards,
My father and I. The whole of Europe
Has passed between us without comment

Down through the years, but mostly sailboats,
Waterfronts, and the polaroid heavens
Reflecting the sea or being reflected.

Only this morning, he sent me
The *Victory* in dry-dock and 3-D,
Second time round. There's the usual

Men's talk about storms and maintenance:
*When it worsened, then I worried would she*
*Drag her moorings, but she rode it well,*

*Her hatches battened.* Is he talking
Marriages or jobs? Or a cabin cruiser
Idling at anchor, five sons and no crew?

Who can tell? Mid-afternoon,
I write him at his hospital
A card addressed to the Ancient Mariner,

Of an island ferry from six months back,
Its lifeboat circled and arrowed:
*The best place to be in a headwind.*

And I post it off from this dusty place,
Thirty miles inland, north of Salonica,
Among chickens and children. Word of thanks,

Word of greeting. This is our way.
We cover our multitudes, he and I,
Our silences carrying over the water.

## AIDAN CARL MATHEWS

# The Death of Irish

The tide gone out for good,
Thirty-one words for seaweed
Whiten on the foreshore.

# Two Months Married

We can tell already
The history of chips in the skirting,
Hammer-marks at the towel-rail,

Or why the asparagus fern
Is housed in the cooking pot
With the hairline crack.

Today, I was cleaning
With the wrong cloth as you hid
Photographs behind photographs.

On the kitchen window there,
Natural Crystal Salt
Flared in a gust of sun;

The marked-down Sage and Mint
From the Nile's source
Unstoppered their genies.

In a room facing south,
A tree-house with the ladder drawn up,
We're home even as we set out.

Foodstore and software,
A clearing and a hideaway in which
We two may be together and alone

With a radio left on
Always, talking of envoys
Going back to a bombed city.

# Spectrum

Everything we stand up in,
Worn long enough, makes one load:
Our warm, discoloured underwear,
The shirts off our backs,
Or the rose-bordered bedsheets
We have made and must lie upon.
On washdays, we entrust it all,
This fabric of our lives together,
To the darkened floodwaters
Of a cycle marked *delicates*.
I think often how you sat up
The first night that we got it,
New to the heavy, heart-like churning
Of its cold wash and its warm wash;
And I think of the silence after:
A turning, a total immersion.
In the reddish glow of the pilot,
Your white hands at the dials.

Tonight the clotheshorse fills
Like the makeshift sails on liferafts
In those B-movies that show
Two stowaways waking
Bone-dry and uninjured
Among cockatoos and banana-crops.
I am trying to say that our lives
Are running into each other
Like the dyes from separates.
You see it in the wash:
My vests the pink of nappy rash
From a royal blue blouse,
And your whitest pair of trousers
Ruined for good, with stains
The colour of flesh and blood

424

AIDAN CARL MATHEWS

From something I slipped in
Among our sustaining garments,
Watermarks water won't budge.

# Caedmon

Because I could sing to High Heaven
The Abbot made me. Marched to the altar
Shotgun style by a scalping party,
My head felt eery, an oval shaved off
As if for delicate neuro-surgery.
What were they thinking beyond in the buttery,
My mates from the shepherds' dormitory
As I bent my neck, as I bent my knee?
'Sing me Creation' says the Master of Students,
The making of matter, a seven-day wonder,
The universe forming from misty gases
Like a disprin dropped in a glass of water;
'Sing me the Exodus out of Egypt',
The sulphur springs of the Promised Land.
And I try with my mouthful of cavities
Among all the statues that throw their eyes
Blindly toward Heaven. I am gargling Latin
Like salt sea water for runny ulcers.
Still, in a month of Sundays, a full church calendar,
I'll never be home here.
                              What I want instead
Is the benediction of words like cabbage
Out in the back where the plot is thickening;
And the lipservice I languish for
Beyond any Latin is the parted mouth
Of my wife with the dental anaesthetic
Turning the other cheek as I kiss her.
Because this is it: when the accurate image
Cools and clears in the sacred mysteries
Like an egg whitening in the pan,
It is her curved spaces in the bed beside me
The sun, the moon and the stars shine out of,
This that I take to my heart and husband
Wholly, wholly, wholly.

# Michael O'Loughlin

## Cuchulainn

If I lived in this place for a thousand years
I could never construe you, Cuchulainn.
Your name is a fossil, a petrified tree
Your name means less than nothing.
Less than Librium, or Burton's Biscuits
Or Phoenix Audio-Visual Systems –
I have never heard it whispered
By the wind in the telegraph wires
Or seen it scrawled on the wall
At the back of the children's playground.
Your name means less than nothing
To the housewife adrift in the Shopping Centre
At eleven-fifteen on a Tuesday morning
With the wind blowing fragments of concrete
Into eyes already battered and bruised
By four tightening walls
In a flat in a tower-block
Named after an Irish Patriot
Who died with your name on his lips.

But watching TV the other night
I began to construe you, Cuchulainn;
You came on like some corny revenant
In a black-and-white made for TV
American Sci-Fi serial.
An obvious Martian in human disguise
You stomped about in big boots
With a face perpetually puzzled and strained
And your deep voice booms full of capital letters:
What Is This Thing You Earthlings Speak Of

# An Irish Requiem

I.M. *Mary Lynch (1897–1983)*

Born in another country, under a different flag
She did not die before her time
Her god never ceased to speak to her.
And so she did not die. The only death that is real
Is when words change their meaning
And that is a death she never knew
Born in another country, under a different flag
When the soldiers and armoured cars
Spilled out of the ballads and onto the screen
Filling the tiny streets, she cried
And wiped her eyes on her apron, mumbling something
About the Troubles. That was a word
I had learned in my history book.
What did I care for the wails of the balding Orpheus
As he watched Eurydice burn in hell?
I was eleven years old,
And my Taoiseach wrote to me,
Born in another country, under a different flag.
She did not die before her time
But went without fuss, into the grave
She had bought and tended herself, with
The priest to say rites at her entry
And the whole family gathered,
Black suits and whiskey, a cortège
Of Ford Avengers inching up the cemetery hill.
Death came as an expected visitor,
A policeman, or rate collector, or the tinker
Who called every spring for fresh eggs,
Announced by the season, or knocks on walls,
Bats flying in and out of rooms, to signify
She did not die before her time

Her god never ceased to speak to her.
Till the last, he murmured in her kitchen
As she knelt at the chair beside the range
Or moved to the damp, unused parlour
For the priest's annual visit.
*Poète de sept ans*, I sat on the polished wood,
Bored by the priest's vernacular harangue
As she knelt beside me on the stone church floor,
And overheard her passionate whisper,
Oblivious, telling her beads, and I knew
That I would remember this, that
Her god never ceased to speak to her.
And so she did not die. The only death that is real
Is when words change their meaning
And that is a death she never knew.
As governments rose and fell, she never doubted
The name of the land she stood on. Nothing
But work and weather darkened the spring days
When she herded her fattened cattle
Onto the waiting cars. It is not she who haunts
But I, milking her life for historical ironies,
Knowing that more than time divides us.
But still her life burns on, like the light
From a distant, extinguished star, and
O let me die before that light goes out
Born in another country, under a different flag!

## *from* The Shards

### 1   *The Bunkers*

Along the great coast south of Bordeaux
The bunkers still stare out to sea
High-water marks of the black wave
That swept up out of the sump of Europe.
Untouched, they stand, undying monuments,
Easter Island heads in cold concrete.
On the side of one I found
Some Gothic lettering, black paint
That hadn't faded in the years of sun and wind.
But the blonde naked daughters
Sleep rough in them during the summer nights
And in the morning run laughing
Into the ocean their fathers had scanned.

### 8   *The Shards*

For months, coming home late at night
We would stop at a traffic light
In the middle of nowhere
And sit there, the engine restless
For the empty motorway
While I looked out at the half-built flyover
That stood in the moonlight
Like a ruined Greek temple
And I suddenly felt surrounded
By the shattered and potent monuments
Of a civilization we have not yet discovered
The ghost of something stalking us
The future imagined past perhaps
Or else the millions of dead
Rising and falling
Into the mud and carved stone

MICHAEL O'LOUGHLIN

The ghost of the beast
Whose carapace we inhabit
Not knowing if we stand
At centre or circumference
Sensing that shards are our only wholeness
Carefully carving their shattered edges.

# Posthumous

Something is pushing against my blood.
From the bus I watch the children
Set fire to sheets of paper
And scatter them, screaming, into the wind.
They burn down to nothing,
A black smudge on the concrete
Bleeding its greyness into the sky.
I think of Siberia, how clean it is.
I move around the city, denounced
To the secret police of popular songs.
A name flares in the darkness.
Moon-sister, twin.
Who are you? I don't know.
My mouth tastes of splintered bone.
I thought I'd left this place a long time ago.

MICHAEL O'LOUGHLIN

# Elegy for the Unknown Soldier

*It is hard to read on the ancient stone . . .*
*In the month of Athyr Levkios fell asleep.*
                                    – Cavafy

One evening in August, the light already failing
An insurance salesman dropped me off at a crossroads
In Cavan or Monaghan, the beginning of the drumlin country
I stood there for a while, near a newly-built bungalow
Watching the green fields darken behind a screen of hedges.
Just where the roads met there was a sort of green
With a JCB parked right up on the verge
And a small celtic cross of grey granite.
I walked over to read the inscription
Peering through the fading light.
'Patrick O'Neill, Volunteer, Third Belfast Brigade
Shot on a nearby hillside. 16 April 1923.'
I can't remember exactly, but that was the gist of it.
By the time I finished reading, it was completely dark.
All the lights were on in the nearby bungalow,
I could see the TV screen through the living-room window.
I heard the engine of a car in the distance,
The cone of its headlights appearing and disappearing.
He stopped and gave me a lift to Cootehill. I didn't look back.

# Glasnevin Cemetery

With deportment learnt from samurai films
I surface in the ancestral suburbs.
My grandmother is older than China,
Wiser than Confucius.
I pace my stride to hers
Soaking in the grey-green air.

Under my name cut in stone
My grandfather lies
Within hearing of the lorries' roar
Out on the main road.
I forget my unseemly haste
To see the Emperor's tomb.

We search for family graves
In the suburbs of the dead.
From the jumble of worn stones
Unmarked by celtic crosses
Like an Egyptologist she elucidates
Obscure back-street dynasties.

We see where Parnell lies buried
Under Sisyphean stone
Put there my father says
To keep him from climbing out.
I am surprised by ancient bitterness
Surfacing among the TV programmes.

The plotters of the nation
Are niched in their kitsch necropolis.
Matt Talbot, Larkin, Michael Collins
A holy graven trio
Shoulder to shoulder enshrined
In the tidy bogomil parlour of her heart.

MICHAEL O'LOUGHLIN

The day flowers sluggishly
From the stone of contradictions.
The trees sway like green Hasidim
I shuffle in a kind of lethargic dance
A sprung sign among the signified
A tenant in the suburbs of silence.

# PETER SIRR

## The Collector's Marginalia

'The range is French and has a mind of its own.
All night long the turf crumbles in the air-tight
Chamber and the hot ash rains on the tray
Yet morning finds the needle stuck at zero
And I come stumbling through the kitchen door,
The last of the true pioneers, arms laden
With firelighters and tins of beans, watching
Through the window the smoke of a dozen
Competent valley fires lean towards Maam.

After breakfast I follow the sunlight
Round the room and copy out my phonemes.
I sit for hours in their homes, a casual
Interloper listening for the square brackets
In the conversation, observing how
The troublesome genitive falls into disuse
In an afterglow of language. Looking up,
I see a trawler heading for the tiny pier,
The white foodmarket stark against the bay

And wonder why I'm here, making coffins
For words. Yesterday I climbed awkwardly
To the top of the hill behind the house
Past two famine cottages and an ageing
White mare looking down into the valley
Like a receding myth, coming at last
To a pile of stones left for someone killed.
When I came down the fire had gone out . . .
On windy days I stay inside and watch

A lone tree grow sideways like something dreamed
Or the idea of a tree, imperfectly grasped,
Which the wind has brought from a country
Where trees are possible. Each hopeful branch
Migrates eastward to where the light falls
The right way up, in orchards, text-book meadows
Or in slow encroaching shadows round hooded
Monastery gardens where night shimmies down
The perfect canopies like an unzipped skirt.

Out on the margins the serious stars
Like drinkers gather, flashing sudden wit
Above the huge, abandoned rocks,
The phone wires lying heavy on the poles.
My aerial's angled to the moon
As I prick my ears to the shaky news:
In three dialects the old people die
And the lights come on in local halls.
A volleyball team is making major strides.'

# Beginnings

'Our city declines, the world is still bleak
and the poems you imagined but couldn't write
have planted themselves in our memory of you:
your lines are stirring again in their folders
with an old hunger. I sit here in the mornings
and begin to understand
the serious business of failure, your weary pride

afflicting our kitchen night after night,
even the air of aesthetic hurt
with which you ate, and how you looked through us
as if we too were the beginnings of a fantasy,
like your folders of drafts, bravura flourishes
trapped forever in their own promise.
I sit here in the mornings

after the children have gone
and forgive your lack of resolution,
your need to wound. That poem I showed you once –
remember? It died then with your laughter
and struggles now with your absence.
I sit here in the mornings
discarding your beginnings, your ceremonies

of silence and the writing desk,
pushing back the dishes just enough to take
the small risk of my copybook, letting the radio work in
its demythifying ache. Listen, I am
trying to come back to you as the line
that ran on, the whole life waiting
like an opened flask . . .'

# Understanding Canada

Tonight
he is understanding Canada
curled up under the standard lamp
with his thoughtful look, eyeing me
like a Whiteoak dreaming of Jalna
or wanting the music down
to explain about the Quebecois poet with the Irish name,
Ukrainians in the open spaces, nights trying to pick
between Greek Orthodox and Greek Catholic.
I have never been to Canada,
he has never crossed the Atlantic
though he sits sympathetically,
his mild gaze an open house
for the Iroquois, the Inuit, and later,
as if our hour had come
he'll turn his head to mine and sigh
with a thin, migratory passion
the last words of our spoken language.

# A Guide to Holland

Audrey Hepburn moons big-eyed on the cover,
a shaded nipple just visible
under the woolly *O* of Holland,
and somewhere between *The Night Watch* and *The Prodigal Son*
the inevitable
grim-faced matron is picking her way
down the stairs, clutching her High Nellie
as if her life depended on it, as it may,
while Father puffs his pipe in a well-lit room.
Land without secrets, heart worn
on the sleeve of Europe . . . near the zoo
a cardboard tiger aims his leap
at an apartment block, and here three months
I borrow the posture, sinking my teeth
in the interior life, matching
each flagrant privacy
with a dry French eye and an oath
for the commissioning editor;
letting the ancient rivalries begin,
the clever nation rescue itself again,
a smell of polders and *jenever*,
a chummy grin for Voltaire's 'infernal phlegm'
a pencil sharpened in a tall hotel
for a final assault on the bourgeois soul . . .

# SARA BERKELEY

## The Parting

### 1

You lower my emotions, sealed in their casket,
To the sea bed, knowing I have nothing to say
Paring down to presence and absence
The sad abstractions of our last day
My throat grows heavy between your hands
My heart gets tossed away.

### 2

A shadow is working hard against the night
Working furiously on a morning wall
The shadow cast by fifteen beams of light
I am a child's bright stone
Longing to be the weapon of your fight
I am the fifteen beams coming straight down.

### 3

In brief moments when a nerve winks out
It seems as though you will always be there
The heart kicks – and then you are removed
You are climbing down the angry white stairs
You are the shadow resting on my skin
And we, a double splash of oars into the still air.

# The Mass is Over

The Mass is over, they have gone in peace
But wind flays the church's sides
I fear my frail cover will be blown
Despite the sunlight on confessional doors,
Desultory coins,
The urgent reaching of the women's prayers.

I have taken refuge from a bitter shower
And find myself at Christ's fire
Yearning for things I've had
And won't have again
Because I have done wrong;
He passes – and a shudder of sparks
Ignites the recognition,
A dark object in a field of light
Where I have come for shelter
And in the warm eye of the wind
My twenty Easters wash me in their milky sun.

# BIOGRAPHICAL NOTES

**Sara Berkeley** was born in Dublin in 1967. She has published *Penn* (1986) and *Home Movie Nights* (1989).

**Eavan Boland** was born in Dublin in 1944. She has published *New Territory* (1967), *The War Horse* (1975), *In Her Own Image* (1980), *Night Feed* (1982) and *The Journey* (1987).

**Ciaran Carson** was born in Belfast in 1948. He has published three collections of poems, *The New Estate* (1976; enlarged 1988), *The Irish for No* (1987) and *Belfast Confetti* (1989), and *The Pocket Guide to Irish Traditional Music* (1986).

**Philip Casey** was born in 1950 and lives in Dublin. He has published two books of poems, *Those Distant Summers* (1980) and *After Thunder* (1985).

**Harry Clifton** was born in Dublin in 1952. He has published four collections, *The Walls of Carthage* (1977), *Office of the Salt Merchant* (1979), *Comparative Lives* (1983) and *The Liberal Cage* (1988).

**Anthony Cronin** was born in Co. Wexford in 1925. His volumes of poetry include *Collected Poems* (1973), *R.M.S. Titanic* (1980), a long poem, *New and Selected Poems* (1982) and *The End of the Modern World* (1989). Other books include *The Life of Riley* (1964), a novel; *Dead as Doornails* (1975), memoirs; *A Question of Modernity* (1966), *Heritage Now* (1982) and *An Irish Eye: Viewpoints* (1985), criticism; and *No Laughing Matter: The Life and Times of Flann O'Brien* (1989), a biography.

**Michael Davitt** was born in Cork in 1950. He has published two collections of poems in Irish, *Gleann ar Ghleann* (1982) and *Bligeard Sráide* (1983), and a bilingual selection, *Selected Poems/Rogha Dánta 1968–1984* (1987).

**Seamus Deane** was born in Derry in 1940. His collections of poems are *Gradual Wars* (1972), *Rumours* (1977), *History Lessons* (1983) and *Selected Poems* (1988). Other books include *Celtic Revivals* (1985) and *A Short History of Irish Literature* (1986). He is General Editor of *The Field Day Anthology of Irish Writing 550–1988* (1990). He lives in Dublin.

**Nuala Ní Dhomhnaill** was born in Lancashire in 1952 and grew up in the Kerry Gaeltacht. She has published two collections of poems in Irish, *An*

*Dealg Droighin* (1981) and *Féar Suaithinseach* (1984), and a volume of *Selected Poems/Rogha Dánta* (1988) translated into English by Michael Hartnett. She lives in Dublin.

**Paul Durcan** was born in Dublin in 1944. His books include *O Westport in the Light of Asia Minor* (1975), *Teresa's Bar* (1976), *Sam's Cross* (1978), *Jesus, Break His Fall* (1980), *The Selected Paul Durcan* (1982), *Jumping the Train Tracks with Angela* (1983), *The Berlin Wall Café* (1985) and *Going Home to Russia* (1987).

**John Ennis** was born in Co. Westmeath in 1944 and now lives in Co. Waterford. He has published three collections of poems, *Night on Hibernia* (1975), *Dolmen Hill* (1977) and *A Drink of Spring* (1979), and a long poem, *The Burren Days* (1985).

**Peter Fallon** was born in 1951. His books include *The Speaking Stones* (1978), *Winter Work* (1983) and *The News and Weather* (1987). He lives on a farm in Co. Meath.

**Eamon Grennan** was born in Dublin in 1941 and now teaches at Vassar College in New York State. His two collections of poems are *Wildly for Days* (1983) and *What Light There Is* (1987).

**Michael Hartnett** was born in 1941 in Co. Limerick and now lives in Dublin. His books include *A Farewell to English* (1975; enlarged 1978), poems in English; *Adharca Broic* (1978), poems in Irish; *Collected Poems: Volume One* (1984); *O Bruadair* (1985), translations from Irish; *Collected Poems: Volume Two* (1986); *A Necklace of Wrens* (1987), selected poems in Irish with facing translations into English; and *Poems to Younger Women* (1988).

**Seamus Heaney** was born in Co. Derry in 1939. His books of poems are *Death of a Naturalist* (1966), *Door into the Dark* (1969), *Wintering Out* (1972), *North* (1975), *Field Work* (1979), *Station Island* (1984) and *The Haw Lantern* (1987). He has also published *Preoccupations* (1980) and *The Government of the Tongue* (1988), essays; and *Sweeney Astray* (1983), a version from the Irish.

**Pearse Hutchinson** was born in Glasgow in 1927 and now lives in Dublin. His books of poems in English are *Tongue without Hands* (1963), *Expansions* (1969), *Watching the Morning Grow* (1972), *The Frost is All Over* (1975), *Selected Poems* (1980) and *Climbing the Light* (1985). A collection of poems in Irish, *Faostin Bhacach*, appeared in 1968.

**Brendan Kennelly** was born in Co. Kerry in 1936. His books of poems include *Getting Up Early* (1966), *Good Souls to Survive* (1967), *Dream of a Black Fox* (1968), *Bread* (1971), *Salvation, the Stranger* (1972), *Love Cry* (1972), *The Voices* (1973), *A Kind of Trust* (1975), *Islandman* (1977), *A Small*

*Light* (1978), *The Boats are Home* (1980), *Cromwell* (1983), *Selected Poems* (1985) and *A Time for Voices: Selected Poems 1960–1990* (1990).

**Thomas Kinsella** was born in Dublin in 1928. His books of poems include *Another September* (1958), *Downstream* (1962), *Nightwalker and Other Poems* (1968), *New Poems 1973* (1973), *Peppercanister Poems 1972–1978* (1980). Recent collections include *Songs of the Psyche* and *Her Vertical Smile* (1985), *Out of Ireland* and *St Catherine's Clock* (1987) and *Blood and Family* (1988). He has translated *The Táin* (1969) and *An Duanaire: Poems of the Dispossessed 1600–1900* (1981).

**Michael Longley** was born in 1939 in Belfast, where he now lives. His collections of poems are *No Continuing City* (1969), *An Exploded View* (1973), *Man Lying on a Wall* (1976), *The Echo Gate* (1979) and *Poems 1963–1983* (1985).

**Thomas McCarthy** was born in Co. Waterford in 1954 and now lives in Cork. His collections of poems are *The First Convention* (1978), *The Sorrow Garden* (1981), *The Non-Aligned Storyteller* (1984) and *Seven Winters in Paris* (1989).

**Medbh McGuckian** was born in 1950 in Belfast. Her books are *The Flower Master* (1982), *Venus and the Rain* (1984) and *On Ballycastle Beach* (1988).

**Tom Mac Intyre** was born in Cavan in 1931. He has published *The Charollais* (1969), a novel; *Dance the Dance* (1970) and *The Harper's Turn* (1982), short stories; *Blood Relations* (1972), translations from the Irish; *I Bailed Out at Ardee* (1987), poems; and *The Great Hunger* (1988), a play based on the poem by Patrick Kavanagh.

**Derek Mahon** was born in Belfast in 1941. He has published six books of poems, *Night Crossing* (1968), *Lives* (1972), *The Snow Party* (1975), *Poems 1962–1978* (1979), *The Hunt by Night* (1982) and *Antarctica* (1985), as well as versions of plays by Molière and poems by Gérard de Nerval and Philippe Jaccottet. He lives in Dublin.

**Aidan Carl Mathews** was born in Dublin in 1956. He has published two collections of poems, *Windfalls* (1977) and *Minding Ruth* (1983), and a collection of short stories, *Adventures in a Bathyscope* (1988). His plays include *The Diamond Body* and *Exit/Entrance*.

**Hugh Maxton** was born in Wicklow in 1947. He has published four collections of poems, *The Noise of the Fields* (1976), *Jubilee for Renegades* (1982), *At the Protestant Museum* (1986) and *The Puzzle Tree Ascendant* (1988). He lives in Dublin.

**John Montague** was born in 1929 in Brooklyn, New York, and raised in Co. Tyrone. His collections include *Poisoned Lands* (1961, 1977), *A Chosen Light*

(1967), *Tides* (1970), *The Rough Field* (1972), *A Slow Dance* (1975), *The Great Cloak* (1978), *Selected Poems* (1982), *The Dead Kingdom* (1984), *Mount Eagle* (1988) and *New Selected Poems* (1989). He has also published two books of fiction, *Death of a Chieftain* (1967) and *The Lost Notebook* (1987).

**Paul Muldoon** was born in 1951 in Co. Armagh. His collections are *New Weather* (1973), *Mules* (1977), *Why Brownlee Left* (1980), *Quoof* (1983) and *Meeting the British* (1987). *Selected Poems* appeared in 1986, as did *The Faber Book of Contemporary Irish Poetry*, which he edited. He now lives in America.

**Richard Murphy** was born in the west of Ireland in 1927. He has published *Sailing to an Island* (1963), *The Battle of Aughrim* (1968), *High Island* (1974), *Selected Poems* (1979), *The Price of Stone* (1985) and *The Mirror Wall* (1989). He lives in Dublin.

**Desmond O'Grady** was born in Limerick in 1935. His books of poems include *Reilly* (1961), *The Dark Edge of Europe* (1967), *The Dying Gaul* (1968), *Sing Me Creation* (1977), *The Headgear of the Tribe: Selected Poems* (1979) and *His Skaldcrane's Nest* (1979). He has translated *Off Licence* (1968) and *A Limerick Rake* (1978) from the Irish and *The Gododdin* (1977) from the Welsh. He lives in Kinsale, Co. Cork.

**Michael O'Loughlin** was born in Dublin in 1958. His three collections are *Stalingrad: The Street Dictionary* (1980), *Atlantic Blues* (1982) and *The Diary of a Silence* (1985). He lives in Holland.

**Frank Ormsby** was born in Co. Fermanagh in 1947 and now lives in Belfast. He has published two collections, *A Store of Candles* (1977) and *A Northern Spring* (1986).

**Tom Paulin** was born in Leeds in 1949 and grew up in Belfast. He has published four books of poems, *A State of Justice* (1977), *The Strange Museum* (1980), *Liberty Tree* (1983) and *Fivemiletown* (1987). His other books include *Ireland and the English Crisis* (1984), essays; *The Riot Act* (1985) and *The Hillsborough Script* (1987), plays. He lives in England.

**Richard Ryan** was born in Dublin in 1946. He has published *Ledges* (1970) and *Ravenswood* (1973). He is Ambassador of Ireland to the Republic of Korea.

**James Simmons** was born in Derry in 1933. His books of poems include *Late but in Earnest* (1967), *In the Wilderness* (1969), *Energy to Burn* (1971), *The Long Summer Still to Come* (1973), *West Strand Visions* (1974), *Judy Garland and the Cold War* (1976), *Constantly Singing* (1980), *From the Irish* (1985) and *Poems 1956–1986* (1986).

**Peter Sirr** was born in 1960. He has published two collections, *Marginal Zones* (1984) and *Talk, Talk* (1987). He lives in Italy.

**Michael Smith** was born in 1942 in Dublin, where he now lives. He has published *Times & Locations* (1972), *Stopping to Take Notes* (1980) and *Selected Poems* (1985), as well as translations of Antonio Machado, Pablo Neruda and Miguel Hernández.

The editors regret that Eiléan Ní Chuilleanáin declined their invitation to appear in this anthology. Her fine poems are available in *The Second Voyage* (1977, 1986), *The Rose-Geranium* (1981) and *The Magdalene Sermon* (1989).

# ACKNOWLEDGEMENTS

Thanks are due to the copyright holders of the following poems for permission to reprint them in this volume.

**SARA BERKELEY**: for 'The Parting' from *Penn*. 'The Mass is Over' from *Home Movie Nights*. Reprinted by permission of Raven Arts Press.

**EAVAN BOLAND**: for 'From the Painting "Back from Market" by Chardin', 'After the Irish of Egan O'Rahilly', 'The War Horse', 'Ode to Suburbia', 'In Her Own Image', 'I Remember' and 'The Oral Tradition'. Reprinted by permission of the author.

**CIARAN CARSON**: for 'Céilí' from *The New Estate and Other Poems*. Reprinted by permission of The Gallery Press. For 'Dresden', 'Judgement', 'Army' and 'Cocktails' from *The Irish for No*. 'Bloody Hand' from *Belfast Confetti*. Reprinted by permission of The Gallery Press and Wake Forest University Press.

**PHILIP CASEY**: for 'Shortening the Road' and 'The Counterfeiter', translated from the Irish of Michael Davitt. Reprinted by permission of the author and Raven Arts Press.

**HARRY CLIFTON**: for 'Monsoon Girl' and 'Death of Thomas Merton' from *Comparative Lives*. 'The Distaff Side', 'Id', 'Euclid Avenue' and 'Eccles Street, Bloomsday, 1982' from *The Liberal Cage*. All reprinted by permission of The Gallery Press.

**ANTHONY CRONIN**: for 'Responsibilities', 'Lines for a Painter', 'Elegy for the Nightbound' and the extracts from 'R.M.S. Titanic' from *New and Selected Poems*. All reprinted by permission of Raven Arts Press.

ACKNOWLEDGEMENTS

**MICHAEL DAVITT**: for 'An Scáthán', 'Ciorrú Bóthair', 'Sean-daoine' and 'An Góchumadóir' from *Selected Poems/Rogha Dánta 1968–1984*. Reprinted by permission of the author and Raven Arts Press.

**SEAMUS DEANE**: for 'Power Cut', 'Return', 'Fording the River', 'Osip Mandelstam', 'History Lessons' and 'Reading *Paradise Lost* in Protestant Ulster 1984' from *Selected Poems*. All reprinted by permission of The Gallery Press.

**NUALA NÍ DHOMHNAILL**: for 'Féar Suaithinseach', 'Geasa', 'Aubade', 'An Crann' and 'An Rás' from *Féar Suaithinseach*. All reprinted by permission of the author and An Sagart.

**PAUL DURCAN**: for 'La Terre des Hommes', 'Ireland 1972', 'She Mends an Ancient Wireless', 'The Weeping Headstones of the Isaac Becketts', 'The Kilfenora Teaboy', 'Going Home to Mayo, Winter, 1949', 'Backside to the Wind', 'Birth of a Coachman', 'Irish Hierarchy Bans Colour Photography' and 'Micheál Mac Liammóir' from *The Selected Paul Durcan*. 'The Pietà's Over' from *The Berlin Wall Café*. 'The Divorce Referendum, Ireland, 1986' from *Going Home to Russia*. All reprinted by permission of Blackstaff Press.

**JOHN ENNIS**: for 'Alice of Daphne' from *Dolmen Hill*. 'Coyne's' and 'A Drink of Spring' from *A Drink of Spring*. All reprinted by permission of the author and The Gallery Press. For 'The Road to Patmos'. Reprinted by permission of the author.

**PETER FALLON**: for 'Winter Work' from *Winter Work*. 'Spring Song', 'The Herd', 'Airs and Graces', 'The Meadow' and 'Himself' from *The News and Weather*. All reprinted by permission of The Gallery Press.

**EAMON GRENNAN**: for 'Facts of Life, Ballymoney' and 'Sunday Morning Through Binoculars' from *Wildly for Days*. 'Wing Road', 'Soul Music: The Derry Air', 'Men Roofing' and 'Conjunctions' from *What Light There Is*. All reprinted by permission of The Gallery Press.

**MICHAEL HARTNETT**: for 'A Small Farm', 'There will be a Talking', 'For My Grandmother, Bridget Halpin' and 'The Person as Dreamer: We Talk about the Future'. Reprinted by permission of the author. For '"I saw magic on a green country road"', 'A Visit to Castletown House', 'Death of an Irishwoman', 'Lament for Tadhg Cronin's Children' and 'The Retreat of Ita Cagney' from *A Farewell to English*. 'An Dobharchú Gonta', 'The Wounded Otter', 'Fís Dheireanach Eoghain Rua Uí Shúilleabháin' and 'The Last Vision of Eoghan Rua Ó Súilleabháin' from *A Necklace of Wrens*. '"Pity the man who English lacks"' from *O Bruadair*. Reprinted by permission of The Gallery Press. For 'Old People', translated from the Irish of Michael Davitt. For 'Marvellous Grass' and 'The Race', translated from the Irish of Nuala Ní Dhomhnaill. Reprinted by permission of the author and Raven Arts Press.

**SEAMUS HEANEY**: for 'Bogland' from *Door into the Dark*. 'Anahorish', 'The Tollund Man' and 'Summer Home' from *Wintering Out*. 'Funeral Rites', 'Punishment' and 'Exposure' from *North*. 'A Postcard from North Antrim', 'Casualty' and 'The Harvest Bow' from *Field Work*. 'An Ulster Twilight' and the extract from 'Station Island' from *Station Island*. 'Clearances' and 'The Mud Vision' from *The Haw Lantern*. All reprinted by permission of Faber and Faber Ltd and Farrar Straus & Giroux Inc.

**PEARSE HUTCHINSON**: for 'Málaga', 'Be Born a Saint', 'Look, No Hands', 'Fleadh Cheoil', 'Gaeltacht', 'Bright After Dark' and 'The Frost is All Over' from *Selected Poems*. 'Amhrán na mBréag' and 'A True Story Ending in False Hope' from *Climbing the Light*. All reprinted by permission of The Gallery Press.

**BRENDAN KENNELLY**: for 'My Dark Fathers', 'The Limerick Train', 'Dream of a Black Fox', 'Bread', 'The Swimmer', 'The Island' and 'Proof' from *A Time for Voices: Selected Poems 1960–1990*. All reprinted by permission of Bloodaxe Books Ltd.

**THOMAS KINSELLA**: for 'A Lady of Quality', 'In the Ringwood', 'Downstream', 'Wormwood' and the extract from 'Nightwalker' from *Selected Poems 1956–1968*. 'Hen Woman', 'Ancestor', 'Nuchal',

'Endymion', 'All is Emptiness, and I Must Spin', 'The Route of the Táin' and 'Death Bed' from *New Poems 1973*. 'Finistère', 'The Oldest Place' and 'Tao and Unfitness at Inistiogue on the River Nore' from *One and Other Poems*. All reprinted by permission of the author.

MICHAEL LONGLEY: for 'Persephonc', 'The Hebrides', 'Wounds', 'The West', 'In Memory of Gerard Dillon', 'Skara Brae', 'Ash Keys', 'Frozen Rain', 'Peace' and 'The Linen Industry' from *Poems 1963–1983*. For 'Remembering Carrigskeewaun'. For 'Aubade', translated from the Irish of Nuala Ní Dhomhnaill. All reprinted by permission of the author.

THOMAS McCARTHY: for 'The Wisdom of AE', 'The Phenomenology of Stones', 'Claud Cockburn', 'Quatrain without Sparrows, Helpful Bells or Hope', 'Toast' and 'The Emigration Trains'. All reprinted by permission of the author.

MEDBH McGUCKIAN: for 'Gateposts'. Reprinted by permission of the author. For 'Lychees', 'The Sofa', 'The Aphrodisiac' and 'The Flitting' from *The Flower Master*. 'On Not Being Your Lover' from *Venus and the Rain*. 'To a Cuckoo at Coolanlough', 'Sea or Sky?' and 'On Ballycastle Beach' from *On Ballycastle Beach*. Reprinted by permission of Oxford University Press. For 'The Bond', translated from the Irish of Nuala Ní Dhomhnaill. Reprinted by permission of the author.

TOM MAC INTYRE: for 'The Yellow Bittern' and 'Sweet Killen Hill' from *I Bailed Out at Ardee*. Reprinted by permission of The Dedalus Press.

DEREK MAHON: for 'In Carrowdore Churchyard', 'Lives', 'The Snow Party', 'A Disused Shed in Co. Wexford', 'Ford Manor' and 'Everything is Going to be All Right' from *Poems 1962–1978*. 'Courtyards in Delft', 'The Woods', 'A Garage in Co. Cork' and 'The Globe in North Carolina' from *The Hunt by Night*. All reprinted by permission of Oxford University Press. For 'Achill', 'Dejection'

451

and 'Antarctica' from *Antarctica*. Reprinted by permission of The Gallery Press.

**AIDAN CARL MATHEWS**: for 'Minding Ruth', 'Letter Following', 'The Death of Irish', 'Two Months Married' and 'Spectrum' from *Minding Ruth*. Reprinted by permission of The Gallery Press. For 'Caedmon'. Reprinted by permission of the author.

**HUGH MAXTON**: for 'An Urgent Letter', 'Ode', 'Elegies' and 'Deutschland'. Reprinted by permission of the author. A later version of 'Elegies' appeared in *The Crane Bag* in 1983.

**JOHN MONTAGUE**: for 'The Trout', 'Like Dolmens Round My Childhood, the Old People', 'Woodtown Manor', 'All Legendary Obstacles', 'King & Queen', 'Last Journey', 'A Lost Tradition', 'A Grafted Tongue', 'The Wild Dog Rose' and 'Herbert Street Revisited' from *Selected Poems* and *New Selected Poems*. 'The Locket' from *The Dead Kingdom* and *New Selected Poems*. 'Deer Park' from *Mount Eagle*. All reprinted by permission of Wake Forest University Press and The Gallery Press. For 'At Last' from *Selected Poems*. 'A Flowering Absence' from *The Dead Kingdom*. Reprinted by permission of the author and Wake Forest University Press.

**PAUL MULDOON**: for 'Hedgehog' from *New Weather*. 'Our Lady of Ardboe' from *Mules*. 'Ireland', 'The Avenue', 'Something of a Departure', 'Why Brownlee Left' and 'Truce' from *Why Brownlee Left*. 'Gathering Mushrooms', 'Quoof' and 'Yggdrasill' from *Quoof*. 'The Wishbone', 'The Lass of Aughrim' and 'The Soap-Pig' from *Meeting the British*. 'The Mirror', translated from the Irish of Michael Davitt. All reprinted by permission of Faber and Faber Ltd and Wake Forest University Press. For 'As for the Quince', translated from the Irish of Nuala Ní Dhomhnaill. Reprinted by permission of the author.

**RICHARD MURPHY**: for 'Sailing to an Island' and 'The Last Galway Hooker' from *Sailing to an Island*. 'Casement's Funeral', 'Slate', 'Rapparees', 'Luttrell's Death' and 'Patrick Sarsfield's Portrait' from *The Battle of Aughrim*. 'Seals at High Island' and 'The

Reading Lesson' from *High Island*. 'Gate Lodge' from *The Price of Stone*. All reprinted by permission of Faber and Faber Ltd, the author and Wake Forest University Press.

**DESMOND O'GRADY**: for the extract from 'The Dark Edge of Europe', 'Professor Kelleher and the Charles River', 'Reading the Unpublished Manuscripts of Louis MacNeice at Kinsale Harbour', the extract from 'The Dying Gaul', the extract from 'Hellas', the extract from 'Lines in a Roman Schoolbook', 'Purpose' and 'The Great Horse Fair' from *The Headgear of the Tribe: Selected Poems*. All reprinted by permission of The Gallery Press.

**MICHAEL O'LOUGHLIN**: for 'Cuchulainn' from *Stalingrad: The Street Dictionary*. 'An Irish Requiem', 'The Bunkers', 'The Shards', 'Posthumous', 'Elegy for the Unknown Soldier' and 'Glasnevin Cemetery' from *The Diary of a Silence*. All reprinted by permission of Raven Arts Press.

**FRANK ORMSBY**: for 'Landscape with Figures', 'Spot the Ball', 'A Day in August' and 'Under the Stairs' from *A Store of Candles*. 'My Careful Life' and 'Home' from *A Northern Spring*. All reprinted by permission of The Gallery Press.

**TOM PAULIN**: for 'In the Lost Province' and 'Anastasia McLaughlin' from *The Strange Museum*. 'Desertmartin', 'Off the Back of a Lorry' and 'Presbyterian Study' from *Liberty Tree*. 'Last Statement', from *Fivemiletown*. All reprinted by permission of Faber and Faber Ltd.

**RICHARD RYAN**: for 'Father of Famine', 'Deafness', 'Winter in Minneapolis', 'The Lake of the Woods' and 'At the End'. All reprinted by permission of the author.

**JAMES SIMMONS**: for 'The Archæologist', 'Written, Directed by and Starring . . .', 'The End of the Affair', 'Stephano Remembers', 'West Strand Visions', 'Claudy', 'For Thomas Moore', 'From the Irish' and 'The Pleasant Joys of Brotherhood' from *Poems 1956–1986*. All reprinted by permission of The Gallery Press. For 'A Long

Way After Ronsard', 'Rogation Day: Portrush' and 'Westport House, Portrush'. Reprinted by permission of the author.

**PETER SIRR**: for 'The Collector's Marginalia' from *Marginal Zones*. 'Beginnings', 'Understanding Canada' and 'A Guide to Holland' from *Talk, Talk*. All reprinted by permission of The Gallery Press.

**MICHAEL SMITH**: for 'City', 'Asleep in the City', 'Chimes', 'Stopping to Take Notes', 'A Visit to the Village' and 'From the Chinese' from *Selected Poems*. All reprinted by permission of the author.

Every effort has been made to trace copyright holders. We would be interested to hear from any copyright holders not here acknowledged.

Quotations from the writings of Patrick Kavanagh in the Introduction are used by kind permission of The Trustees of the Estate of Katherine B. Kavanagh, c/o Peter Fallon Literary Agent, Loughcrew, Oldcastle, Co. Meath, Ireland.

# INDEX OF FIRST LINES

# READ MORE IN PENGUIN

# READ MORE IN PENGUIN

## A SELECTION OF POETRY

**James Fenton**   Out of Danger

A collection wonderfully open to experience – of foreign places, differences, feelings and languages.

**Geoffrey Hill**   Canaan

'Among our finest poets, Geoffrey Hill is at present the most European   in his Latinity, in his dramatization of the Christian condition, in his political intensity' *Sunday Times*

**Generations**   Edited by Melanie Hart and James Loader

Every poet was once a child. In this collection they write of the mothers and fathers they worship or resent, love or mourn, and poets who are parents describe the joy and pain of bringing up children.

**Tony Harrison**   Selected Poems

'Brilliant, passionate, outrageous, abrasive, but also, as in his family sonnets, immeasurably tender' Harold Pinter. 'The poem 'v.' is one of the most powerful, profound and haunting long poems of modern times' Bernard Levin, *The Times*

**Spike Milligan**   Hidden Words

Everyone knows and loves Spike Milligan for his amazing comic genius. This collection of his poems, however, reveals other sides to him that we may not have met before.

**U. A. Fanthorpe**   Selected Poems

'She is an erudite poet, rich in experience and haunted by the classical past . . . fully at home in the world of the turbulent NHS . . . and all the draughty corners of the abandoned Welfare State' *Observer*

**Craig Raine**   Clay. Whereabouts Unknown

'I cannot think of anyone else writing today whose every line is so unfailingly exciting' *Sunday Times*

# READ MORE IN PENGUIN

## A SELECTION OF POETRY

**Octavio Paz**  Selected Poems

'His poetry allows us to glimpse a different and future place ... liberating and affirming' *Guardian*

**Allen Ginsberg**  Collected Poems 1947–1985

'Ginsberg is responsible for loosening the breath of American poetry at mid-century' *New Yorker*

**Jules Laforgue**  Selected Poems

During a tragically short life, Jules Laforgue created a poetic persona so powerful it decisively influenced the work of T. S. Eliot and Ezra Pound, marking him out as one of the founding fathers of modernism.

**Roger McGough**  Sporting Relations

'McGough's knack, as the Peoples' Poet Laureate, is to be relevant and contemporary; to achieve popularity without patronising' Clare Henry, *Glasgow Herald*

**Fernando Pessoa**  Selected Poems

'I have sought for his shade in those Edwardian cafés in Lisbon which he haunted, for he was Lisbon's Cavafy or Verlaine' *Sunday Times*

**John Updike**  Collected Poems 1953–1993

'Updike's eye comes up very close ... yet eschews the gruesome, keeps life vivid and slippery and erotic' *Observer*

**Craig Charles**  No Other Blue

Actor and comedian Craig Charles reveals yet another talent with his first collection of poetry.

**Penguin Modern Poets**

This highly influential series celebrates the best and most innovative of today's poetic voices.

# READ MORE IN PENGUIN

## A SELECTION OF POETRY

American Verse
British Poetry since 1945
Caribbean Verse in English
Chinese Love Poetry
A Choice of Comic and Curious Verse
Contemporary American Poetry
Contemporary British Poetry
Contemporary Irish Poetry
Earliest English Poems
English Romantic Verse
English Verse
First World War Poetry
French Poetry
German Verse
Greek Verse
Hebrew Verse
Imagist Poetry
Irish Verse
Japanese Verse
Medieval English Lyrics
The Metaphysical Poets
Modern African Poetry
New Poetry
Nineteenth Century American Poetry
Poetry of the Thirties
Restoration Verse
Scottish Verse
Surrealist Poetry in English
Spanish Verse
Victorian Verse
Women Poets
Zen Poetry

# READ MORE IN PENGUIN

# READ MORE IN PENGUIN

## POETS IN TRANSLATION

Penguin Classics now publishes a series that presents the best verse translations in English, through the centuries, of the major Classical and European poets. With full introductions and explanatory notes, the Poets in Translation series is a unique addition to the wealth of poetry within Penguin Classics.

*Published or forthcoming:*

| | |
|---|---|
| **Baudelaire in English** | Edited by Carol Clark and Robert Sykes |
| **The Bible in English** | Edited by Gerald Hammond |
| **Catullus in English** | Edited by Julia Haig Gaisser |
| **Dante in English** | Edited by Eric Griffiths and Matthew Reynolds |
| **Homer in English** | Edited by George Steiner |
| **Horace in English** | Edited by Donald Carne-Ross and Kenneth Hayes |
| **Juvenal in English** | Edited by Martin M. Winkler |
| **Lucretius in English** | Edited by Christopher Decker |
| **Martial in English** | Edited by John Sullivan and Anthony Boyle |
| **Montale in English** | Edited by Harry Thomas |
| **Ovid in English** | Edited with an Introduction by Christopher Martin |
| **Petrarch in English** | Edited by Thomas P. Roche |
| **The Psalms in English** | Edited by Donald Davie |
| **Rilke in English** | Edited by Michael Hofman |
| **Seneca in English** | Edited with an Introduction by Don Share |
| **Virgil in English** | Edited by K. W. Gransden |

# READ MORE IN PENGUIN

## A SELECTION OF ANTHOLOGIES

**The Penguin Book of Caribbean Short Stories**
Edited by E. A. Markham

Spanning the history of the genre, this major anthology reflects the enormous diversity and richness of Caribbean writing. The great figures of the Caribbean short story are included with works by Jean Rhys, Roger Mais, V. S. Naipul and Earl Lovelace.

**Trilogy of Death**  P. D. James

Contains the three classic novels *An Unsuitable Job for a Woman*, *Innocent Blood* and *The Skull Beneath the Skin*. 'She writes like an angel. Her atmosphere is unerringly, chillingly convincing. And she manages all this without for a moment slowing down the drive and tension' *The Times*

**Night Thoughts**

Poems and prose, either about the world of darkness or with the flavour of late-night composition form a loose but beguiling genre. This book celebrates the great tradition of 'night writing' – the extraordinary inner dialogue provoked in the late hours when 'the world's whole sap is sunk'.

**The Second Penguin Book of Modern Women's Short Stories**
Selected and Introduced by Susan Hill

'Constantly surprising, sometimes hilarious and often moving ... every single story, without exception, is good ... a collection to read over and over again' *Scotsman*. 'There are some marvellous stories here' *Observer*

**The Third Rumpole Omnibus**  John Mortimer
Savour a third helping of Rumpole, the Old Bailey hack from Equity Court with a talent for scathing sarcasm, standing up for the underdog and proving a fly in the ointment of judges everywhere.